"You are being extremely rude."

"And you're actin' like a goddamn saint, I suppose?"

"Uncivilized and boorish," she continued without a pause. Her finger rap-tapped on his breastbone with each word. "You pay no attention to anything I—"

Will grabbed her shoulders. She twisted away from him, but he held her fast. "Let me set you straight on somethin', princess."

Again she tried to free herself. Will gave her a little shake and stepped in close. "Stop wiggling, dammit. Let me explain something."

Without moving, she looked up at him. She just stood there, gazing up as if she'd never seen him before. A question formed in her eyes, but before she could voice it, something in Will boiled over. The next thing he knew he was hauling her against him and dragging his mouth over hers....

* * *

The Ranger and the Redhead
Harlequin Historical #773—October 2005

LYNNA BANNING

The RANGER and the REDHEAD

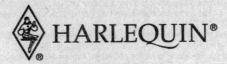

HARLEQUIN®

TORONTO • NEW YORK • LONDON
AMSTERDAM • PARIS • SYDNEY • HAMBURG
STOCKHOLM • ATHENS • TOKYO • MILAN • MADRID
PRAGUE • WARSAW • BUDAPEST • AUCKLAND

ISBN 0-373-29373-9

THE RANGER AND THE REDHEAD

Copyright © 2005 by The Woolston Family Trust

This edition published by arrangement with Harlequin Books S.A.

® and TM are trademarks of the publisher. Trademarks indicated with
® are registered in the United States Patent and Trademark Office, the
Canadian Trade Marks Office and in other countries.

www.eHarlequin.com

Printed in U.S.A.

Available from Harlequin Historical and
LYNNA BANNING

Please address questions and book requests to:
Harlequin Reader Service
U.S.: 3010 Walden Ave., P.O. Box 1325, Buffalo, NY 14269
Canadian: P.O. Box 609, Fort Erie, Ont. L2A 5X3

For Yvonne Mandarino Woolston and David Woolston

With grateful thanks to:
Tricia Adams, Suzanne Barrett, Kathleen Dogherty
and Brenda Preston

Chapter One

Nebraska, 1861

The column of black smoke spiraled into a noon sky so blue it looked painted. Will reined in his mare and watched the smoke dissipate in the hot wind. Seven, maybe eight miles ahead, he calculated.

He didn't have time to ride out of his way, but he had to know. McCray's orders would have to wait. Might even save him a few hundred miles of tracking a man through sage scrub and dried-up water holes. He nudged the mare forward across the scorching plain.

By the time he reached the smoldering remains of the wagon, he'd pulled his neckerchief up over his mouth and nose to block the acrid smell.

No horses. No oxen. Just the sheared-off leather lines where the reins had been cut. Sioux, most likely. Must be a wagon train up ahead; stragglers didn't last long out here.

He dismounted and prodded the piles of blackened cinders with the toe of his boot. Nothing. No bones, anyway. The wagon occupants must have fled on foot.

Will remounted, pulled his hat low to shade his eyes from the sun and scanned the flat plain in a slow circle. A person on foot would head west, toward water. Will turned his horse in that direction.

The old man lay facedown about four miles from the trail, an arrow in his back and a strip of his scalp missing. Poor bastard. Will slid off the horse and dragged the corpse into the shade of a cottonwood, untied his camp shovel and sweated for an hour digging a shallow grave.

He had just shoveled the last spadeful of dirt over the body when something caught his eye. A bit of white fabric fluttering on a branch of sage. He strode toward it with a sinking feeling in his gut.

Lace. A scrap of white lace, maybe torn off a petticoat. A cold chill crawled up his back. A woman.

He thought over the possibilities. If they'd wanted her dead, she'd be lying alongside the man, an arrow in her back. If they'd taken her alive, they'd use her for ransom or trade or…worse.

He mounted and rode in widening circles until he found another piece of lace trapped against a tumbleweed and the tracks of an unshod horse. They were moving north. Sioux country.

By the time he'd traveled another hour he'd recovered three more bits of white petticoat and the horses were easy to track. He figured it had to be White Eagle's band, and now he knew exactly where they were taking her.

Hell and damnation. That's the last thing he needed now, a dustup with White Eagle. But he spurred the horse forward anyway.

The air inside the stifling tepee smelled of dust and something dark and smoky. With each choking breath Charlotte thanked God she was alive and tried not to think about the fate of Mr. Thomas. Tried desperately not to think about her own fate, after the Indian had unceremoniously dumped her off his pony and shoved her inside the deer-hide structure.

Would they kill her? Charlotte swallowed. How did Indians kill their captives, starve them to death? Torture them?

Or would they force her to… She shut her eyes. Surely this was not the sacrifice Papa had meant when she'd told him of her plans. Why, *why* had Mr. Thomas not stayed with the wagon train? A weakened axle, he had said. When the Indians had swept toward them, the old man shouted for her to run.

She managed to get only a few hundred yards before she was snatched off her feet and tossed onto a hot, almost bare lap. By the time the Indian slowed the horse to a walk, her stomach felt as if it had been pounded with a sledgehammer. Unable to help herself, she had vomited onto the horse's withers, and the brave had backhanded her. Her jaw still ached.

It felt unreal, like a terrible nightmare. As if she were sleepwalking, not thinking or feeling, just sitting here like a trapped animal, trying to force her lungs to draw air in and out. Her mind felt as sluggish as cold molasses. And she was tired, so tired.

How long had she been here? From the heat inside the tepee, and the amount of light filtering in through the stretched skin wall, she guessed it was late afternoon. No one on the wagon train knew what had happened. No one would even know where to look for her.

Her throat was parched. Her belly was knotted, whether from hunger or terror she didn't know. It just hurt. Oh, God, what was going to happen to her?

She crept to the door flap, pushed it aside and peeked out through the crack. An old woman, her spine bent like a twisted hairpin, labored slowly across an open area surrounded by other tepees. She disappeared into the largest tent and did not reemerge. Charlotte's heart sank. Weren't they going to feed her? She would give anything for a sip of water.

Dropping the flap, she slumped down on the pile of buffalo robes stacked opposite the door flap and tried to pray. *Dear God, I feel so alone. Please, please help me to be brave.*

The buzz of insects in the stifling interior made her head pound. She rubbed her forehead to ease the dull ache.

An hour went by, she guessed. Maybe two. Lord help her, was she going to die here in an Indian camp? Would her life end before she had a chance to put her dreams to the test?

A faint scratching sound behind her turned her blood to ice water. A pause, then another *scritch-scritch* on the tepee wall, as if a fingernail were scraping over the tight deerskin. Then came a voice, speaking so quietly Charlotte wasn't sure she really heard it.

"Ma'am? Are you in there?"

She moved toward the voice, pulling her arms tight over her belly. "Who are you?" she whispered.

"Name's Bondurant. Followed your trail."

Charlotte felt a sudden urge to cry. The strips of petticoat she had torn off and dropped along the way had worked. Someone had seen them, followed them to the camp. She clamped her teeth shut over a sob.

"Ma'am? Are you—" he hesitated "—all right?"

No! She wanted to scream out the word, but caution held her tongue in check. "I am unharmed," she murmured. "But awfully thirsty. Have you come to take me away from here?"

"I've got a plan. Can you hold on a little longer?"

A plan! Oh, thank the Lord, the man had come to rescue her. "Y-yes, I can," she replied.

"Okay, listen up. I'm gonna circle around and ride straight into the camp."

Charlotte sucked her breath in. "You can't be serious. They'll kill you!"

She thought she heard a tired sigh. "Don't talk, ma'am. Just listen."

She nodded, then realized he couldn't see her.

"Whatever you see or hear, don't do anything. Don't react in any way, no matter what."

Again she nodded. "I understand, Mr. Bondurant."

She huddled in the airless enclosure, reminding herself to stay calm for what seemed like another hour, until an outcry of voices rang through the camp. Creeping forward, she again pushed aside a corner of the door flap.

A tall, hard-looking man in a black hat banded in silver conchas stepped a dark horse into the center of the camp. Children grabbed at his boots, his stirrups, screaming with excitement.

The man waited for some minutes, his hands folded loosely on the pommel, his face unsmiling. Gradually the commotion died away, and then an imposing Indian with a regal air about him approached. He waved the children away with a sweep of his arm and stalked toward the sinewy man on horseback.

Charlotte squeezed her lids shut. She couldn't watch one man murder another. Killing went against everything she believed in.

When she heard no scuffling sounds, no cry of aggression or pain, she opened her eyes and peered out. Five fierce-looking Indians were now gathered behind the chief—at least she thought he must be the chief since his beaded neckpiece was the most ornate. They studied the tall man with sullen faces.

The man—Mr. Bondurant, she remembered—raised one hand and spoke an Indian word. The chief did the same. Mr. Bondurant dismounted, but he kept his hands on the reins. She heard more Indian words, and then a guttural snarl as the brave who had captured her gestured toward her tepee, then touched his fist to his bare chest.

Bondurant shook his head. The chief barked something and the tall man unbuckled his gun belt, dropped it over his saddle and began to unbutton his shirt.

The chief pulled a wicked-looking knife from his

belt and offered it to the tall man. The brave who had spoken strode forward, touched the point of his own knife to the tall man's blade, and then the two men crouched and began circling each other.

In an instant Charlotte understood. They were going to fight for her! Her stomach roiled. Men—Indian or white—were brutal. She opened her mouth to cry out, but Mr. Bondurant's words came back to her. *Whatever you see or hear, do nothing.*

Through a haze of terror, she watched the Indian brave and the white man leap and plunge at each other. She wished for no man's death, but dear God, Mr. Bondurant had to win. He had to!

Dust from the men's scrabbling feet puffed into the hot air. Both fighters gleamed with sweat, breathing heavily through open mouths.

She turned her face away. She couldn't bear to watch.

A scream tore through the still air, and she jerked her head back to the tent opening. She couldn't *not* watch.

The white man, Bondurant, had sliced the Indian's chest. The brave lurched forward crazily, his knife arm flailing. She saw Bondurant's arm come up from below at the same instant the Indian's blade slashed into the white man's neck where it joined the shoulder.

Charlotte gripped the deer-hide flap and stared in horror as the brave's blade flashed again and met skin. Mr. Bondurant staggered as the Indian fell on him, his weapon lifted. But the brave's body slumped suddenly, slipped down the length of the white man's torso and crumpled at his feet.

A great shout went up. The chief stepped forward and

made a sign with his hand, and the white man nodded. Tears stung her eyes.

Footsteps came toward the tepee and stopped. "Ma'am?" a raspy voice said.

"I'm here," she called. Her jaw ached when she spoke and she realized she'd been clenching her teeth.

"Let's go." He moved the flap aside and waited.

She tried to rise, but her legs trembled uncontrollably. "Now? I am not sure I can."

"You can," he snapped.

She moved forward, her legs shaking under her weight.

Will opened his mouth to hurry her up just as she stepped through the opening. *Jupiter and Jesus, would you look at that!*

She had red, red hair, tangled wildly about her shoulders, and she wore a blue dress with a ruffle at the hem. The sight of her took whatever breath he had left clean out of him. Any second now he'd remember how to inhale, and she'd disappear in a puff of conjure-man smoke.

What the hell was a woman like her doing on a wagon train? Hell, an Indian would kill her just for her hair!

"Come on, ma'am." He shrugged into his shirt and pivoted toward his horse. "Stay close," he ordered.

He reached his hand behind him, felt her cold fingers wrap tight around his knuckles. When he reached the mare, he dropped her hand and strapped on his gun belt. He mounted, favoring his right arm, then reached his left down to swing her up behind him.

She stood looking at him, her upturned face white as his grandma's drawers. And her eyes. So wide and frightened, he wondered if she was going to faint. *Another damn Eastern female. Weak in body and frail in spirit.*

She didn't faint, just stood there clasping his elbow. Then he noticed her eyes again, and the spit went right out of him. They were a soft, dark gray, almost black, and the expression in their depths made him hungry for something he couldn't even begin to name.

Joseph, Mary and Jupiter, too! For a moment he forgot the stinging pain in his shoulder, the dust caked in his nostrils, and simply stared at her. In the next instant he bent to haul her up behind him.

"Wait! My skirt will tear."

"Ruck it up between your knees."

Without another word Will hoisted her behind him, signed to White Eagle and walked the mare slowly out of the camp. He held the steady, slow pace until they were out of sight. "Hang on," he said over his shoulder, then kicked the animal into a gallop. The woman made a little sound and grabbed him tight around the waist. For some reason he didn't want to think about, he didn't mind.

He rode until he was sure they weren't followed and the sun dipped below the horizon. His throat cried out for water and her head drooped against his back in exhaustion. In half an hour it would be full dark; better find a place for the two of them to bed down for the night.

Chapter Two

For hours Charlotte's backside bounced on the horse, her tailbone jolting hard against the animal's spine. Lord, how the man rode, as if the devil himself were chasing him. She could feel the muscles in his back flex under her cheek, but *his* body wasn't jouncing up and down as hers was. He moved as if he were part of the horse.

The animal's breathing grew labored, but the man holding the reins remained quiet as a stone. Suddenly he pulled up, and the mare danced sideways. When the man slipped off, Charlotte had nothing to hold on to.

She flopped forward, grabbing the saddle in desperation as he strode off into the brush. "Wha-what are you doing?" she gasped.

He didn't answer. A necessary stop, she reasoned. What a good idea!

She let her tired body slide off the back end of the horse and headed for a clump of bushes in the opposite direction. Scrunching down behind a stunted gray-green tree, she waited until she was positive only her head could be seen and then hoisted her petticoat and untied her muslin drawers.

When she rose from her sheltered spot, Mr. Bondurant was already mounted, watching her. She snatched up her drawers and dropped her petticoat over her knees.

His eyes looked amused, but his lips formed a straight slash across his suntanned face. She'd wager he never smiled.

"Finished?" he asked in a matter-of-fact voice.

"Quite."

"Mount up, then." He reached his left hand toward her.

"Where are we going?" she asked as she arranged her skirt to cover as much of her spread knees as possible.

"To make camp."

"Soon?" Relief made her voice wobble. She ached all over and her nerves were stretched like a too-tight clothesline, so taut she felt she might snap at any moment. When he didn't answer, she asked another question. "Where?"

His head tipped to the right. "Yonder."

Charlotte saw nothing that looked like a camp. No trees. No creek. Just a lumpy mass of huge, gray boulders tumbled over the hard earth, as if some giant hand had spilled them out of his palm, like marbles.

The man guided the horse straight toward the rocks. In a quarter of an hour she saw that the circle of stones enclosed a small space of bare ground.

Surely this wasn't the camp he referred to? Out here in the middle of nowhere? But when he lifted his leg over the horse's head and swung off the animal, she knew she was wrong. This *was* the camp.

She studied the area with sinking spirits. No privacy. No source of water. And only the hard ground for a bed. This was even more primitive than the camping arrangements with the wagon train.

She slid off the animal's back and groaned aloud at the pull of muscles in her back and thighs.

"Build a fire," he ordered. "Use buffalo chips."

Charlotte's stomach tightened. Of all the tasks she'd been assigned on the wagon train, gathering an apron full of dried buffalo excrement was the worst. She pressed her lips together, turned toward the plain and ordered her legs to carry her forward past the circle of boulders.

When she returned to the campsite with the front of her skirt full of dried buffalo dung, she found Mr. Bondurant squatting on his heels next to a small ring of stones he'd apparently rolled into place. She dumped her load of fuel on the opposite side.

"You ever dig a fire pit?" he rasped.

"N-no. Mr. Thomas, the man who drove my wagon, did that. However, I did do the cooking."

"My camp shovel's over there, next to that rock. Sorry I can't do it, but my shoulder feels like a lightning bolt's dancing over it and I'm right-handed."

"I will manage." *Just as soon as my knees stop shaking.* She tried not to think about the ordeal she'd been through, just concentrated on the shovel. She was lucky to be alive.

"Could you tell me about Mr. Thomas?" she asked hesitantly.

"Your driver? He's dead."

Her hands flew to her cheeks. "Dead! Oh, the poor man. How did he—"

"Sioux arrow," he said shortly.

After a long moment she asked, "And the wagon?"

"Burned. Nothin' left but cinders. What the hell were you doing out there alone, anyway?"

Charlotte choked back a sniffle. "We were the last in line, and when the wheel started thumping, Mr. Thomas dropped out. We were so far back the rest of the train didn't see us."

She said nothing, but the tears gathering under her lids spilled over. Her whole life, everything she had in the world was in that wagon—her mother's good china, her sewing machine, the trunk of work skirts and shirt-waists. And, most important of all, her precious books. Now she had nothing but the clothes on her back, not even a hairbrush! With a little moan, she let go of the shovel and suddenly sat down right where she stood.

"I'm right sorry, ma'am."

Charlotte bent her knees, clasped her arms about them, and began to rock back and forth. She couldn't stop trembling. "I can't believe it," she whispered. "One minute you're alive and the next you're—" Her voice cracked.

Mr. Bondurant shook his head. "Can't be helped now. Nothin' to be done but move on."

Move on? What was he talking about? She guessed it made sense in a rational way, but inside, where her heart hammered, she felt raw and bloody. "Move on," she murmured.

She wasn't sure she could do it again, gather up the remnants of her life and start over. It had been six months and she still woke up sweating with the same nightmare, her father and mother trapped inside the blazing rectory.

"I don't think I can move on," she said.

"For starters, get a fire going and boil some water."

"Water! Where would I find water out here on this plain?"

"In my canteen."

She retrieved the shovel, carried it to the rock circle. On her first try at digging the fire pit, the shovel head skittered uselessly over the hard-packed ground.

"Get down low and dig sideways." His voice sounded tight.

She knelt and scraped the shovel back and forth until she'd made a depression the depth of her clenched fist. Then she rose unsteadily and filled it with a mound of buffalo chips and dry grass.

He leaned forward with his tinderbox, but he couldn't strike a spark left-handed. After his fourth try, he held the steel out to her.

"Canteen's in my saddlebag, over there," he said, gesturing behind him with his head. "Couldn't lift the saddle off, though. Think you could? I'd sure like to rest my mount."

Charlotte nodded. At the moment, the flint and steel occupied all her attention. At last a spark caught and she bent low to puff her breath on the tiny finger of flame.

"Good," he offered.

At least he had some measure of civility; every word he'd spoken up to now had been an order.

Before she could draw breath, he issued another one.

"Boil the water. Kettle's in my saddlebag."

"Should I not retrieve your saddle first?"

"My shoulder's hurtin', lady. I'd like to deal with that first." She noted the raspy edge in his voice.

"Very well." She stepped past two of the largest boulders to where the horse stood, rummaged for the kettle, dumped in half the contents of his canteen and balanced the vessel on the circle of rocks surrounding the now-blazing fire.

"Anything else?"

"My knife, in the deerskin sheath. Whiskey."

Charlotte wrinkled her nose. Spirits had never been used in her home. Not surprising, since her father had been the minister of the Marysville Methodist Church. She had never tasted or even smelled whiskey.

She handed him the knife and a quart bottle of something labeled Red Wolf Bourbon. She could see he was in pain. Sweat stood out on his forehead, and his breath hissed in through stiffened lips.

"Drop the knife in the kettle and get my shirt off."

Suddenly she understood. He wanted her to doctor his wounded shoulder. Her stomach floated up into her rib cage and turned over. She didn't know how! Mama had let her roll bandages for the hospital guild, but Charlotte had never tended a patient in all her twenty-three years.

"I—I'm not sure I know what to do."

"Don't worry about it, ma'am. I'll talk you through."

Will watched her face turn white as a snowfield. With his uninjured arm, he uncorked the whiskey, downed a healthy swig and wiped his mouth with the back of his hand.

"Don't worry, I'm not gonna die. Just need to clean this gash out so it won't fester. That's what the knife's for, to—"

Her knees buckled. "I can't. I can't bear to hurt things."

"Better than gettin' gangrene and havin' some citified sawbones take my arm off."

She closed her eyes tight. "Isn't there another way? We could ride to a town, find a doctor."

"I can't gamble on finding one in time. Sorry, lady, but you're it."

He half expected her to keel over into the fire pit, but while her body swayed, she managed to stay upright. Will gulped another mouthful of Red Wolf and handed the bottle to her.

"No, thank you," she said. "I do not…"

Will shrugged. "You ready? It's getting dark. Won't be able to see much longer."

She nodded. "Tell me what to do," she said in a small voice.

Damn. He hated to saddle her with this, after what she'd already been through, but he guessed he didn't have a choice.

"If you're gonna faint, lean away from the fire," he instructed.

"I shall not faint."

She talked pretty brave, he thought. Like a lot of females. But when the road got rough, they turned tail and ran.

"Okay, now. Unbutton my shirt."

She bent her head and her small hands worked the buttons free one by one. A light, sweet fragrance rose from her tangled red hair, and Will took his time drawing the scent deep into his lungs. He held it there, like tobacco smoke, letting it soak into him. Even better than tobacco. This did something to his insides deep down.

He lifted his arm so she could slip his bloodstained shirt over his shoulder. It hurt like hell, and he sucked in a breath. The wound was so close to his neck he couldn't see it. "How does it look?"

"Dreadful." She wadded up the shirt and laid it to one side.

"Dreadful, how?"

"Well, it's crusted with dried blood. And down inside the cut it's black with dirt. It's red and swollen here—" she touched her forefinger to his skin "—and it feels hot."

Will groaned. Infected. He'd bet a month's pay Five Feathers had purposely spit on his knife blade.

"Gotta clean it out," he said.

"Oh, no." Her face went even whiter.

"Use the knife to scrape it clean. Take it slow and don't miss anything."

For a moment she looked like she was going to throw up all over his chest. He pressed his fingers against her cheek and turned her face to one side. "If you feel sick, aim the other way," he said dryly.

"I will not be sick."

He would have laughed at her bravado, but he knew it would hurt too much.

"Wrap your hand in something. The knife handle will be hot."

She reached under her blue skirt and he heard fabric ripping. A band of white muslin appeared, which she wound around her hand. Then, using a small twig, she fished the knife out of the bubbling kettle and grasped the handle.

He flinched when the blade touched his skin, worked to keep his body from jerking as she traced the point along the length of the cut. "I'm sorry," she said in a hoarse voice. "I'm so sorry."

"Just keep cutting," he said between gritted teeth. "Use the blood to wash the dirt out."

He watched her small white teeth bite down onto her lower lip as she probed. Sweat broke out on her forehead, but her eyes stayed focused as she leaned over him.

Will clenched his jaw hard. He'd think about how good she smelled instead of the line of fire crawling along his neck. About how her hand shook, gripping the knife. How her breath hitched whenever the least sound escaped his clenched teeth. Hell, she was green as grass and scared to death. Women always thought they could stand up to anything. Damn few even came close.

"How're you doing?" he managed between strokes of the blade.

"Fine," she said with no inflection. She unwound the strip of fabric from her hand and blotted at the welling blood. "How are *you* doing?"

"Fine," he lied.

"I'm almost finished." She glanced up into his face. Her gray eyes were hugely dilated, and tears rolled over the film of grime on her cheeks.

"I hate hurting you." The words sounded choked.

Will swallowed painfully. "I'm kind of enjoying it," he lied again. "Don't stop. Finish it up."

"I always finish what I start, Mr. Bondurant." Her voice shook, but her knife hand had steadied some. "There's an awful lot of blood…"

"Damn right," Will joked. "Might be enough left over to keep me alive."

She surprised him with a soft laugh. Then she drew the knife along what felt like his shoulder bone. "Shall I tear up some bandages?"

"Yep," he said when he could talk. "When you're ready."

"I'm ready."

"One last thing," he said. "Pour some of that whiskey into the cut."

"Won't it sting?"

Will stuffed down a snort of laughter. "Yeah, like hell. Don't waste any."

She upended the bottle, and he hissed and squirmed and swore under his breath until the worst was over.

"I'm finished now," she said softly. Again she flipped up the hem of her skirt and ripped wide strips off the white petticoat underneath. The sound was raw and gritty, like his shoulder felt.

"Won't have much of that petticoat left at this rate," he managed.

"It is of no consequence." She looped a strip of muslin around his shoulder and bound it.

"Tighter," he ordered. She tugged the band with all her strength.

"Tighter," he repeated.

"I cannot. I am not strong enough."

"Spirit-wise or body-wise?" The words leaped out before he could stop them. There was no call to needle her. No call whatsoever.

She looked directly into his eyes. "I would like to think my spirit is strong, Mr. Bondurant. My arm, however, is a woman's."

She wrapped his wound with the remaining bandages, then sat back to survey her handiwork. "Well," she said in a pleased tone. "I guess that wasn't so bad after all."

Will rolled his eyes. "You're speakin' for yourself, I imagine."

"I wasn't sure I could do it," she murmured.

"Lady, you're a lot tougher than you look." He lifted his good arm and downed another slug of whiskey.

"Well, it's a little like diapering a baby."

Will coughed until he choked. And damn, did that hurt!

"You have a child, ma'am?"

"No, I do not."

"Married?"

"No."

"What were you doing on that wagon train?"

She lifted the whiskey bottle out of his grasp and tipped it to her lips. Her eyes watered, but she didn't cough or carry on. "I am traveling to Oregon territory. An Indian school near the Warm Springs Indian reservation. I am a teacher."

She was a spinster, Will supplied silently. But she sure didn't look dried up and flat-chested like most of them he'd known in Texas.

"I will retrieve your saddle now." She marched a bit unsteadily to his horse, loosened the cinch, and pulled the leather contraption toward her. Staggering under its weight, she managed to manhandle it over near the fire and drop it where he pointed.

"Good," he said. "Now we've only got two problems left."

She turned slowly and studied him in disbelief. "What problem could there possibly be after those we have already met in the past twelve hours?"

Will took his time answering. No use scaring her. No use riling her up, either. "Well, for starters, we're short of food and just about out of water. And if that isn't enough, it gets cold at night and we've only got one blanket."

Chapter Three

Will rested near the fire, not wanting to move his throbbing shoulder, while the woman—hell, he didn't even know her name!—dumped a handful of coffee into the kettle of water and began to lay out their meager supper. A sharp prairie wind kicked up, curling into their small boulder-sheltered camp, and by nightfall he was shivering. He prayed it was from the cold, not infection.

With his left hand he draped the blanket around his shoulders, but he still couldn't get warm. By the time he wrestled his sheepskin coat out of his saddlebag and drew the sleeve on over his good arm, he felt dizzy. The whiskey, he guessed. And an empty stomach.

She divided the single strip of dried beef into two portions, handed him one, then poured some sandy-looking coffee into the single mug. Hunkered before the fire, they ate in silence, making each bite of beef last as long as possible and sharing the overboiled contents of the coffee mug.

"Mr. Bondurant," she said at last. "I am extremely grateful for your rescuing me, but I do wonder about something."

"Yeah? What's that?"

"What are you going to do with me?"

He'd been wondering the same thing. Every hour he spent dallying around a fire pit was an hour lost on a trail growing colder. "Tonight, keep us warm as best I can. Tomorrow, try to catch up to the wagon train."

She swallowed the last of her dried beef and turned to face him. "Thank you for what you did, Mr. Bondurant. I am in your debt."

Will sighed inwardly. He didn't have a choice, really, once he'd spotted those bits of petticoat lace. A man just couldn't ride on, no matter what business he had elsewhere. He knew more than he wanted to about White Eagle and his renegade braves. They stole horses, burned wagons, murdered settlers and captured women and children. They even harbored outlaws on the run.

But in the years he'd been crisscrossing this territory, White Eagle had also supplied him with valuable information and saved him from at least one wild-goose chase. Often they marked a horse they'd traded to an outlaw on his way to Canada so Will could identify it.

The woman looked at him with expectation in her steady gray eyes.

"Yes, ma'am? You say somethin'?"

"I asked you why you did what you did today. Why you fought that Indian?"

"Only way I could bargain you away from him. The

Sioux, and the Comanche, too, they put a lot of stock in one-upping their enemies. Counting coup they call it."

"You mean by attacking each other?" She straightened her spine and sniffed. "That is barbaric."

"Maybe. But to get you away from Five Feathers, I had to lower his status to where he owed me something. Something of value, like horses or… " He left the obvious unsaid.

Her eyes widened into two slate-colored pools. "But you risked your life! And you don't even know me!"

"Five Feathers figured you were worth it. He didn't want to give you up, so I had to force the issue." Will swallowed and then looked off into the night. "I told him I had the right. I told him you were my woman."

If she was gonna pitch a fit, she'd do it now. He braced himself.

She leveled a cold look at him. "So you lied. The Lord frowns on that."

"You think you'd be sitting here if I'd told that Indian the truth? That I'd never laid eyes on you before? Didn't even know your name?"

"Oh. I see." Will waited, but she said nothing more.

Will studied her. That's the sum total of her anger, that he'd lied? She sure thought like an Easterner. Things were either black or white, right or wrong, with no in-between. A Bible-thumper, with perspective only as long as her nose. Pretty enough, but closed minded. Hell, she wouldn't last a week in an Indian school. He'd best push his advantage while she was still so reasonable.

"No, you don't see," he growled. "The West is no place for a woman like you."

A thoughtful look came over her face, a little frown creasing between her dark eyebrows. "On the contrary, Mr. Bondurant, I believe the West is just what I need. And I believe I may be just what the West needs."

"Huh!"

"You think me rigid, is that it? Narrow-minded?"

He gulped. She'd all but read his mind. "Aren't you?"

"I am trying hard not to be. That is one reason I am going out West."

"What's the other reason?"

"One I am not prepared to discuss at this time," she said in a prim voice.

Will stared at her, then hitched his jacket up over his unsleeved shoulder and changed the subject. "You're gonna need a hat to shield your face from the sun tomorrow. Maybe a clean shirt. Your dress is bloodstained."

"And," she said with a sigh, "a hairbrush."

He gazed at the tangle of red curls tumbling past her shoulders. "Not sure Fort Laramie will have a hairbrush. That's where your train was heading, right?"

"Yes. We embarked from Independence three weeks ago. My home is—was—in Hardin County, Ohio."

"We'll try to catch up to them tomorrow."

She stood up suddenly, plunged her hands into her skirt pocket and drew out a ragged-looking cookie. "Oh! I just remembered this!"

With care she broke it into two pieces and offered him one. "It's a molasses cookie. One of the women on the train baked day before yesterday."

Something about her gesture, sharing what might be

the last morsel of food she would see for a day or two, made him swallow hard. He nibbled the edge of the cookie, taking his time about it because he couldn't think of a thing to say. He watched her do the same, eating slowly with her cupped hand underneath to avoid losing even a crumb.

Before he'd swallowed the last hint of molasses, she startled him with a question. "How shall we sleep tonight?"

"Under the blanket." He wondered why he growled the words at her.

"Together?"

"Close together. To keep warm. We'll use my saddle for a pillow."

She eyed the hard leather object and her frown deepened. "It looks…uncomfortable."

"It is uncomfortable. Can't be helped. Unless you'd rather put a rock under your head?"

"Please do not joke, Mr. Bondurant. I am aware of our…um…unusual situation out here on the prairie. I quite appreciate your candor."

Will released the tension in his chest he hadn't known he'd carried. He'd half expected her to break down in hysterical wails or protest her womanly virtue or some such rot, but she'd surprised him. Again. She wasn't thrown off stride by what had to be done.

He'd thought for sure she'd pass out cold when she'd cut into his wound and the blood welled out, but she hadn't. Now she accepted the sleeping arrangements with neither artifice nor argument.

He'd have to roll that around in his mind some. He knew one thing, though, now he'd thought about it. He was looking forward to it.

Night on the plains brought a velvety blackness so thick a man couldn't see a foot in front of his face. To-night Will thanked God for the dark; moonlight would outline the silhouette of his horse, and he'd rather not put temptation in the way of an Indian on the prowl. Even the fire the woman had built was a risk; the darker it grew, the farther the glow would be visible.

He rose to kick dirt over the flames.

"What are you doing?" she shot.

"Dousing our fire." He couldn't see her face, but he could imagine her expression. Wary as a fox and twice as skittish.

"Do we have to put it out? I mean, it's so warm and comforting to have a fire."

"Yep. Sorry." He kept scraping his boot across the ground, kicking the gritty earth over the hot coals. He waited a minute to let his eyes adjust to the dark. When he could distinguish her hunched form from one of the boulders surrounding them, he reached for the single blanket he'd laid beside him.

"We'd best get some sleep."

The dark form didn't move. Will pondered how to say what had to be said. Finally he knelt next to her. "I don't mean for this to sound rude, ma'am, but we've got a decision facing us."

"Yes, I know. The wagon train."

"Tomorrow, yes. Right now it's more, well, personal."

"Please explain, Mr. Bondurant."

Will waited for a minute to get his words in order. "The decision is, are you gonna bed down with me, or am I gonna bed down with you?"

Here it comes, he thought. The Outraged Female reaction. Well, go on, lady. Get it over with.

But again she surprised him. "Is there a difference?"

"If you sleep with me, it's on my terms."

"Your terms? Whatever do you mean?"

"I pick the spot, and I decide how the blanket gets shared." He waited, giving her a chance to make a speech about propriety and then lay out her proper-lady objections.

Again she surprised him. "I shall sleep with you, Mr. Bondurant. After all, it is your blanket."

Will blinked. No protestations? No false modesty? This was one practical woman. One down-to-earth, no-pretense woman. A very rare breed, in his experience. Suddenly he wondered what her name was.

He rose. "Come on, then." Using his left hand, he found his saddle where she'd dropped it and spread out his saddle blanket. On top of that he laid his sheepskin coat, woolly side up, and unrolled the single blanket.

His right shoulder throbbed every time he moved. He lowered himself onto the coat, tucked the blanket over his back and rolled toward her on his good side.

"Come on down here next to me. Put your backside into my...uh...put your spine against my chest. Then flap over your side of the blanket to cover you."

She hesitated only a moment, then crouched beside

him and without a word, not even a hitched breath, she stretched out as he had instructed, with her back against his chest.

Will dropped his arm over her waist as far as he could with the stiffness and pain from his wound gnawing at him. When she pulled the blanket over herself, it wrapped them in a snug woolen cocoon. Already the heat of her body penetrated his, and he knew he was warming her, as well. Something about that made him feel good. Made him feel...necessary. Needed.

Whoa, boy. Look at this head-on. It's nothing but a sensible solution to a chilled, windy night in the open, and that's all. They could keep each other warm. Period.

He closed his eyes. Her breathing sounded slow and even. Her rounded bottom was tucked tight into his groin. She might be bloodstained and travel-sore, but she damn well felt good next to him. The scent of her hair mingled with dust and the smell of the doused fire. Roses and ashes.

"Mr. Bondurant?"

"Yeah?" He kept his eyes closed.

"Thank you for sharing your blanket."

"Get some sleep," he muttered. He tightened his arm about her, and with a sigh she snuggled closer. Lordy lord, this was the best thing he'd felt in years.

Charlotte lay next to his hard, warm body in a haze of exhaustion. All the difficulties of these past weeks, the hollow ache of uncertainty, the fear, all of it faded into the background. She'd never thought that life could so quickly narrow down to just the essentials—food, shelter, warmth. Companionship.

It had been a horrible day, almost as bad as the day her father's rectory had burned. But for some reason she felt happy. Almost joyful. She had learned something: the more simple and elemental one's needs, the more satisfaction in meeting them.

She had survived. She had filled her stomach. And in a moment or two she would drift off into sleep.

God is good.

And Mr. Bondurant was right up there with Him.

Chapter Four

Charlotte lay motionless beside him for some minutes, listening to Mr. Bondurant's gravelly voice muttering something, but she couldn't make out the words.

The huge boulders surrounding their camp looked like brooding gray animals, waiting and watching while overhead a new moon rose and the stars winked like tiny silvery eyes. A coyote cried out in the distance.

Deliberately she eased her body out from under his heavy arm over her waist, and began to edge away from him and scoot free. He grumbled and flopped over onto the space she had left.

As quietly as she could, Charlotte got to her feet and walked to the perimeter of the boulder circle, drinking in the sharp, clean air of the sagebrush-dotted plain.

The air was much colder than she'd expected. The wind cut, and her unprotected ears began to ache. She took a single step beyond the edge of camp and a low voice froze her in her tracks.

"Just where the hell you think you're goin'?"

"I, um, thought I heard something."

"Probably a coyote."

A rustling in the direction of their shared bedroll told her Mr. Bondurant had turned over. Or perhaps he had sat up and at this very minute was watching her.

"You gonna hunt it down all by yourself?" Amusement colored his sleep-roughened voice.

Her cheeks burned with embarrassment. Thank heavens there was no illuminating moonlight. "To be frank, Mr. Bondurant, I intended to make a trip to the…necessary."

"Out here we call it a latrine, ma'am."

Another rustle. She guessed he had stretched out once more. She turned away and headed for the biggest of the boulders, one she could squat behind and remain unseen. Again, his voice stopped her.

"If you're goin' beyond camp, take my sidearm."

"Oh, no, I—" The thought of a revolver in her hand, even a ladies' derringer, raised the hair on her neck.

Something thudded at her feet. "Be careful, it's loaded."

Charlotte sprang backwards, lost her balance and sat down, hard.

"It's not *that* loaded," he said in a dry voice. "Pick it up."

She patted her hand in a tentative circle. When her fingers met the cold steel, she sucked in her breath. It was a machine for killing, and killing was wrong. That commandment had been drummed into her for as long as she could remember.

"Pick it up," he repeated. "You got a pocket in your skirt, don'tcha?"

"Y-yes."

"Then slip the pistol in there and forget about it. Unless you need it," he added. She heard a muffled chuckle.

"And don't forget to release the safety before you fire. You know what I'm talkin' about?"

"Of course," she lied. She lifted the heavy metal object as gingerly as she would a scorpion. Its weight in her hand seemed to press on her heart; she could never, never take the life of a living creature, even a coyote. She dropped the loathsome object into her pocket, then rose and stepped outside the circle of boulders. The pistol's bulk was a constant reminder of man's evildoings in a sinful world. Somehow carrying it on her person made her feel sinful, as well.

Just as she hiked up her skirt, his voice floated over the rock to her. "If you're not back in ten minutes, sing out so I'll know you're okay. Otherwise, I'm comin' after you."

The brusque way he issued orders annoyed her. She finished her business and stalked back to the bedroll to find him sitting up, waiting for her.

"You get chilled out there?"

"My backside did," she said without thinking. Again she was grateful he couldn't see her face; it was so hot he could probably feel the glow.

He chuckled. Then chuckled again, louder.

"Oh, for mercy's sake, it was just a slip of the tongue!"

"Good one, too," he said. "Made me laugh for the first time in the last seven days. You're good company, Miss…?"

"Greenfield. Charlotte Greenfield."

She dropped to her knees beside him and touched the gun barrel against what she hoped were his ribs.

"Here's your pistol. I think that safety thing is still on."

"You *think?* Jesus, lady—"

"Please, Mr. Bondurant. Do not take the Lord's name in vain."

His hand groped over her skirt, found her fingers and lifted the weapon from her grasp. She heard him slide it under his side of the saddle. Then his hand closed around her forearm and he gave it a gentle tug. "Come on and get warm."

She let him guide her down beside him and she curled up with her spine pressed into his chest. When she bent her knees, his legs followed, to rest against hers.

She had never been this close to a human male. Never dreamed such a juxtapositioning of bodies could feel so good. So warm and comforting and…just good.

Charlotte Marie, have you lost your senses?

Quite the contrary, she answered with a little shiver of fear. Today she had been through hell—*oh Lord, forgive me for using that word, but I am glad, glad, glad to be alive.* It did not matter that the muscles in her thighs screamed every time she moved, or that her stomach rumbled with unsatisfied hunger. Or that her dress was bloodstained and her wind-burned skin grimy with dirt.

She was aware of the fine line between life and death in a way she had never been before. It mattered only that she was safe, protected by a brave and courageous man.

She sent a silent prayer of thanks up to the starry sky and closed her eyes. Her last thought was about his arm, how warm and solid his arm felt snugged about her waist. Surely, a man was one of God's better creations.

Will's lids opened to find a pair of slate gray eyes studying his face, her gaze so unswerving he began to sweat. He knew he had a four-day whisker shadow, that his lips were dry and cracked from the sun. His hair must be awry and grown too long anyway, and he hoped to God the expression in his eyes was friendly. He'd been so gun-shy around females for so long he figured his gaze was none too civilized.

She just kept staring at him with that imperturbable expression in her eyes. Then she gave him a smile that made her whole face come alive.

What was she so damn happy about?

"You are a nice man," she said softly. "A friend."

Her face turned the color of scarlet paintbrush. "I mean," she said, staring down at her knotted fingers, "that I have never—" she hesitated "—had a friend who was a man."

Will swallowed over a choking sensation.

He swallowed again. Time to change the subject. "Ma'am, could you take a look at my shoulder? It feels like my whole arm's on fire."

She straightened as if someone had jabbed her spine with a hatpin. "Yes, of course."

She untied the outer bandage and lifted the folded inner pad to peek underneath. "Hold still." Frowning, she bent closer.

"It's red. Swollen."

"Damn." He rotated his shoulder and swore again.

"Button it up," he instructed. "We've got some hard riding ahead of us."

Will heated the remains of last night's coffee over a tiny fire, and they gulped it down scalding hot, again sharing the speckled tin mug. All too aware that his last provisions were used up, he tried not to mention the words *bacon* or *breakfast*.

They packed up the kettle and the bedroll, and Charlotte wrestled the heavy saddle onto the horse just as the rose-peach tint of dawn faded into the piercing blue of a midsummer sky.

He patted the hard leather saddle. "Up there," he ordered. "Put you in front today, be easier on your...easier on you."

"That is most considerate."

"Trouble of it is, ma'am, I can't lift with but my left arm, so...you think you could mount up first?"

She stepped into the stirrup and swung her right leg as high as she could manage. She couldn't lift it high enough. When she tried a second time, Will stepped close and boosted her up with his good hand on her rump.

And wished he hadn't. He could feel the curve of her hip, the soft swell of her buttocks. At this moment he didn't feel anything like a "friend." He just felt like a man.

Charlotte felt the horse shift as he swung up into the saddle and settled himself behind her. Heavens, her backside and his...well, their proximity was awfully close. Even closer than last night, when he'd curled his body around hers. To keep them warm, she reminded herself. Now, because there were two of them and only one saddle, their touching like this was inevitable.

His forearms brushed her breasts on either side as he took up the reins. Propriety dictated that she pull away, but as she was practically sitting on his lap, there was nowhere to pull *to*. Besides, she liked sitting within the circle of his arms. She felt safe. Protected. If she leaned her head back, it would rest against his chin.

Oh, she couldn't do that! Her hair was full of dust and would smell wood-smoky, if not downright rank. Right this minute he was no doubt smelling it. Her. The thought made her cringe.

Her dress was filthy, perspiration-soaked and blood-stained, and her petticoat must be even worse. As the horse moved under her, she tried to decide which she wanted more, a hairbrush or a bath. A willow-twig toothbrush would be nice, as well; her teeth felt positively fuzzy when she ran her tongue over them.

He didn't say a word for at least an hour. After a while, his hand lifted to his neck, and he fiddled with something. Finally he laid a wrinkled blue bandanna on her lap.

"We're riding straight into the sun. Drape this over your face."

"What about you?"

"I've got a hat. You don't."

She fashioned a loose kerchief over her head and pulled it forward to shade her nose. After another quarter hour she wished she could shade her mouth, as well. Her already windburned lips felt sun-parched and cracked. No amount of tongue-licking seemed to help; the unrelenting hot, mouth-parching wind under the merciless sun sucked the moisture away in an instant.

Her throat ached for water, but she knew she could not beg a drink from the half-empty canteen. Not yet. Not until they were desperate.

"Sometimes it helps to suck on a pebble," he said. He reached into his vest pocket and pulled out a handful of small, smooth stones. "Here." He pressed one into her hand. "Might not find water right away."

Charlotte surveyed the barren plain head of them. The grass was seared, the heat shimmered and danced into mirages.

"How will you find water?"

"Look for somethin' green, a tree maybe. Better yet, two or three trees. Leafy ones."

The thought of water became an obsession as the morning stretched on. They stopped every hour or so to rest the horse, and Charlotte noticed how he patted the animal's nose and talked to it, apologized for not providing feed or water.

"How're you holding up, Miss Greenfield?"

"Just fine," she rasped. "The pebble helps."

"Kinda magic, in a way, gettin' water from a stone. Like Jesus makin' wine out of a pitcher of water."

At the biblical reference, Charlotte came to attention. "You are a religious man, then, Mr. Bondurant?" It was not a question she could have asked in polite society—but joined together in a struggle for survival, social conventions didn't seem to matter.

"Nope. The Good Book's a good book, all right. But out here a good horse and a gun make more sense."

"You are quite wrong, Mr. Bondurant. Out here the teaching of the Bible should be foremost in a man's—

or a woman's—mind. It is nothing less than the difference between savagery and civilization."

"I don't have enough spit to argue it now. Maybe after we find water."

"Won't we run into the wagon train soon? They will have water."

"Not soon enough. We're gonna need to drink first."

Charlotte sighed. "And a hairbrush. And a clean dress. I must smell like a…like a moldy old cheese."

He sniffed at her hair. "Nope. More like a smoked ham."

She laughed, and the pebble in her mouth flew past her teeth. She shoved it back inside with her fingers.

"Shall I tell you what you smell like?" Without waiting for an invitation, she turned her head to one side, pressed her nose against his shoulder and inhaled. He smelled of leather and sweat and something smoky. She rather liked it.

"You smell…good."

He snorted. "Better pull that bandanna down farther, lady. Your nose is dying."

"You have to admit, smelling each other helps to keep our minds off water."

He exhaled so forcefully the back of her head tickled. She guessed he was trying not to laugh.

The thirstier she got, the harder it was to think clearly. Thoughts drifted in and out of her consciousness, swirled together and came out all mixed up.

The sun, for instance. The higher it rose in the sky over their heads, the whiter it grew, the hotter the wind, the more numerous and wavery the mirages. Twice she pointed at what looked like a sparkling lake on the horizon, only to have it disappear as they drew closer.

Mr. Bondurant rode at the same slow, steady pace and did not alter their direction. Apparently he knew where he was going. She knew only that Fort Laramie lay somewhere ahead of them, because that's where her wagon train was heading. She prayed there would be a sutler's store at the fort; she desperately needed to replace some necessities.

To keep her mind off her parched throat, she thought about what kind of hairbrush she would purchase. Not silver-backed, like her mother's. Too expensive. And not—

Mr. Bondurant touched spurs to the horse and it jolted forward. "Trees ahead," he said in a hoarse voice. "Cottonwoods."

Charlotte's heart thudded. Cottonwoods must mean water, a stream, maybe even a river. She tried not to think about tumbling off the mare and splashing into a deep, cold pool.

Will circled around to one side of the water hole, stepped the mare into the leafy brush and pulled up. He'd watch a minute or two, just to make sure it was safe.

Listening to the trickle of the spring feeding the shallow pool of water was almost as maddening as rocking along on a horse with a woman's buttocks riding his thighs. No way to assuage the temptation.

"What are we waiting for?" she whispered.

"Don't know. Just…something." Will scanned the horizon and stiffened.

Yep, something. Two riders, heading straight for them.

Chapter Five

The closer the two riders came, the tighter Will's jaws clamped together. The man riding an underfed dun-colored mare laid his quirt into the obviously exhausted animal. Strings of foamy saliva dribbled from the animal's mouth, and Will's stomach clenched. He hated to see an animal pushed beyond endurance.

The second man, taller and leaner, wore his hat pulled so low Will could see only a dark chin. Will slid off the mare and helped Miss Greenfield dismount, then carefully removed Sandy's bridle and laid it on the ground.

The woman stared at him. "Why did you do that?" she whispered.

Will pressed her down behind some scrubby bushes and hunched beside her. "The bridle jingles every time the mare moves her head. They'll hear it."

"But why must we hide at all? Surely there is plenty of water for all of us?"

Will spoke in low tones, keeping his gaze on the approaching horsemen. "It's not the water I'm worried about." With the flat of his hand he pushed her shoulders to the ground, then stretched out prone beside her.

"Don't say a word until they leave. And don't make any noise."

She nodded obediently and lay belly-down, her chin resting on her folded arms. Will removed his hat, settled it over the bright tangle of red hair to hide it. First chance he got, he'd have to find her a bonnet. Maybe from one of the ladies on the wagon train.

He watched until the riders drew up at the edge of the water hole, then silently lowered his face close to hers and propped his chin on one hand.

The tall man dismounted and scooped up water in the crown of his hat. Will saw now that he was an Indian. Peeking out from under his hat, Charlotte noticed it, as well, and touched his arm.

"Not Sioux," he breathed. "Comanche."

He figured the red man was tracking for the other; maybe came up from around Texas. Odd that a Comanche would ride this far out of his home territory; could the smaller man be another Ranger on a hunt? Will wondered what—or who—they were looking for.

When the short man removed his hat to drink, he felt Charlotte's body stiffen. Hell's bells, did she know the man?

The two men guzzled their fill, dipped in their canteens, then let the horses drink. The sound of water being slurped up made Will's tongue swell until it felt like a bone-dry washrag. It was torture to hear that wet, trickling noise and not be able to drink. His throat was so clogged with dust he could hardly swallow.

He glanced sideways at Miss Greenfield. She'd scrunched her eyelids tight shut, and as he watched, she ran her small pink tongue over her dry lips. Too bad she couldn't close her ears to those seductive sounds.

Will knew they were both so thirsty they could do something foolish like bolt for the water hole. He'd bet a month's pay she'd never suffered this kind of deprivation before; to her credit, she lay motionless, as he'd instructed.

The Indian still squatted at the water's edge, studying the muddy perimeter, while the smaller man tore off his shirt and denim trousers and immersed his long-john-encased torso in the small pond.

Will wrinkled his nose at what the filthy underwear would do to the water, and immediately discarded the possibility that he might be a Ranger. A Ranger would never foul a water hole.

The splish-splashing went on until Will felt a scream building in his throat. *Don't waste it, for God's sake. Leave some for us.*

He cut his gaze to Miss Greenfield. Eyes still closed, she had clenched her hands into fists. A small black spider was crawling across her cheek. She had to feel the brush of its legs, had to guess what it was, but she neither cried out nor moved to brush it off.

Will tried to flick it off, but the insect lodged in the hair at her temple. With stealthy movements, he nudged his left hand under her hat and squashed the insect against her skin to kill it. She gave a little shudder, and he saw her mouth tighten. She was trying not to scream, too.

He almost laughed out loud. Hell, they made a good team. She followed orders without objection, and he issued them without hesitation. Like Uriah the Hittite and King David. Except he didn't much like what he remembered about King David.

Listening to the watery noises coming from the pond was tangling up his thoughts. He looked over at Charlotte.

The remains of the spider were smeared over the skin near her temple, but she hadn't moved an inch. Her sunburned face showed a single, irregular wet streak through the dirt on her cheek. Tears? After all she'd been through she was crying over a spider?

His heart made an odd half-flip and folded into itself. If she had moisture enough to cry, her body wasn't so water-starved she couldn't last another twenty minutes until Long John and his Indian friend got back on their horses and rode on. Even so, he couldn't help feeling sorry for her. She'd already been through an experience no lady should have to endure, and they hadn't even reached Fort Laramie yet.

A guttural shout brought his attention to the Comanche, now mounted and obviously anxious to be moving. Long John splashed out of the water hole, pulled on his pants and draped his shirt around his neck.

When the two men rode out, Will rose without making a sound and watched the direction of their dust trail. Their route led away from the tracks Sandy had made; with any luck, they'd seen the last of the Comanche and his friend.

He tried to wet his lips and groaned. With any luck, there'd still be a swallow of drinkable water left in the pond.

"They're gone," he said. "Let's go."

Without looking back at her, he stepped out of the brush and whistled for Sandy.

"You think a horse that thirsty will obey you?" The doubt in her voice made him smile.

"These plains could flood all the way to Texas and Sandy would be there when I whistle. Horses are easier to train than people." It was one of the few things Will still believed in. That and his rifle.

A long silence fell while she apparently considered his statement. "I wonder why," she said finally.

With a whicker the animal trotted up to him, then stepped down to the water hole and lowered its head. Will untied the canvas-covered canteen and filled it while Sandy slurped at the pond's edge. "Wish I had some feed for you, girl," Will murmured. "You've earned it."

He picked his way through the scrub toward the water hole. Behind him he heard the crunch of dry leaves as Charlotte scrambled to her feet. Her steps drew closer, until they were right on his heels, and then she marched past him, her long stride determined.

When she reached the water, she waded straight in up to her hips, then flopped forward to float full length in the wet. Facedown, she gulped huge mouthfuls, choking when she couldn't swallow fast enough.

At first her blue skirt belled up around her, but as the fabric soaked up moisture, it drooped into the water like a gunnysack full of wet hay. Will watched while she pushed her skirt and petticoat under the surface and then plunked her backside down on the muddy bottom. Water reached to her neck, sloshed under her chin.

Hell, he was thirsty, but he sure didn't want a bath. He moved around the perimeter until he found a place where the water looked reasonably clear and knelt to drink. He tried not to think about Long John's sweaty underwear, concentrated instead on sluicing cool water over his head and neck.

When he looked up, she was alternately scrubbing at the bloodstains on her chest and scraping her wet hand against her skin where he'd mashed the spider. Just like a woman. They'd go through hell without a whimper, but they can't wait to get clean afterward.

He watched her try to stand up and suppressed a snort of laughter. Her sodden skirts kept her off balance, and no amount of dragging them to one side or the other made any difference. When she finally regained her footing she found she couldn't pull the weight of her skirts through the water. At the rate she was inching forward, she'd be pond-walking all day.

Will ran his hands over his face and neck, shook the water out of his hair, and shucked his boots. With a swallowed grumble he started toward her.

"Next time you go wadin', take off your skirt." He looped his good arm around her waist and pulled her forward.

"I will surely remember that. Thank you."

He sent a covert glance to the front of her dress. The rusty-looking bloodstains were still visible, but she didn't look half-bad with that sky-blue fabric clinging to her form. Not bad at all.

They splooshed out onto dry ground, water streaming off their garments. Miss Greenfield tried to wring out her skirt by twisting the hem into a spiral. The tighter she twisted, the higher both skirt and petticoat rose, until he could see all the way up past her knees to her lace-edged knickers.

Will turned his back. At last she gave up and let the soaked material drop to the ground with a soft plop.

When they were mounted and on their way once more, Will let himself relax for the first time. They had water, and a good horse. His shoulder still hurt, but now that he was cooled off and some rested, it didn't bother him so much.

"I doubt we're gonna catch your wagon train before nightfall. Tomorrow we'll take a shortcut to Fort Laramie."

She said nothing.

"Ma'am?"

Still nothing.

"Miss Greenfield? Anything wrong?"

"Those two men at the water hole," she said. "Who were they, do you think?"

Will tipped his head to one side, trying to see her face. She was frowning, and her mouth had straightened into a narrow line.

"Dunno. Does it matter?"

"I am not sure. One of them looked…familiar."

A nerve jumped in Will's jaw. "Yeah? Which one?"

"I must be mistaken. I haven't seen one single face I recognized since I left Ohio."

"Which one?" Will pursued.

"The short one."

"Long John. He looks like a lot of *hombres*, kinda

shifty-eyed and underweight. Probably a city fella. I reckon that Comanche is trackin' for him."

She sucked in air as though she hadn't drawn a breath in a while. "Tracking? You mean he—the short man—is after someone?"

"Could be. Could also be that he's a stranger to the country out here and needs a guide to, say, find a ranch he's fixin' to buy."

She relaxed at once, releasing the tension in her shoulders along with a shaky sigh. "I am sure you are correct, Mr. Bondurant."

The nerve in his jaw twitched again. All of a sudden Will was not so sure.

Chapter Six

Mr. Bondurant nudged Charlotte's shoulder. "Look, up ahead."

Her first sight of Fort Laramie loosed a swarm of flutters in her belly. They were still a mile or so away, but even from here she could see the gleam of white canvas sails in the noonday sun, and dark dots that must be teams of oxen. The wagon train!

Inexplicably, she began to cry. The whole terrible ordeal—the Indian camp, the heat and dust, the thirst—it was over. She was safe. Safe!

"Tonight, Mr. Bondurant," she said in a choked voice, "we will fill our stomachs with meat and hot biscuits. And," she added, her voice rising in excitement, "we will sleep warm, all night!"

"But not together," he said under his breath.

She mopped at her eyes with her bandanna. "I am alive at this moment because of you, Mr. Bondurant. You must know how grateful I am. How much I am in your debt, and always will be."

"Don't want a debt obligation," he said brusquely. "Look there, they've spotted us. Sending a rider to investigate."

Charlotte waved one arm over her head, then thrust both arms into the sweet-smelling air.

"He sees you. Stop jumping around, you'll spook Sandy."

"I am quite sure Sandy is better trained than that," she replied with a grin he couldn't see. "You told me she never spooks."

He pressed a hand down on her shoulder. "She's never been bounced on before."

"Hello!" Charlotte shouted at the approaching horseman. She dropped her arms to her sides. "I'm sorry, Mr. Bondurant, what were you saying?"

She heard him chuckle deep in his throat. "It'll keep."

The rider, a young, fresh-faced lieutenant, widened his eyes at the sight of her. "Beg pardon, ma'am. With that neckerchief over your head I thought you might be an Indian squaw." He turned his horse in to ride beside them.

"I came much closer to that fate than was comfortable. Mr. Bondurant rescued me and has brought me back to connect with my traveling party. I was afraid we would miss the wagon train."

The lieutenant's head came up. "Bondurant? Will Bondurant?"

"Reckon so," Will said.

"Well I'll be— Captain heard you were dead."

"Reckon not." His low voice at Charlotte's back sent a shiver up her spine. "Your sutler about?"

"He'll be back this afternoon. Captain has the key, though, in case you're in a hurry to stock up."

"Afternoon's fine."

Charlotte laid a hand on his arm. "Oh, but Mr. Bondurant, I do need a few necessities. A hairbrush, and a new apron." Oh, but she had no money! She would have to ask for credit.

"And a hat," he said near her ear. "A blue one." The last words he murmured so only she could hear. It gave her the oddest twinge of pleasure to think of Mr. Bondurant noticing that she wore blue. "Tell Henry to put it all on my tab."

The two horses entered the parade grounds, where a dozen wagons had been pulled into a loose circle. Charlotte slid her leg over the mare's neck and dropped to the ground. Emigrants poured out of the conveyances to investigate, and as word spread, women flocked to her, enveloping her in suffocating hugs, wiping their eyes and peppering her with questions.

"Are you all right, child?"

"Yes, Essie, I am quite all right." She squeezed the thin woman's hand.

"Did you…?" The older woman leaned closer. "I mean, were you captured by the Indians?"

"I was, yes. Mr. Bondurant here came to their camp and…rescued me."

"The men found your wagon," a plump woman in a crisp white apron said. "You lost all your possessions, even your clothes." She studied Charlotte's stained blue dress.

"Is there anything you need, dearie?"

She looked up at Mr. Bondurant and suddenly remembered his injury. "Yes, there is. We, Mr. Bondurant that is, needs the doctor!"

"Doc Warburton's wagon is on the end," a woman chirped.

Will touched his hat to the ladies and stepped the mare forward in the direction indicated. As he approached the big Conestoga, he began to think about saying goodbye to Miss Greenfield.

He didn't want to say too much. Hell, he didn't know what to say to the woman he had ridden with and slept beside the last two days. But...something. He wanted to say some words to her before he rode out.

He thought about it while he sat in the doctor's wagon, smelling hot dust and carbolic acid. The gray-bearded man unwrapped the bandage and inspected the knife wound in Will's shoulder. "What'd you use to clean this?"

"Blood. Some whiskey."

"Hmm." He poked a gnarled forefinger around the cut. "Hurt?"

"Yeah."

The doctor chose another spot. "Here?"

"Yeah. Worse."

Dr. Warburton doused the wound with disinfectant, put on a clean bandage and stepped back. "You're a lucky man, Bondurant. The knife missed an artery, and you can still move your arm. But the wound's infected. I'd recommend some hot poultices and a few days rest."

"Nope." Will pulled the sleeve of his shirt up his arm and began buttoning it. "Gotta move on."

"I'd like to keep an eye on that shoulder. You joinin' this train?"

"Nope. I'm ridin' west." He shook the older man's hand carefully; his right shoulder still smarted. "What do I owe you, Doc?"

"Nothin'. You brought the Greenfield girl back to us, that's payment enough. One of our scouts found what was left of the wagon. Too bad about the driver, Aaron Thomas."

Will said nothing. Might be better if the wagon train party didn't know the exact details of Mr. Thomas's end.

The doctor's wife bustled into the wagon. "You'll stay to supper, won't you? You and Miss Greenfield? Then we're holding a meeting to find her a place."

"Sure, ma'am. Thanks." It wasn't just the promise of a hearty meal after two days of skimpy rations. He wanted to see that Charlotte got settled.

"Miss Greenfield's over at the sutler's," Mrs. Warburton said. Will nodded. He knew she'd repay him when she reached Oregon and took up her teaching position. She was that kind.

He liked that about her. Seemed kinda funny, considering his own checkered background, but he liked the notion he got when he looked into her clear gray eyes and felt he could see all the way through her and then some. Innocent, that was the word.

He turned Sandy into a roped-off corral with a dozen other horses and fed her oats from the crown of his hat until she turned her head away. Then he strolled over to the sutler's, just in case Miss Greenfield wanted his opinion on a new bonnet.

She looked up the instant he stepped through the doorway. "Mr. Bondurant, how is your shoulder?"

"Doc says you did a fine job." She looked so pleased with herself Will had to laugh. "We're invited to supper."

"I have purchased a new dress and an apron. And," she added with a wide smile, "a new hairbrush set. I cannot wait to comb the snarls out of this tangle."

"Too bad there's no water hole around, so you could have a bath," he joked.

"Oh, but there is! I mean, I can have a bath. That nice lieutenant arranged for it in the captain's quarters. The captain is not there at the moment, but his wife is. She thought it a splendid idea. Oh, everyone is being so awfully kind."

Will wondered if their generosity would extend to offering her food and shelter when it came down to it.

Before suppertime, Will walked over to the Warburton's wagon to find Miss Greenfield bending over a blackened Dutch oven hung over a cook fire.

"Charlotte." He'd never used her given name before; it just slipped out.

She turned, an oversize metal spoon in her hand. "Hello, Mr. Bondurant. Are you hungry?"

"Yeah, I reckon so."

She dipped the spoon into the Dutch oven contents. "It won't be long, now."

"Can you stop for a minute?"

"Yes, I suppose so." She laid the spoon aside. "Is anything wrong?"

"I came to say goodbye. I'll be leavin' tonight and, well, I wanted it to be private."

She smiled in a way that tightened his throat. Damn, this was harder than he'd thought.

Charlotte moved toward him and extended her hand. "Thank you for all you have done, Mr. Bondurant. I will never forget you."

"It was a pleasure, Miss Greenfield. Charlotte." The truth of his statement surprised him. Despite the hardships, it *had* been a pleasure. He grasped her hand and held it. It felt small and warm in his, and he was suddenly afraid to squeeze it too hard. No woman he'd ever known had shaken his hand.

Her grip tightened, then eased as she withdrew her fingers from his grasp. "Goodbye, Mr. Bondurant," she said softly.

Will swallowed. "There's somethin' I want to say."

Her head came up, her face expectant. "Yes?"

"Uh, well, just that you're not like, well, most females."

She laughed. "I've been told that all my life. I hope I haven't been too much of a trial?"

"Nope. I meant it. About the pleasure, I mean."

"You are very kind, Mr. Bondurant." She stretched on tiptoe and brushed her lips against his cheek. "Thank you. That's the nicest compliment I have received in years."

Will's eyes burned.

"I can't let the stew scorch," she said quickly. "I told Mrs. Warburton I would watch it."

He watched the swirl of her skirt as she spun back to the cook fire, caught a flash of a snow-white petticoat. She'd put the credit he'd offered her to good use. Damned practical woman. And she sure smelled good.

When the meeting commenced after supper, wagon master Abraham Ludlow got himself caught in Will's craw. First, he proposed that Charlotte wait for the next wagon train through Fort Laramie instead of "crowding up on this one." Just now, Ludlow had presented the idea of a lottery.

Neither idea sat well with Will. A man didn't just shove a woman around like she was a sack of cornmeal.

Will stood next to Charlotte and listened to the arguments back and forth until he'd swear he'd been nibbling jimsonweed. "Folks are already doubled up after they lost two wagons crossing the Platte," someone said. "Taking on needed supplies in Fort Laramie means no extra room for passengers." It went on and on until the anger boiled up inside his gut. Without thinking, Will stepped forward.

"Are you saying none of your wagons has room for one more passenger?"

The wagon master spoke to Will's question in a clipped, sure-of-himself voice. "Well, yes, mister, that's the way I see it. All of our wagons are loaded to the limit. Shouldn't be too surprising, as most folks are carryin' their whole lives out to Oregon. That's why I suggested a lottery."

"Might be better to find someone among you that would welcome her, even with the crowding, 'stead of dumpin' her on someone that might not?"

Out of the corner of his eye, he watched Charlotte as he spoke. Her skin glowed and her red hair, caught up in a ribbon at the back of her neck, shone coppery-gold in the firelight. But her lips were pressed together and her shoulders were hunched up tight.

All through supper she'd seemed edgy about something. Maybe she guessed what was coming—a lottery to see who got stuck with her.

Now she stood motionless, the wagon master on one side and Will on the other, while they dickered over her fate.

"Mr. Ludlow," she said at last. "This is ridiculous. I will find my own passage among these good people." She spun to face the group of emigrants gathered around the Warburtons' cook fire.

Will saw her swallow, and then her head came up. "I can cook and tend children. Teach them their letters. I have no belongings to burden your already heavy wagons, only the garments I wear and some personal necessities, and I am willing to wash clothes and sleep under a wagon. Now, who among you needs a helpful woman?"

A long, awkward silence fell. People shuffled their feet, but no one spoke up.

Charlotte's cheeks turned pink with embarrassment. "None of you?" Her voice trembled. "Not even one?"

"I'm awful sorry, Charlotte," Essie Walker whispered. "But with the new baby…"

"I'll take 'er," a scratchy voice shouted. A giant of a man in a ragged plaid shirt and stained trousers stepped out of the crowd. "I'd kinda fancy havin' a pretty woman along. An' she won't hafta sleep under no wagon, neither."

Charlotte edged a step closer to Will. Even without touching her, he knew she was shaking. She smelled so sweet and flowery it muddled up his insides.

"That wouldn't be at all proper," the doctor's wife protested. "A young, unmarried woman with a big unmannerly oaf like you, Harve Jenkins? I should say not!"

"Well, no one else wants her," the giant said. "Least-ways nobody spoke up for her, now did they? And I'll make her right welcome. I already said she could sleep in the wag—"

Suddenly, Will toppled the man to his knees with a two-handed punch square into the side of his whiskery jaw. He felt the impact all the way up to his shoulder, like a hot coal had been shoved into his armpit, but he was glad he did it anyway.

The giant got to his feet and swayed toward Charlotte, who stood without moving. Will turned to one side, nursing his arm and waiting for the pain slicing into his shoulder to ease. He wanted to punch the man again, but he didn't think he could do it.

When he turned back, Charlotte was moving away, toward the doctor's wife. Before she reached the plump woman's side, she swung around to look at him.

He started toward her. When he reached her side, she pivoted suddenly and without a word fell into step beside him.

"I can't let you do it," he said in an undertone.

"I must. I must reach my school in Oregon."

"Yeah, I know that."

"No, you don't, Will. It's all I've ever wanted to do, ever since I was a little girl. And especially now that Mama and Papa are…" Her voice choked off. "Papa ministered to his congregation, and Mama ministered to the sick. I need to do something with *my* life that matters. I've prayed and prayed on it, and it's what I must do."

"I guessed as much."

They walked a few yards away from the crowd, and

then Will stopped. "I want you to be careful around Jenkins."

"I am careful around any man, Mr. Bondurant."

"Charlotte, there's men and then there's men."

"I haven't a choice, Will. It's like a hunger inside of me, to be useful. I have waited all my life for this. But I will be careful, I promise." She tipped her head up. "Will I ever see you again, do you think?"

"Most likely not. I'm tracking to the west, but…"

"I see," she said, her voice quiet. "Our paths will not cross again."

Will disliked the sound of that. "Where's your school, exactly?"

"I don't know, *exactly*. All I know is that it's an Indian school in a place called Christmas Lake Valley."

"Where will you live while you're teaching?"

"The Indian agent promised me a small cabin of my own. Why are you asking all these questions? Saying goodbye is harder than I thought." She gazed at him with tear-shiny eyes. "Oh, Will."

"Dammit, don't cry," he said. "Makes it worse."

"I—I know." She snuffled, then fished in her apron pocket for a handkerchief. "I feel quite…close to you."

"Not sure why that should be. We've had hard travelin'."

"It's because we are friends, Will."

For a moment he couldn't speak. "Yeah," he said at last. "Sure thing."

"I will always be glad of that," she said softly.

"I've gotta ride out tonight." Sure was hard talking over the lemon-size lump in his throat.

"Yes," she murmured. "I thought you would."

They stood facing each other in silence while the sounds of the camp fell away. Neither moved for a long minute and then Will bent and brushed his mouth over hers. Deliberately he kept his hands in his pockets, afraid if he touched her he would pull her hard against him.

"Goodbye, Charlotte," he breathed against her lips.

She made no response, merely looked at him, her eyes shimmery.

Will turned and walked quickly away.

Chapter Seven

For the first hour on the trail, his mare was more fractious than Will had ever seen her. Outside of an occasional soothing pat, he wasn't paying much attention to his horse tonight; he couldn't stop thinking about Charlotte.

Hell, he missed her already. The rub of her slight spine against his chest as they rode together had just plain felt good. Now the space between his belly and the saddle horn yawned cold and empty.

Okay, so he missed her. And he couldn't stop worrying about her. Like Charlotte, a hunger gnawed at his gut, but his was for revenge, pure and simple. No amount of praying would change it.

He couldn't give it up. The thought of revenge on his half brother had gotten him through the black hell of the past year, had kept him going when everything he had loved had been destroyed. The only time it hadn't eaten away at him was these past two days with Charlotte.

Yeah, he missed her. She was an overeducated, Bible-quoting Easterner with her head in the clouds. She was closer to some kind of holy mission than she was to hardscrabble reality. He still couldn't stop thinking about her.

What if Jenkins bullied her?

No concern of Will's if he did. He had his road before him, and Charlotte had hers. He couldn't spare the time to guide a greenhorn to Oregon. Not with the score he had to settle with Luis.

What if Jenkins worked her too hard?

So what if he did? Charlotte had a mind of her own; she could sure enough stand up to Jenkins.

What if he put his hands on her?

Will clenched his teeth. Don't think about it. Charlotte could take care of herself. She would be all right. He'd already lost three days, and the trail grew colder with every passing hour. He had to keep going.

What if Jenkins forced himself on...

He drew rein so hard Sandy stumbled. With a muttered curse, Will turned the mare and headed back toward Fort Laramie.

When he caught sight of the shadowed outline of the Fort Laramie encampment, he kicked Sandy into a gallop. Passing through the parade ground perimeter, he headed for the cluster of canvas-bonneted wagons. Where would she be sleeping?

He dismounted, preparing to go from wagon to wagon until he found her. He hadn't taken a dozen steps before he spotted the tall figure of a woman a ways from camp. Jesus, must be near three in the morning; what was she doing out there?

She stood with both hands propped on her hips, staring up into the star-scattered sky as if giving God a piece of her mind. Will moved toward her, and she turned at his step. He halted an arm's length away.

"Will?" The disbelief in her voice made his heart jump. He stepped in close and their gazes locked. In that split second, it all came clear to him.

"I've got business elsewhere," he said. "I can't hardly believe what I'm doin'."

"Nor can I."

"It'll be hard travelin'."

"I know. I will manage."

"Well, then, I reckon we'll need another horse."

In the morning, Will looked over Captain Cutter's personal remuda and picked out a gray mare with good lines for Charlotte, then talked Mrs. Cutter into a saddle and bridle, as well. "John knows I'm good for it," Will said.

"He'll be sorry he missed you."

"I'll be back this way, Nora. Look for me before winter."

Now he stood with Charlotte in the sutler's store for the second time in two days. From the look on her face he thought it might be the last he'd see of her.

"Trousers?" she demanded. "A man's trousers?"

"And a shirt," Will said to the sutler. "Two shirts. Make 'em green plaid. Boots. A hat. That one." He pointed to a gray felt with a wide brim. It would match her eyes. At least it would when they weren't dark as slate and shooting sparks the way they were now.

Charlotte propped her hands on her hips. "Mr. Bondurant."

"Two of those blue bandannas," Will added. "Got any good wool blankets, Henry?"

"Mr. Bondurant," Charlotte said again.

"Then we'll need some provisions—coffee, bacon, couple boxes of cartridges." He turned to Charlotte. "Anything special you'd like?"

"I'd like to be listened to!"

"Okay. I'm listenin'."

"I…well, I cannot wear trousers and a shirt! Those are men's garments. It is entirely improper for—"

"Yeah, you're right."

"Well, then." She turned to the sutler with a smile. "Instead of trousers, I would prefer—"

"Wrap 'em up, Henry."

"Sure, Will. Anything else?"

"Cigarette makins'. And, you got any cigars?"

Charlotte spun. "You wouldn't! The smell of a cigar is perfectly noxious."

"You're right, I wouldn't. They're for you."

He thought about stepping out of the way, but there wasn't room enough in the aisle for her to take a good swing at him. And anyway, she didn't try, just stared at him, her eyes snapping.

"Listen, princess, there are a few things we'd better settle before we ride out."

"I should think so!"

"One, it's a long, hard trip to Oregon from here."

"Any schoolchild knows that, Mr. Bondurant."

"Two, you'll be safer on the open trail if you look like a man."

She opened her mouth to protest, but he cut her off. "Third, I'm the boss. You do what I say or you stay here at Fort Laramie."

"Yes, *sir*," she snapped. She was mad as a wet cat, he could see that plain enough. What he hadn't expected was the sheen of moisture in her eyes. He could out-muscle her, but he couldn't deal with tears.

"Dammit, don't cry."

She turned blazing wet eyes on him. "Is that an order, *sir?*"

"Yep."

"Very well." She mustered a trembly smile at the sutler. "The blue shirt, if you please. Not the green."

Then she stunned Will by starting to laugh. The sutler looked from her to Will, shrugged his shoulders and joined in. At that, Charlotte laughed all the harder.

Will eased the tension in his chest with a choked guffaw. Lordy, the look on her face. She looked like a fluffed-up banty chick that would sooner peck his eyes out than eat. To him, just the expression on her face was funny; but he did wonder what had set Charlotte off into a fit of giggles in the first place.

He signaled Henry to package up the garments. She might not like wearing the duds, but she'd see the sense of it sooner or later. In the meantime, he hoped she was smart enough to take his word for it.

Well before sunup, Charlotte crawled out from under the quilt Mrs. Warburton had provided. Careful not to wake the older woman, she stood up in the wagon and quietly pulled on the new denim trousers and the man's shirt Will insisted she wear.

The trousers gaped at the waistline, but she cinched them up with a boy's leather belt the sutler had thrown in. The shirt hung off her shoulders, but at least she could tuck it in. The boots, however, fit tight enough to pinch. No wonder cowhands would ride rather than walk even a short distance; walking was positively crippling.

Last, she twisted her hair into a knot, secured it with seven precious tortoiseshell hairpins Mrs. Warburton had given her and clapped on her new gray felt hat. Thank the Lord Elda Warburton had no mirror. Charlotte had an uncomfortably clear idea what she must look like.

She couldn't think about that now. If this is what she had to endure to do what she'd set out to accomplish, then she would do it. She might look outlandish, and she might be uncomfortable, but at least she knew she would be safe with Mr. Bondurant, and she would reach Oregon before fall.

She peeked through the canvas into the silent circle of wagons. Good people, mostly. But she wouldn't be sorry to leave Harve Jenkins behind. In the middle of the night, he'd tried to sneak into the doctor's wagon where Charlotte lay sleeping. Mrs. Warburton had smacked him with the heavy wood coffee mill.

Her only regret was that she could not be entirely truthful with Will. At least not yet. She wouldn't lie. Lying was against her principles. She just wouldn't mention the matter until the time came.

Will appeared riding Sandy and leading a gray mare,

saddled and ready. She watched him dismount and lift a saddlebag from the back of the gray. Moving quietly, he stepped to the back of the wagon and spoke in a low voice. "You awake?"

"Yes."

"Dressed?"

"Y-yes."

Will handed the empty saddlebag through the bonnet opening. "Load up whatever you're bringin' with you. Your bedroll and foul weather coat are already tied on your horse."

Charlotte folded up her old blue dress and her new one, two petticoats, a change of undergarments and the extra man's shirt Will had talked her into. Then she rolled her new hairbrush set into her apron and stuffed everything into the leather pouch. The other half of the bag already clanked with a speckled enamel mug and a matching plate, a spoon and a worn pocketknife with initials carved into the handle. It had to be Will's.

"I'm ready," she whispered. She tossed the loaded saddlebag down to Will, then knelt beside Mrs. Warburton's pallet and touched her shoulder.

"I'm going now, Elda. Please don't worry about me."

The older woman sat up and clasped her arms around Charlotte. "I'm not worrying about you, my girl. You've got plenty of spunk. It's that man you're traveling with."

"Mr. Bondurant?"

"His shoulder's infected. My Samuel says it might get worse, so you watch him close, you hear? Won't do to lose your guide."

"I will watch him, I promise."

"God bless you, child," the woman said with a sniffle.

Charlotte kissed her soft cheek and rose. When she stepped out onto the driver's bench, she stood for a moment, peering through the gray shadows at the man mounted on the handsome black mare. She wondered why Will called the animal Sandy.

Dr. Warburton was shaking Will's hand and saying something, and then Will's face turned in her direction. In the peach-colored dawn light she saw his eyes widen.

Of course. She knew she looked ridiculous. Not only that, dressed as a man she found she did not know how to move or sit or even stand naturally. She never realized how much of her identity depended on the garments she wore, the ruffles, the constricting corsets and especially the soft lace-edged smallclothes underneath, where no one could see them.

She took a deep breath, managed to plunk her new boots down onto the ground and wobbled unsteadily toward her horse. Dr. Warburton boosted her up into the saddle and laid the reins in her hands.

"Good luck to you both," the doctor said gruffly. "Take care of each other."

Will clicked his tongue and reined Sandy away. Charlotte fell in beside him and they stepped their mounts away from the wagons, across the parade ground, and headed west just as the first blush of rose-pink washed the sky.

Will waited until it was full light before he turned his head to study the woman riding next to him.

God damn. What he thought he saw when she first stepped down from the wagon was sure enough what he'd seen. She looked no more like a man than a horse looked like a camel. The oversize shirt covered her breasts, all right. As long as she kept it buttoned up to her chin so no one could glimpse the swell of white skin below her neck.

He'd purposely chosen trousers that would fit loose, but even so, beneath the baggy denim the curve of her hip screamed female. Not only that, he thought with an inward groan, at the first river they forded the denim would shrink to a formfitting garment he didn't care to think about at the moment.

The hat looked good, though. Pulled down over her hair like it was, that tangle of red curls wasn't visible. Soon as it got a bit dirty, it'd look a lot more natural. But what the hell was that straggling down the back of her neck?

A shiny copper curl spiraled just below her earlobe. "Damn."

She sent him a frown. "Whatever can be wrong?"

"You look too...female."

"Impossible. The trousers are so stiff and heavy I can scarcely bend my legs, and the shirt..." She glanced down at her chest. "The shirt is too big and floppy, and I feel positively flat without my corset!"

"Not near flat enough," Will growled.

She turned scarlet. "Few men would study my chest as thoroughly as you are doing, Mr. Bondurant."

"Think so, do you?" She knew less about men than she knew about trail travel. "You'll look a lot less clean and shiny with a layer of trail dust."

Maybe she was right about her chest. He knew what

was underneath the blue plaid shirt; anyone they chanced to meet on the trail wouldn't. A stranger would take her at face value.

He hoped. But one more look at her chest convinced him. He shrugged out of his buckskin vest and handed it over. "Wear this."

"Whatever for?"

"It'll cover your...cover you better."

She gave him a sideways glance, but pulled the vest on over her shirt.

"Better," he said. "You ever try smoking?"

"Certainly not. My father preached against both spirits and tobacco."

"Can't help that. I want you to learn."

"Really, Mr. Bondurant, I hardly think—"

"I'll teach you how when we stop for our nooning."

He watched her mouth tighten into the stubborn line he'd seen before. "I have a feeling, Mr. Bondurant, this journey is going to be far more educational than I ever dreamed."

He reined up short. "You want to go back? Call it quits?"

"Certainly not," she replied instantly. "I would much prefer what I will learn from you to what I might have learned from Mr. Jenkins."

Will nodded. "Good enough. First lesson—get your face dirty." He spurred Sandy into a trot and swung in ahead of her, purposely letting her eat his dust. When he looked back, she had pulled the blue bandanna at her throat up over her nose and mouth.

Will wheeled the horse, rode back and pulled it down

below her chin. "Just give it five minutes, princess. Let the dust settle over you."

Her mouth thinned even more, but she nodded. He spurred ahead again, and when he reined up a few minutes later, letting her catch up to him, her face looked good and grimy.

"Now, rub the dirt in."

"I beg your pardon?"

She looked outraged. Her thin, aristocratic nose shone through the layer of grime like a pink beacon. If he opened his mouth he knew he'd laugh, so he clamped it shut, reached over and rubbed the dust and grit into her skin with his thumb. Jupiter, those gray eyes of hers could shoot arrows right through a man.

He couldn't stop now. He brushed off the excess dirt with her bandanna. Something must have shown in his eyes, because all at once she was laughing.

Will stuffed her bandanna into her vest pocket. "What's so damn funny?"

"You are," she gasped. "When your thumb moves, your jaw moves in the same way, as if you were grinding oats."

"Yeah?" He didn't feel the slightest bit amused.

"Like this." She demonstrated with her own thumb on *his* cheek, her own jaw waggling with each movement.

Will caught her hand, pushed it away from his face. "Best ride on, we're wastin' daylight."

"Yes, *sir!*" Charlotte snapped her spine straight. "But it *was* funny."

The look on his face, unsmiling and dark as a thundercloud, told Charlotte she had gone too far. One did not tease a man, she guessed. Especially if he was a friend.

Twisting in the saddle, she took a long look back at the trail behind them. Puffs of dust marked their route over the flat, dun-colored ground. Ahead rose gentle hills and beyond them she knew were mountains and high valleys. Surely she was doing the right thing?

She turned her face up, breathed in the sweet morning air, scented with sour grass and sage, and a rush of exhilaration swept over her.

"What are you smiling about?" His question startled her.

"I am smiling because…because I love the goodness of the earth," she announced. "I see the Lord everywhere, Mr. Bondurant. In every living thing. Don't you?"

"Nope."

"Are you not a believer, then? Do you not love the Lord?"

"Dunno how you can love in the abstract, Miss Greenfield. Love's more than an idea."

Gracious! Charlotte stared at the lean, dark face of the man riding beside her. Something told her this man carried secrets that would make hers seem very small and insignificant indeed.

Chapter Eight

They made their nooning in the shade of a stream-fed stand of ash and juniper trees. Will's shoulder hurt, but he managed to build a small cook fire, boil up some coffee and lay out their meal—strips of jerked venison and a couple of apples the sutler had tossed in when Will had picked up the supplies.

Charlotte stretched out full length on the sandy creek bank, pillowed her head on her folded arms and gazed up into the green branches. "Where are we, exactly?"

"On the banks of La Bonte Creek. Under a juniper tree."

"How do you know that, the name of the creek, I mean?"

"I've ridden this country before. Got an uncle built a trapper's cabin in the mountains yonder." He settled himself a few yards away, positioned his hat over his face and closed his eyes. Maybe she would take the hint.

"What were you doing out here before, riding this country?"

Will kept his eyes closed. "Chasin' a man."

"An outlaw?" Her voice tensed with excitement.

"Kinda, yeah."

"You mean you didn't know for sure?"

"Not 'til I caught up with him." From under his hat brim he watched her raise up on one elbow, her quick breaths fluttering the blue shirt that outlined her breasts. How come she was so full of questions?

"And then what happened?"

"I shot him."

For some reason he enjoyed her shocked intake of breath. He liked teasing her.

"You didn't," she said in a hushed voice. "You couldn't."

"Could and did. He drew on me." Will smiled under his hat. She was easily surprised; the trip west wouldn't be dull.

She sat bolt upright. "But…but that's murder!"

"No, it isn't," he said. "It's killing, but it's not murder. Not out here."

"I fail to see the diff…" Her voice trailed off and then her eyes sharpened with interest. She peered at him so intently it made him squirm.

"You are a lawman of some sort, are you not? A marshal or something?"

"Was," Will said after a moment. "Texas Rifles. This is Nebraska, not Texas, so out here I'm on my own."

"Are you chasing someone now? An outlaw? A bank robber?"

He gave up trying to catch a nap. All he wanted to

do now was shut her mouth up any way he could. He pushed his hat off his face and got to his feet.

"Time for your smoking lesson." He had a purpose in mind, but he didn't want to alarm her by explaining.

She sat bolt upright. "Smoking is a dreadful, smelly habit. And it's practically a sin. Why must I learn?"

"Because I say so. In your right vest pocket you'll find a packet of papers and a tobacco pouch." He tried not to grin at the look of distaste that came over her face.

Her fingers scrabbled where he directed. "The paper looks awfully…flimsy."

"It'll do the job. Dump some tobacco out on one of the papers. Hold it in your palm, like this." He cupped his hand under hers. Instantly she lifted her fingers away, but he caught her wrist and spread them open again. Her palm felt like wet silk.

Frowning in concentration, she shook out a hefty pinch of the fine-cut leaf while Will tried to control his breathing.

"Try not to spill too much, the stuff's expensive."

"W-what now?"

"Take it and roll it up into a little sausage. Now lick the open edge, press it and twist the ends closed."

Her pink tongue came out, working up and down the paper, and he swallowed hard. Storm clouds were gathering in her eyes.

"Now," he directed, "put it between your lips."

He watched her gingerly rest one twisted end of the cigarette on her lower lip, then close her mouth over it. Good, he thought. No more talk.

"In the other vest pocket you'll find a tin box of sulphur matches. Take one out and scratch it on something rough—that rock by your foot'll do."

She made three swipes at the stone surface and suddenly the match flared up in her face. With a little cry, she dropped it onto the sand where it fizzled out. The cigarette followed.

Will shook his head. "We could spend all day at this, at the rate we're goin'."

"It was your idea," she snapped.

"Pick it up," he ordered.

She bent to retrieve the cigarette, brushed sand off the end, and poked it between her lips again. Without moving her mouth, she enunciated a careful "I'm ready."

Will walked forward, dug another match out of the tin and scratched his thumbnail across the head. Cupping his hand around the guttering flame, he held it toward her.

She drew back, eyes wide. Will reached his good hand to the back of her neck and held her steady as he moved in closer. The flame blackened the twisted cigarette tip and he sucked in the pungent scent of tobacco.

"Breathe in," he instructed. The end smoked, then bloomed red, and he knew she'd inhaled. He braced himself.

He remembered his first draw on a cigarette. Luis had howled with laughter and pounded him on the back to stop his coughing. It was Will's tenth birthday; Luis had learned to smoke when he was seven.

Charlotte didn't cough or carry on as he'd expected. Instead, her eyes reddened and filled with tears. He plucked the cigarette from her lips and drew on it himself. Damn good tobacco.

When he held it out to her again, she swallowed hard and pinched it between her thumb and forefinger. "I would prefer not to continue," she said in a quavery voice.

"I know you would. This time don't breathe in too deep. If it comes right down to it, you can fake it."

She looked up, her eyes darkening. "Mr. Bondurant, you pay no attention to me at all."

"Oh, yeah, I do. Maybe not the kind of attention you'd approve of, but you're a hard woman to ignore."

Her eyes widened. "Nonsense! Men have always ignored me. Papa scarcely heard a word I said, and you are no different."

Will opened his mouth to argue, then changed his mind. She was right. She didn't want to do this smoking thing, and he was pushing her. Best stick to the cigarette business; she'd cool down when it was over.

"Like I was saying, to fake it, just hold the cigarette there in your lips, and every so often flick off the ash at the end. Like this." He pantomimed removing the cigarette from his lips, holding it in the curve of his hand and thumping it lightly to drop the ash.

She mimicked his movements exactly, her gaze holding his in an unspoken challenge.

"Yeah, you got it. Good." His voice came out raspy.

She sniffed, then grinned, and with a flourish stuck the cigarette back between her lips. Will patted her shoulder. "I think you'll do fine, Charlie."

"I think," she said, her pinched tone indicating she held a cough at bay, "my Methodist father must be spinning in his grave."

Will packed up the coffeepot and kicked dirt over the

fire. He watched her surreptitiously, half expecting her to turn bone white from the smoking lesson and toss up her meal.

But she didn't. She was a fast learner, all right. She climbed back on her mount, and still Will kept his eye on her. Damned if she didn't smoke her first cigarette all the way down to a butt.

Again he stifled a grin. The preacher's daughter didn't approve of smoking, but she could sure as hell rise to a challenge.

Then, when they trotted out of the shade and picked up the trail, Will noticed something else. She took extra care not to brush against his sore arm. Damn square of her.

Will half dozed in the heat, hoping she was too drowsy to talk as the merciless sun beat down. Within ten minutes, her voice dashed that thought.

"I certainly do not mean to pry, Mr. Bondurant, but you have not yet answered my inquiry. Who are you chasing?"

Jesus, she was like that mutt he and Luis had adopted, the one that never gave up until he'd gnawed a leather boot into pieces.

"I know you don't mean to pry, Miss Greenfield, but you are."

She pursed her lips. "You don't know who the man is? Or you do know but you won't tell me?"

"None of your business."

Charlotte blinked at him. "If anyone in Marysville, Ohio, spoke so bluntly, and with such a grumbly voice, why I'd…I'd…pass the collection plate right by them!"

Will laughed. "What for? Annoying the preacher's daughter?"

She shot him a startled look. "Well, yes. Partly. And partly because I feel...left out."

Will barked a laugh. "Left out? Hell, there's only the two of us. Feeling left out simply means you want to know everything that's going on." He gazed out over the plains. "Sometimes it's not smart to know everything."

Charlotte felt her neck prickle. "But knowing things is educational!"

"Not some things."

My goodness, the man did try her patience. For starters, he didn't talk much, and when he did, it was not the least bit conversational. Not like Papa, who used beautiful poetic phrases and flowery terms. Instead of *It's not smart to know everything,* Papa would have said, *Daughter, the good Lord has added some devilish aspects to life on this earth.*

But she wanted to know all about Will Bondurant, and about the outlaw he was chasing, as well. "Why is the man you are after none of my business?"

"Should be obvious," he growled.

She waited for more, but he was, as usual, annoyingly spare with words. "It is not obvious to me. Do you not believe that a burden shared is a burden eased?"

He turned sideways in the saddle to face her. "Hell, no, I don't."

Her heart gave a little jump. In his eyes she saw something that made her insides turn over. It was as if two smoky-blue stones were beginning to smolder; any minute now they would shoot sparks.

"Mr. Bondurant, I have an active mind. I have to think about *something!*"

"Keep your mind on the trail and your mouth shut."

"Well, really! You issue orders as if you were some kind of king. I agreed that you were the boss on our journey, but you could at least say 'please.'"

He made no reply, just spurred his horse ahead.

She rode another quarter hour without saying a word until she couldn't stand it any longer. Biting her lip, she drew abreast of his mare and twisted her head to look at him. "I am storing up a string of things I would like to say to you. None of them flattering."

"Starting with?"

"Starting with, you have a maddening habit of—" Her eye caught a dust cloud moving toward them and she broke off.

Will saw it, too. Horse, coming fast. One rider. Dark-skinned. In one swift movement he lifted his rifle from the leather scabbard and laid it across his lap.

"Don't say anything if you can avoid it," he instructed. "And keep your hat low."

Her eyes went wide with fear. He wanted to say something to ease her apprehension, but the rider came on at a gallop and there wasn't time.

The stranger pulled his horse up in a cloud of dust, and sidestepped the panting animal toward them. Silver jingle-bobs on his spurs, Will noted. Black vaquero hat, but no lasso and no war bag that Will could see. What he did see was a pair of ivory-handled pistols, worn low on his hips in a gun belt of shiny tooled leather.

"*Buenos días,*" Will offered.

"I speak English," the man said. "Your name?"

"Yours?" Will shot back.

"Julio Eduardo Velez."

"Will Bondurant."

The man nodded. "And the young one?"

Charlotte's mouth opened, but Will cut her off. "That's my nephew. Name's Charlie." He heard her teeth snap shut and winced inwardly.

Will leaned forward, casually resting his left wrist on the pommel. All he had to do was slip his right hand off his thigh and over the trigger and the rifle would be in position. "Where you headin' in such a hurry?"

"Fort Laramie. I bring news to the *capitan.*"

"That'd be Captain Cutter," Will said.

"*Sí.* Maybe so you know him?"

"Maybe so."

The man's black eyes studied Will's face, then fastened on Charlotte. "I theenk you maybe take shortcut through the hills." He gestured northward.

"Why's that?"

"Indians, *amigo.* The Sioux and the Cheyenne, they are on the warpath."

"What's new about that? They've been enemies for generations."

"Soon they will fight, near to this place. I must reach *Capitan* Cutter and tell him."

Charlotte's gasp sounded so unmasculine Will figured it would give her away. He watched the Mexican's face, but his expression showed nothing.

Will touched his hat brim. "Thanks for the tip, *señor.*"

"*De nada.*" The man's horse began to sidle away.

"Eef I was you, *amigo,* I would take your…nephew and vamoose quick as you can."

"Much obliged."

The Mexican reined away and spurred his mount on down the trail. Will nudged Sandy forward and waited for Charlotte to catch up. "Much as I hate to lose the time, it'd be a lot safer to do what the man says and ride north."

"What would you do if you were alone, Mr. Bondurant? If you didn't have me to concern yourself about?"

"Keep going and take my chances. With you along I can't do that."

"I am truly sorry to delay you, but—"

"There's a cutoff north of here. Kinda rough ridin', but the vaquero's right about avoiding the fight. Think you can hack it?"

"Was it the Sioux who attacked my wagon and killed Mr. Thomas?" she asked in a quiet voice.

"Yep."

Her face went as white as bleached granite. "Then I will manage."

Chapter Nine

The gray mare jolted up yet another steep outcropping of jagged rocks and Charlotte gritted her teeth. The bone-jarring pace and the trail—what there was of it—pummeled her frame until her spine felt as brittle as a dry twig. Ahead of her, the hind end of Mr. Bondurant's black mare disappeared around another turn, and she groaned aloud.

"Wait!" she called. "Please slow down."

"Can't," he yelled back. "Try to keep up."

Keep up? She could scarcely stay in the saddle! All the soft parts of her body ached with bruises she knew would be purple and green by nightfall. If she could manage to last until nightfall.

Her horse half scrambled, half slid down a gravelly incline, and Charlotte's stomach flew up into her throat. How *he* stayed seated with no apparent effort was a mystery. The man and his horse moved as if they were one being, but she wasn't that experienced a rider. At every dip and chuckhole and steep descent, she clutched the pommel with both hands until her fingers burned from gripping the leather knob.

She could *not* keep up. Just when she decided she wouldn't even try, she rounded the next bend to find him waiting for her. "Doin' all right?"

Charlotte unclenched her jaw. "Perfectly well, thank you."

He chuckled and shook his head. He'd guessed she was lying. Well, not lying, exactly. Lying was a sin. She was…just not speaking of her discomfort.

What good would it do if she *did* speak out? It surely wouldn't slow him down, so why add trouble to an already mind-numbing ordeal?

This is what you wanted, remember? To strike out for Oregon ahead of the wagon train.

Yes, it was exactly what she wanted. She would keep her mouth shut and her bottom in the saddle for as long as it took.

Will altered his pace, not so much that she'd notice it, just enough to save her pride. And her backside. Even so, she'd be pretty stove-up by dark.

He hadn't heard one word of complaint, and he had to admit he admired her for it. Most Eastern women would let him know right quick when they didn't like something. This one was sure different.

He noticed other things about her, as well. The more uphill the trail, the quieter she grew. The tireder she got, the straighter her back. He'd lay a bet she'd ford the river ahead sitting her mount stiff as a green trooper, even if her stomach was tied into a knot.

By the time they reached the top of the pass, Sandy's breathing was labored. When he looked back, he saw the gray's sides were heaving in and out like a bellows. Charlotte rode with her hat pulled down against the late afternoon sun, the blue neckerchief covering her mouth and nose.

He reined in and turned to watch her come toward him. With her hat tipped forward like that, a few curls of red hair escaped down the back of her neck. It made her look dangerously female.

She rode up to him and halted. "Why are we stopping?"

Will pointed at the green and gold valley below, where the Platte meandered through stands of cottonwoods and chokecherry. "Every so often I come up here just to have a look-see from the top of the world. Back there's Nebraska and Kansas. That way's Oregon territory."

She peered in the directions he indicated. "We're traveling north, is that right?"

"Northwest. Down below us, to the east, is Indian territory. Sioux mostly. Cheyenne and some Nez Perce."

He heard her quick intake of breath. "Are…will we encounter Indians?"

He glanced at her, then looked away. "We might see some, but I'm tryin' hard *not* to encounter any."

"Are all Indians hostile, Mr. Bondurant?"

"Wouldn't you be if somebody overran *your* land and just took what they wanted?"

"Yes, I suppose you are right. I didn't think of it that way. That is why I chose to come West. I intend to help the Indians. The children, I mean. They must give up their savagery and learn our ways."

Will snorted. "When you've been out here in the West for a while it's not real clear who the savages really are."

"Nevertheless, I have determined what I will do."

"You make this decision back in Ohio?"

"Yes. After my parents died. I didn't want to waste my life—they would not have wished that. I wanted to put my days to some good purpose."

Will said nothing. He'd wanted the same for his own life, but it hadn't worked out that way. Now he was trying to pick up the pieces. He touched his boot heel to Sandy's side. "We'd best head down to level ground. We'll make camp after we cross the river."

The mud-brown Platte flowed swiftly, but it looked widespread and not too deep. Will studied it for a long time before he picked a fording place. At a shelving bank where the water licked the rocks, he started across.

"Let's go," he called over his shoulder. "Whatever you do, don't let go of the horse."

Charlotte was too frightened to argue, and much too frazzled by the steep trail they'd just stumbled down against the blinding sun to even think clearly. The water shone like a silver mirror where the slanting rays of the sun hit it. It looked so solid she imagined she could slide off her horse and walk upon the surface.

A half dozen yards out, Will twisted to look back. White-faced, she gripped the reins in one hand, the pommel with the other. The gray splashed into the water and Charlotte shut her eyes.

"What're you doin'?" he shouted.

"Praying."

"Do it with your eyes open!"

She snapped her lids open. "Yes, *sir,*" she shot back.

"For heaven's sake, don't you ever say 'please'?"

"Not often, no."

The gray sloshed on at a steady pace, and Charlotte clung to the rocking animal with all her strength.

Will waited until the gray's nose reached Sandy's tail. "Sit still," he barked. "You're weaving in the saddle."

Exasperated, Charlotte's mouth popped open of its own accord. "Oh, shut up!"

First she caught her breath at the audacity of what she'd said, then suppressed the grin that threatened. The thunderstruck look on his face was worth her lapse of manners.

The horses slogged on toward the opposite bank, and suddenly Will's mount sank into the river until only her head showed. The mare began to swim.

Charlotte guided her gray to one side. Water splashed over her thighs, and she squealed. Will looked back. "Hold on tight," he shouted.

At that instant his own mount hurtled up onto a small island in the middle of the river, and Will tumbled off backward with a splash. He sank, came up swearing, and sank again.

Charlotte laughed until her stomach hurt.

"Goddammit, help me!" he gurgled when he reappeared. This time his head stayed above water long enough to see his hat float by. He snaked his arm out and snagged it.

Charlotte nudged the gray in close to him. How she would love to hear "please," at the end of his command, but now wasn't the proper time to press the point.

Will caught the gray's tail, and Charlotte towed him to shallower water, where he stood up, slapping his hat at the water sluicing from his britches. Sandy left the island and swam straight to the opposite shore, stepped up the bank and shook off the water droplets, while Will splish-splashed on across, sometimes swimming, sometimes wading hip-deep. From the look on his face when he stumbled up the bank, Charlotte decided it was again time for a prayer. She closed her eyes. *Dear Lord, help me not to laugh.*

Will plunked himself down on the bank and proceeded to inspect the wet revolver he carried in his holster, wiping it down with a handful of dry grass. Then he remounted, trotted forward a half mile without looking back and picked a campsite. Within twenty minutes he'd built a fire and begun to strip off his wet clothes.

Too dazed with fatigue to move, Charlotte sat on a rock, watching him. First his shirt, which he tossed to the ground in a sodden mass. Then he unbuckled his gun belt, dropped it next to the shirt and reached for his waistband of his pants.

"You gonna turn your back?" he grumbled.

That did it. No "please." Not even a friendly tone. "No," she said calmly. "I am not. Watching will be educational."

"Suit yourself." He shucked his boots, unbuttoned his pants and drew them off, taking his soaked underdrawers down with them.

His skin was bronze all over, his back, his legs, even his buttocks. And lean, with sinewy muscles. She had never seen a man undressed before, never imagined a body could look so…purposeful. Not one ounce of flesh was wasted on this man, and when he moved…oh, my, he was beautiful to watch.

She swallowed hard and turned away, her cheeks hot, while he stalked around naked, propping his wet garments on stick frames next to the fire.

"You educated yet?"

"Oh, yes. Your…you are very interesting to look at." She rose. Deliberately keeping her back to him, she moved to the horses and busied herself untying his bedroll and tossed it to him. He shimmied the blanket out of the leather ties and wrapped it around his shoulders, Indian style.

It didn't cover near enough. Charlotte decided she'd better occupy herself unloading the saddles, as well. Especially since Will couldn't lift with his right arm yet. Maybe she'd feed the horses, too. And brew some hot coffee for him.

She watched him hunch close to the flames, saw that he was shivering. She was wet, too, but only up to her hips. Her trousers would dry off just standing next to the fire. She could see the chill-bumps on his arms. She slipped her own bedroll blanket free and draped it over his shoulders.

"Thanks," he muttered. "Damn cold."

"I'm making coffee, Mr. Bondurant."

"How about callin' me Will, like everybody else does?"

"I am not everybody else."

"You sure as hell aren't," he muttered.

Charlotte ignored the comment. "Are you sure you want me to use your Christian name? I get the impression you don't like me very much."

"Nothing could be farther—" He snapped off the rest of the sentence. "Yeah, call me Will. I've been calling you Charlotte in my head for some time."

She stopped spooning coffee into the pot. "Without my permission?"

"Do I need your permission, out here a hundred miles from anywhere?"

The question hung in her mind. He was blunt, but he had a point. They were alone, just the two of them, far from civilization and the rules of society. She was completely dependent on him. Dependent on his care of her. On his treatment of her. He could call her anything he wanted.

He could *do* anything he wanted.

She set the coffeepot on a flat rock. He reached his right arm forward to shift the container closer to the fire and she heard his breath hiss in.

"Wrong arm," he muttered. "Hurts like… Charlotte, take a look at my shoulder, will you?"

The extra blanket apparently didn't help. Even the mug of hot coffee she pressed into his unsteady hand and watched him gulp down didn't stop the chills. He needed food and dry clothes.

She peeled the wet bandage off his wound and her heart sank. The skin of his neck and upper shoulder was fiery red and hot under her fingers. A yellow liquid seeped from the wound itself.

He downed the last of his coffee. "Infected?"

"Yes."

"Damn. Is it bad?" He twisted his neck to see, but the knife wound was out of his range of vision.

"Yes. Did Dr. Warburton give you anything to put on it?"

"Salve. In my saddlebag."

She found it after a few moments, a small fat jar labeled Peppermint Oil Carbolic. She also discovered a brown paper packet of what looked like moss and dried herbs.

"For poultices," Will said when she showed it to him. "Doc thought I might need—"

"Yes, you do need," Charlotte interrupted. "Right now."

She laid more dry branches on the fire, filled a kettle with water from the small stream that fed into the Platte and set it on the fire pit rocks to boil.

"See if my clothes are dry," he ordered.

Charlotte bit her lip. "Please," she muttered under her breath. But she checked the garments. "Your shirt and drawers are dry. Your trousers are still damp."

She rearranged them on the framework of stripped branches he had devised, this time with the back side toward the fire.

"Help me get my shirt on."

His frame shook with chills, and his face looked ashen. She slipped the sleeve over his left arm, drew the fabric up over his left side. She left the right side exposed to apply the poultice.

He managed his drawers on his own, even though his good hand trembled and he could only fumble at the buttons.

"Leave them undone," Charlotte said at last. "I won't look." She wrapped his lower torso in one blanket, then searched his saddlebag for a pair of clean socks. His boots wouldn't be dry before morning, but his feet had to be covered with something.

When the water came to a boil she dumped in half the packet contents and stirred the odd-looking mixture around with a twig. The herbs sank to the bottom; the moss floated on the surface. She would need cloth for a poultice.

She eyed his drawers. No, he needed all the warmth he could get.

Her petticoat, then. The new one, in her saddlebag. With a sigh, she ripped off the ruffle at the hem and began tearing strips of muslin from the skirt.

Will tilted his head. "Your underclothes dòn't last long, do they?" When she did not respond, he gave a shaky laugh. "No offense."

"None taken," she said, her voice crisp. She dropped a length of fabric into the bubbling kettle, stirred it around, then twisted it between two sturdy twigs to wring out the excess water.

The moss went on the wound first. He sucked in air. "Hot," he rasped. She dropped the folded square of hot muslin on top of the moss.

Will flinched. "You havin' fun?"

"After a fashion." Gingerly she pressed the poultice against the wound, careful not to scald her hand while he tried to control his breathing.

While the hot cloth steamed on his skin, she fished in his saddlebag for a tin of beans and a tin of tomatoes for their supper. She could heat the contents right in the cans, and they could just spoon it out.

"You know," she said in a conversational tone, "I

worried all day about my poor horse stumbling and going lame. It never entered my mind that you…" She lifted the muslin away from his shoulder and dumped it back into the kettle. "You would be my biggest source of distress."

"I am?" His voice checked as she dropped the steaming muslin back onto his shoulder.

"Oh, my, yes. I quite prefer it. If my horse goes lame, we can always get another. But if something happens to you…" She dropped another poultice onto his wound.

"Yeah? Ouch! Damn, that's hot! If something happens to me, what?"

"There would be no way to replace you, Mr. Bondurant. So I am going to doctor your shoulder, cook your supper and save your life!"

She sounded so pleased with herself Will had to chuckle. She was enjoying this, being able to boss him around.

"You know," he said in as normal a tone as he could manage, "you have all the makings of an army colonel. Matter of fact, you remind me a bit of one Josh McCray, down in Texas."

He watched her pry the tops off the cans with the pocketknife she now carried in her jeans. He almost cheered when she managed it without cutting herself.

"I don't see how anybody, male or female, could grow up not having a pocketknife. How the hell do you cut up meat?"

"With a silver dinner knife."

A silver knife. Oh, boy. He should have guessed. But

he'd known all along that she was Eastern. And a lady, oh, my, yes. Miss Greenfield was a tenderfoot Bible-bouncer going West to civilize the Indians. And he was an edgy hombre trying like hell to kill one.

She kept dropping the hot cloths on him, but he grew colder and colder. Even the extra blanket didn't help. His shoulders quivered, his calf and thigh muscles danced uncontrollably. If he opened his mouth, his teeth chattered. Kinda funny to keep shivering when you feel like you're burning up.

"Supper," she announced. "Beans and tomatoes. Which do you want?"

"Is it one or the other? Or are we sharing?"

"Sharing, of course." She folded his cold fingers around a spoon handle and passed him a scorched-looking tin of beans. "You eat some, then we'll trade."

Made sense. "You're learning fast."

"Why, thank you, Will."

"If it wasn't—ouch!—for these damn boiled-up petticoats you're slingin' around, you'd be a fine trail companion."

She sat down and traded tins with him. "You are quite wrong," she said crisply. "I am already a fine trail companion."

"Think so, do you? Think there's nuthin' more for you to learn?"

Oh, hell. She was more than fine. She was the best damn company he'd had for years. When she bent over to lay the poultice in place, he could see right down her shirt front. Smell her skin, kinda sweaty and sweet at the same time.

Don't think about it. Think about tinned beans and tomatoes and feed for the horses and…

She sure looked soft and white underneath her shirt when she worked over him. His manhood, the only part of him that wasn't shivering, swelled and grew hard.

He shifted under the blankets, praying she wouldn't notice. He sure as hell didn't want her to stop.

Chapter Ten

Charlotte continued to lay the hot poultices on Will's wound until she could scarcely raise her aching arms. Each time she touched his shoulder he flinched, and she sucked in her breath. She hated hurting him.

Will grew quieter and quieter. His chin drooped toward his chest, and whenever she removed the square of hot muslin, he swayed toward her. On top of his fatigue, Will was fighting infection. When it grew dark, she knew she had to think about how to care for him through the night.

"Will," she murmured. "Are you feeling warmer?"

"N-no. Not m-much."

Oh, Lord, what was she to do? *Keep him warm and dry,* a voice said. *Make him drink.*

She dumped out the coffeepot and filled it with fresh water. Before she set it on the hot rocks, she poured a scant cup into his speckled mug. "Will, you've got to drink this. Your body needs water."

"My body needs…" He raised his head suddenly. "Yeah. Whiskey in my saddle—"

"No, not spirits. Water." She tipped the mug to his lips. His hand closed over hers, steadying it against his mouth. His teeth rattled against the metal rim.

She had to get his trousers back on him, had to get some covering over his legs. He needed all the warmth he could get.

She lifted his pants off the makeshift frame next to the fire and felt the material. Warm but damp. They would have to do.

"Will, stand up."

"What for?"

"To get your trousers on. Stand up."

He lumbered to his feet and stood unsteadily in front of her. "Stand up. Hold still. Drink this. Damn, l-lady, don't you ever s-say 'please'?"

Charlotte laughed. He gave her a lopsided grin, then his shaky legs folded under him and he sat down abruptly.

"Please, Will. Try again."

He dragged himself upright and she managed to get his left foot into the trouser leg. When he gave way this time she could pull the pants leg up to his knee. Almost against her will, she noted how muscular his limbs were, the fine dark hairs on his calves.

"Put your other foot in this side." From a sitting position he stuck out his right leg and she drew the trousers up both his trembling legs.

"Now, stand up."

"Already did," he protested.

"Do it again. Please," she added. He wobbled to his

feet, and she knelt next to him. He grasped her shoulder with one hand to steady himself while she slid the trousers over his knees, up to his thighs, then up to…

"I'll take it from here," he said.

She turned away while he tugged the denim over his hips. "Can't do up the buttons," he muttered.

"Leave them undone," Charlotte said, her back still to him. Looking at him half-dressed gave her the strangest feeling in her belly, a low ache she'd never felt before. She pulled her mind back to what had to be done. "Now, one more poultice."

Will groaned. "One more. That's it."

She laid the steaming cloth against his shoulder, then unrolled both bedrolls and eyed them thoughtfully. Together, she decided. It was the best way to keep him warm.

She dragged his saddle close to the fire, laid out both saddle blankets and retrieved her own tight-woven wool covering. Quickly she made a cocoon-style bed and tugged Will down on top of it.

"My gun," he said.

She found it and slipped it under the saddle. How could a man sleep in peace with an instrument of violence under his pillow? It must give him dreadful nightmares.

She lifted the last poultice away and pulled the blankets over him. "Boots," he murmured.

"I put them next to your saddle, away from the fire."

"Good. Lotta heat makes 'em stiff."

When she had straightened up the camp and hung the poultice material up to dry, she pulled off her own wet boots and socks, spread the socks on a warm, flat rock and set the boots next to Will's.

She ran her fingers over her own denim trousers. Dry, thank the good Lord. She crawled in next to Will, curled her warm body around his still-shivering form, and pulled the doubled blankets over them both. Even suffering, as he was now, he felt good. Strong and, well…good. Little by little, Will's shaking eased.

She felt so proud of herself! She was saving a man's life. Or at least his arm. She smiled up at the stars overhead, then jerked to a sitting position.

Merciful heavens, it was his right arm she had worked so hard over. His gun arm. The arm he used to take other men's lives. How could she ever face herself after helping him to continue such an endeavor? She really had no choice, though; he would die if she did *not* help him.

She flopped down next to him again. Perhaps her actions mattered less than she thought. God gave him the arm. What Will chose to do with it was up to him.

Much later she woke to his muttering. Nothing intelligible, just a word here and there. "Door." Then something that sounded like "dark." Then "son of a bitch."

Charlotte gasped. Oh! Was that what her father meant by language that would make your ears burn? She guessed she was hearing some of it now.

Will must be dreaming, so he actually couldn't be held responsible for what he said. She scooted toward him, wrapped her arm over his middle. Suddenly she remembered his trousers were still unbuttoned. And his drawers, as well.

Just never you mind about his drawers, Charlotte Marie.

She nuzzled her face into his broad back and drew in her breath. The man was burning up! She touched her fingers to his forehead, then his neck. His face was so hot she could feel the heat rise from his skin.

Fever! After chills came fever. A man could die of fever. But, dear God, not *this* man. Not the man who would guide her to Oregon.

She tried to think. They were miles from a town, even more miles from Fort Laramie. Maybe she should build a signal fire.

No, you goose. That would alert every Indian for a hundred miles.

What had the hospital guild ladies said about fevers? She tried desperately to remember, but not one thing came to mind. She would have to figure it out on her own.

Sweat it out of him, she guessed.

She rose to pile more wood on the fire and filled his cup with water. When she returned to the pallet, she found he had thrown off the blankets. She drew them close around his body and held the cup to his lips.

He brushed it away, and the contents splattered onto the ground. Tightening her lips, she trudged back to the kettle to refill the cup.

"You must drink," she ordered.

More mumbling. "Door...Pa. Pa." She dipped her finger in the cup and moistened his lips. "Drink!"

His tongue came out to lick the water off her finger, and that gave her an idea.

Once more she arose, this time to tear another strip from her new petticoat. She dunked the scrap of muslin in the water cup and held it to his mouth. He sucked at it eagerly.

She did it again. And again.

As she fed him driblets of moisture, she studied him. His tanned face and chin were dark with whisker growth. His hair, unkempt and black as coal, was overlong, down to his ears in front, longer in back. Maybe he didn't visit the barber too often. Or maybe he preferred it that way, to keep his neck from getting sunburned. She wished she could wear her own hair down for the same reason.

His face, often carefully expressionless, now twisted into a grimace, his lips pulled back as if baring his teeth. He groaned and spoke a word. "Master." Oh, no, it was "bastard." And he sucked and sucked on her muslin water teat.

Would blankets and water be enough to keep him alive?

She racked her brain to recall the ladies guild teatime conversations at the parsonage. Sweating, that was it. To break the fever she had to make him sweat.

Again she climbed out of the pallet, found his dry socks, and her own. Into each one she stuffed the largest fire-heated rock she could find, folded down the top and laid them at his back. Crawling in beside him, she forced her bottom against his groin, her spine against his chest. Lord, he was hot!

He began to thrash. Charlotte rolled over and pinned his flailing arms. Heat radiated from his skin. Even his hair was hot!

Each time he opened his lips, she dribbled a bit of water into his mouth. She replenished the hot stones until she ran out of rocks, and still he burned.

Out of his head with fever, he suddenly clutched her

shoulder, digging his fingers into her flesh and muttering something. A name. "Alice...don't. Don't." When she bent over him, he flung his elbow out, smacking into her cheekbone.

Hours passed. She didn't know how many, only that the moon rose and set while she smoothed the matted hair off his forehead and dripped water past his dry lips. A coyote howled some distance away and a shivery chill went through her.

I am alone. Completely on my own. And I am frightened to death!

She leaned over Will's fever-contorted face. "Don't you dare die, Will Bondurant! Can you hear me? Don't you dare!"

He groaned and flung his arm up. "Alice," he murmured.

"Not Alice!" She surprised herself by shouting. "Alice is not here. *I* am here. Charlotte. And I insist that you not die and leave me alone out here. Don't die!" She shook his uninjured shoulder. "Do you hear me? Don't die. That's an order!"

She dropped her forehead onto his chest. *God in heaven, please. Please.*

She dozed off and when she woke, her cheek felt damp. Wet, as if... She raised her head and stared down at him.

Perspiration poured off his face; his bare chest glistened with it. He was sweating! The fever had broken.

Charlotte dropped her face into her hands and wept with relief. *Thank You, Lord. Thank You! My heart is full of gratitude.*

And with something else, but she didn't know what. Just that she was so happy Will was alive.

Will opened his eyes to a clear blue sky and a campsite bathed in sunshine. Had he slept through breakfast? He pulled on his boots, noticing that his right arm hurt less. When he stood up, he also noticed he was light-headed. Not surprising, since he hadn't eaten since last night, and judging from the sun's position it was now near noon.

Charlotte lay curled up on the pallet, apparently oblivious of the hour. He prodded her hip gently with the toe of his boot. She moaned and rolled over, still asleep. He touched her again.

"Go 'way," she mumbled. "I'm sleeping."

"Not anymore, you're not. It's late. Get up."

"Been up all night," she muttered. "Still tired."

Will gazed down at her with a frown. She never complained of being tired. She could spend all day in the saddle and she'd never say she was tired. What the hell was wrong with her?

He knelt beside the pallet. "You sick?"

She moaned again.

"Me, I'm feelin' pretty good this mornin'. Guess that bath in the Platte did me some good."

Charlotte opened her eyes and looked at him as if he'd sprouted curly green whiskers. "You don't remember last night?"

"Yeah, I remember some of it. You got my pants on and then I fell asleep. If you were smart, you'd have done the same."

She stared at him in disbelief.

"Nothin' like a good night's sleep." He bent to peer at her more closely. "You've got a bruise on your cheek."

"Do I?" She sat up so fast he had to dodge out of her way. "Do I, indeed?"

Her voice sounded as crisp as overfried bacon. Something was wrong.

"How'd you get that mark on your cheek?"

"How do you think?" she snapped. "Someone hit me. Then someone woke me up and started asking me a passel of questions." She flopped back onto the pallet.

Will stood up, shaking his head. Someone? What someone? Her only companion was…

"Jesus, did *I* do that?" A small part of the night's events filtered into his memory. Poultices. Sucking water. Dreaming. He must have tossed some in the night and accidentally pasted her a good one.

"I'm sure sorry, princess."

She closed her eyes and curled up under the blankets.

He headed for the coffee and bacon in his saddlebag, stirred up the fire and started breakfast. He even mixed up a pan of his special trail biscuits—edible, but not so tender they didn't travel well.

He let her sleep until the bacon sizzled and the coffee smelled about right. When everything was ready, Will hunkered down beside her motionless form. "There's coffee," he said. "And bacon."

She murmured something and folded herself into an even tighter ball. Hell, she was acting like a goddamn porcupine this morning.

"Charlotte? Miss Greenfield?" He laid one hand on her shoulder and she swatted it away.

"What?" she said without opening her eyes.

"Are you praying?"

"Not exactly." She rose up on one elbow. "I was thanking the Lord for a few precious hours of sleep. And," she added in a softer tone, "for your life."

Will rocked back on his heels and stared at her. So that was it. He felt good this morning because she'd stayed up most of the night tending his shoulder. No wonder it felt better. He reached to his neck, ran his forefinger along the cut. Still sore, but not swollen and not oozing pus. She'd probably saved his skin. "Princess, you get breakfast in bed."

"No, I—"

"I'm boss, remember? Do as I say."

In unison they both spoke a final word. "Please."

He brought over two mugs of hot coffee, then strips of bacon he'd threaded on a slender branch and broiled close to the fire. Last came the browned trail biscuits. Seated beside the pallet, he ate in silence, studying her.

"You are one surprising woman." He didn't realize he'd spoken out loud until she looked up, a question in her eyes.

"Your hands," he said. He pointed to the mug she cradled in her fingers. "Your hands don't look strong enough to crochet lace doilies, but they've lifted saddles, spread out bedrolls, slapped on poultices, even pulled up my trousers."

"What is so surprising about that? I simply did what was necessary."

Will tossed away the dregs of his coffee. "Those

poultice things kept me from havin' a crippled-up arm. Maybe even kept me from dyin' of blood poisoning."

"Yes, I think that is so. It wasn't easy, but I am glad I did it."

So she was glad, was she? Did that mean she liked his company?

Nah. More likely she didn't want to be left alone out here; that's why she'd worked all night to doctor him. He should be grateful.

Well, hell, he was grateful. The little hole in his heart was because…because…

He looked off into the distance. He wished she'd done it because she liked him, not because she'd be helpless without a guide.

While Charlotte went down to the stream to wash up, Will split the rest of the trail biscuits with his pocket-knife and slipped in thick pieces of leftover bacon. It'd do for their nooning. Then, studying the angle of the sun, he realized that noon was past. Okay, supper maybe.

He packed up the horses, even hefted his own saddle, and once again acknowledged his debt to the delicate-looking woman with the soft gray eyes.

By midafternoon they had climbed a good number of miles up into the hills and stopped to rest the horses at a spring. Charlotte gazed down across the flattest expanse of earth she had ever seen, so brown and bare it looked like another planet.

"Pretty, isn't it?" Will said beside her. He handed her a bacon-stuffed biscuit.

"The land looks like it's waiting for something."

"Yeah? What?"

"I don't know exactly. Fields of corn. Towns. Even iron railroad tracks. Don't you think someday there will be people living down there?"

"Already are people living down there."

"Where? I see nothing but dry grass and sagebrush."

"That land is Indian land. Belonged to the Sioux before the white man had a Constitution." He bit into the dry biscuit, washed it down with a gulp of water from his canteen.

"Look there." He pointed ahead of them.

Charlotte studied the landscape and caught her breath when a dust cloud bloomed in the still air. Will spotted it at the same moment.

"Looks like our Mexican friend was wrong. The Indians aren't south of us, they're here. Dead ahead on the other side of this butte."

He turned his mount toward the rocky bluff above them and signaled Charlotte to follow. It wasn't a trail, just an occasional foothold for a steady horse who didn't mind heights. Will could smell the dust now, sweet and rich, like burning leaves. When he reached the top, he reined up. Sioux.

Quickly he dismounted, motioning Charlotte to do the same. "Stay here and keep low."

He picketed both horses well away from the rim of the butte, then crept forward on his belly and peered down at the scene below.

Charlotte crawled after him, and when she reached the edge, Will pressed her down flat. "War party. We've stumbled into the middle of an Indian set-to."

Chapter Eleven

Charlotte choked on a mouthful of biscuit.

"Just keep down and lie quiet. They won't see us."

She did not believe that for one minute. She forgot all about her biscuit and crunched her body as flat as she could to the ground. But she couldn't resist peeking.

The dust cloud moved to the south, and within minutes a band of Indians trotted into view. Their skin looked shiny, as if smeared with grease; faces and chests, even the horses, were painted, and every man carried a lance and a boldly painted round leather shield.

"What are they going to do?" she whispered.

Will belly-crawled to the rim and peered down at the scene below. "Find some Cheyenne and have a not-too-friendly powwow."

Braves in war paint and older warriors in feather headdresses lined up on horseback facing an identical line of mounted Indians across a flat stretch of ground. Will spotted the renegade chief, White Eagle, on a magnificent roan horse. A dozen of his followers clustered near him, including Five Feathers. Will heaved a sigh. Guess he hadn't killed the brave after all.

"If the Sioux have asked for White Eagle's help, they must be desperate. Or outnumbered." He scanned the double row of mounted Cheyenne warriors, their faces striped with red and yellow paint. Lances held upright, they looked into the sun.

"The Sioux have the sun at their backs. It'll be close to a draw. Or a massacre. Whatever it is, it's gonna happen fifty yards below us."

"What will we do?" Charlotte asked in a small voice.

"Nuthin'. They won't see us as long as we stay flat. They're getting ready to fight."

"But why?"

"Instinct. These two tribes have been enemies for generations."

"Can you not stop them?"

Will jerked his head sideways to stare at her. "Are you crazy? They hate the white man worse than they hate each other."

"Will they kill each other?"

"Damn right. And we're gonna keep quiet and watch."

"It's wrong," she murmured. "The Bible forbids it. 'Thou shalt not kill,'" she quoted.

Will turned his attention back to the field of battle. "Indians don't read the Bible."

The opposing lines began to move forward, the ponies stepping slowly at first, then trotting as the two lines drew closer. At the point of contact, the horses on both sides hurtled forward to meet with a sickening crunch and then screams.

Shouts rose. Men fell, arrows protruding from chests and bellies. Beside him, Charlotte shuddered and buried her face in her hands.

It went on until the sun slanted toward the mountains, and then as Will watched, White Eagle's roan plunged into the roiling sea of animals and men and disappeared. Will watched for a minute, then edged back from the bluff and went for his rifle.

When he crawled back into position, he saw that the renegade chief was alone and unmounted. A Cheyenne brave was riding hard toward him.

Will raised the Sharps and sighted down the barrel.

Charlotte clutched his sleeve. "What are you doing?"

"Evening the odds."

The brave swung to White Eagle's unprotected back and raised his lance. Will knew he shouldn't take sides; next time around he might owe a debt of honor to a Cheyenne chief. All he knew was that White Eagle had saved Will's life years ago, and he couldn't just stand by and watch—

"Will, don't!"

His forefinger squeezed the trigger, and the attacking brave catapulted headfirst over the neck of his horse. In the melee of battle no one seemed to notice the gunshot. Only White Eagle looked startled for a moment, but just then Five Feathers raced up with the roan and White Eagle remounted.

Will released his breath and wiped the sweat out of his eyes.

They spent the rest of the day hugging the rocky ground in silence until the sun sank behind the mountains and long shadows crept over them.

Charlotte hadn't let out a peep for hours. Now she laid her hand on his arm. "You killed a man."

"It's not the first time."

She stared at him as if he'd suddenly sprouted buttercups on his nose. "Don't you feel any remorse?"

He answered her with a question of his own. "Should I have let White Eagle die?"

Charlotte just looked at him.

"If I let myself take time to feel sorry for every bullet I've sent into a man, someone would have shot me long ago. If you're gonna make your life in the West, you might as well get used to it, princess."

"I am not going to give up my principles," she said in a small but determined voice.

Will snorted. "Principles! We don't have much law out here. What we do have is usually backed up by a forty-four."

"I will never get used to that. Never! That is why I must teach, so the Indian and the white man can learn to live together."

He shook his head. "Don't think you'll live as long as it'd take, Charlotte. New ways come slowly. Men change even slower than that."

"But I could make a start. I could try!"

Will studied the plain below them. When he spoke he didn't look at her. "You'd be wasting your life."

The Sioux were withdrawing, maybe to regroup. He shifted the rifle to one side and removed his hand from the stock. "Don't try to Jesus-save me, Charlotte. It's too late."

"H-how could I waste my life if I am doing the Lord's work?"

"How come you're so sure you know what the Lord has in mind for you?"

"What do you mean?"

"There's other things for a woman. Like, well, marryin' a man. Raisin' some kids?" He wished like hell he'd bit his tongue off rather than poke that at her. Most spinsters he'd known hadn't had the choice.

Her face closed up like a morning glory in the rain. "I have had enough of love." Her voice was dull with pain. "I loved Papa. And Mama. Now I love God."

"And that's enough?"

"It is."

"You ever wonder if there's more to it than that?"

She edged to one side, away from him, and covered her eyes with her bent arm. "No, I do not wonder those things."

"Maybe you oughtta look inside yourself a bit deeper. If you've got the guts."

She said nothing and he dragged his attention to the dispersing Indians. "We've got to get out of here."

"Will they see us?"

"Don't think so. They're movin' south, we're ridin' north."

She gave a little moan. ·

"We'll leave soon as it gets full dark." He rolled over onto his back and pulled his hat over his face. "Good time to catch a nap."

Charlotte gaped at him. A nap! How could he sleep with marauding savages only a short distance away?

She lay beside him a long time, her chin propped on her fists, watching the Indians retreat and their dust dissipate in the wind. She closed her eyes and tried to pray.

And then Will was poking her shoulder. "Time to move," he said.

Charlotte blinked. She had fallen asleep. Below her a dozen small campfires glowed. Indian campfires.

"Mount up," he said in a low voice. "I've muffled the horses' hooves. We've got to get past their camp before the moon rises."

Charlotte's entire frame jerked. "Dear God in heaven, we're going to ride right by them?"

"Can't be helped. If we leave the trail and skirt around, we might run into the Cheyenne camp."

Charlotte bit down hard on her lower lip. She was caught between the devil and... How, *how* had she come to such a pass?

She shook her head in disbelief, then mounted and prepared to follow Will's black mare down off the butte.

Chapter Twelve

On muffled hooves, their horses skirted the Sioux encampment, at times moving so close to the glowing campfires that individual warriors' features were clear, and their soft language carried to Charlotte's ears. Crouched against the gray's neck, her cheek brushed the animal's coarse hair. She did not dare close her eyes.

Ahead of her, Will hunched low in the saddle, picking his way along the faint trail barely visible in the blackness. Except for the breathing of their horses, they made no sound.

Tension drew her shoulder muscles tight. Was it possible that the sharp-faced warriors could eat and talk by their fires while two white travelers rode past only a few yards away? Charlotte kept her head down, peering sideways to reassure herself that they were not seen and prayed that the red man could see in the dark no better than the white man.

A brave not twenty yards to her left stood up from

his fire and swung toward them, looking out into the
night. Charlotte's heart stopped, then skittered into an
irregular pounding. Should they stop or keep moving?

She couldn't voice the question; her only option was
to do exactly what Will did. She gripped the pommel
with one hand in case Will broke into a gallop, but his
black mare moved stealthily on.

An owl hooted so close she automatically ducked
her head. Or perhaps it wasn't an owl. Perhaps it was
Will, signaling her to keep going. Holding her breath,
she watched the Indian brave scratch himself, then drop
to his haunches and reach toward something over his
cook fire.

The owl called again, and she resumed breathing.
Grasping the reins so tight her fingers ached, she followed
Will through the darkness at the same plodding pace.
Drops of perspiration rolled down the back of her neck.

Will halted and waited for her to come alongside.
"You all right?" His voice was barely audible.

"I am frightened to death," she murmured.

"We're past the main camp. Another few hundred
yards and we can dig in our spurs."

"Won't they hear us?"

"I wrapped the hooves to deaden the sound."

"Wrapped?"

He didn't answer, just stepped his horse forward.
Charlotte clenched her teeth to keep from screaming.
Why would he never answer her questions?

*Because there is something he doesn't want you to
know.*

She shivered. The man kept himself hidden. Was he

really what he said, a lawman chasing someone? Was *he* on the run, as well?

She would satisfy her curiosity when they reached safety. If they did. She had another question, too, one that just this minute popped into her head. *Was he sorry he'd taken her on?*

Sandy broke into a trot, and Charlotte stiffened. Glancing back, she noted campfires far behind them. She thought she saw an Indian mounting a horse, but she couldn't be sure. She jabbed her boot heels into the gray's side and rode like the wind to catch up to Will.

He headed straight for a stand of trees silhouetted in the moonlight. They rested for a short time, then rode on through the night, stopping every hour or so to water the horses. When it grew light, Charlotte saw what Will had used to silence the hoof beats. Around each of the animal's legs was tied a length of ruffled lace which held padded muslin booties in place over the iron horseshoes.

"My petticoat!"

"We'll talk about it when we get to Oregon." But he smiled when he said it. At least she thought he did; Will's face was hard to read, even after days on the trail, living practically in each other's pockets.

Farther on, Will picked a campsite hidden in a copse of ash and thornberry and immediately set about digging a fire pit. At Charlotte's questioning look, he grinned. "Firelight won't show if the flames are below ground level," he explained.

She stared at him. "But we have passed the Indian camp."

Will snorted. "You think Indians are our only problem?"

Her large gray eyes narrowed. "Is someone chasing *you?*"

He hesitated. "Maybe. Most times it's the other way around."

She didn't say another word until their supper of hot beans and bacon and canned peaches was ready, and by then she was too busy spooning the food into her mouth to fuss at him.

"Problem is," he said when they had washed up the two tin plates and sat by the fire nursing their coffee, "you don't know enough about life out here in the West to question every damn thing I do."

Her eyes snapped sparks at that. Will winced. Maybe he'd gone too far. When she opened her mouth to speak he stifled an impulse to dodge.

"That is true, as far as it goes. However, I am learning quickly. And I intend to keep on learning. *And* asking questions."

"'S'long as you don't forget who's the—" He broke off. A dozen yards away a branch rustled. Will edged toward Charlotte and continued talking without changing his tone. "Charlie? I think we're gonna have company."

"What do you mean? Oh!" Her mouth opened into a large round O.

Another swishing noise. Closer.

Will leaned away from her, drew his revolver from under his saddle, and leveled it across the campfire, aiming chest-high.

A horse whickered.

"Indians?" Charlotte whispered through stiff lips.

"Don't think so. Too noisy."

"Will, I'm scared."

"Just follow my lead," he murmured.

A man strode into the firelight, leading a horse. At the sight of Will's revolver, he raised his hands. "Do not shoot, *señor.* It is me, Julio Velez."

Will fingered the trigger. "Velez."

"You will forgive me please for frightening you and your nephew. I am happy to have find you."

Will gestured the man to sit. "Why is that, Velez?"

The Mexican rubbed his plump belly and eyed the coffeepot, his black eyes lighting up.

"You hungry?" Will asked.

"No, *señor.* I eat beans and tortillas an hour ago, but some coffee…"

Will tossed away the remains of his mug and filled it for the Mexican. "Only got two cups," he explained.

"*Gracias, amigo.* It is a generous man indeed who shares his coffee. And his cup."

"You been following us?"

Velez gulped a mouthful from the mug. "*Sí.*" He shifted his gaze to Charlotte and Will came to attention. Carefully he edged one finger onto the trigger. "Care to tell me why?"

"*Sí.*" The Mexican drank again, wiping his bushy black mustache with the back of his hand. "I bring a message from Capitan Cutter. He say to tell you that two men come to Fort Laramie, and they are looking for a woman. A woman with red hair."

Charlotte's breath gusted in. Will managed to cover it by clearing his throat. "A woman, huh?"

"*Sí, señor.* There was such a woman on the wagon train, but it pull out before these men arrive. The *capitan,* he tell the men this. Then he tell me to find you pronto, so you will know."

"Much obliged, Velez. We'll keep our eyes peeled, won't we, Charlie?"

Charlotte grunted.

"Red hair, huh?" Will whistled. "Those two men— what'd they look like?"

"One is Comanche. Tall. The other is a small man. Americano."

"What do they want with this redheaded woman?"

Velez slurped up the last of the liquid in his cup and studied Charlotte. "Maybe so this woman, she run away?" He looked directly at Charlotte. "I wonder why would she do such a thing?"

Charlotte shrugged and said nothing.

"The Americano, he say he must find her."

"Roll me a smoke, Charlie," Will said quickly. "*Señor?*"

Velez raised one hand. "No, *señor.* I thank you, but the Americano cigarettes, they taste too strong."

"Charlie, roll one for yourself, too." He watched Charlotte fumble in the vest pocket for the makings and the tin of matches. "Or maybe you'd rather chew on a ceegar?" He clapped her on the shoulder.

Charlotte's hand jerked, but she managed to grunt a "nope" out of the side of her mouth. Will caught Velez staring at her.

"My nephew just took up smokin'. Kinda too bad, I reckon. His momma gonna whup him good when he gets back to Texas."

Charlotte handed over a loosely rolled cigarette and followed with the match tin. With a long-suffering look, she started rolling another one for herself. Will couldn't wait to see her smoke it.

Velez sat for another hour while the fire burned down to coals and Charlotte smoked two cigarettes, drawing her breath in slowly and carefully and flicking off the growing ash at the tip with a hand that trembled slightly. Only once did she glance at him; her eyes looked stricken.

Will wondered whether she'd be sick. He also wondered if they were fooling the Mexican. Something about the man made him uneasy. His tooled leather boots, maybe. Or those expensive side arms with the pearl handles. Why would Captain Cutter's messenger carry such fancy weapons?

Finally, Velez heaved his heavy frame onto his feet. "I have other messages to deliver, *señor*. I will bid you—" he touched the wide brim of his hat "—and your…nephew good night."

Will rose, walked around the fire pit and extended his hand.

The Mexican grasped it. "Eef I was you, *amigo*," he said in a low voice, "maybe so I would cut your nephew's hair. Not many Tejanos grow a long red curl down their back."

"I'll do that," Will said quietly. *"Gracias."*

"Go with God. Both of you."

* * *

Charlotte woke to the faint sound of splashing water. Surely she must be dreaming? The only water they had was carried in their canteens. But there it was again, a soft plop, followed by the rippling noise and then a long silence.

She opened her eyes to a deserted camp. "Will?" She sat up.

"Unnhh."

She peered behind her. He stood splay-legged before a shallow enamel bowl, his face lathered with frothy white soapsuds. A small mirror hung from a leather thong he'd hooked over the end of a stubbed-off limb, and in his hand—his right hand, she noted with satisfaction— he held a straight razor with a tortoiseshell handle. Just as he raised the blade to his chin he caught sight of her.

"Mornin'." The razor scraped away a swath of foam.

"Good morning." She couldn't take her eyes off his hand, deftly sliding that wicked-looking blade over his skin. One slip and he could slice his throat.

His shirt hung on the tree limb next to the mirror; the skin of his bare chest was bronzy in the morning light, with a sprinkling of dark hair punctuated by dark nipples. Lord, he was so…male.

He straightened, swirled the suds-laden blade in the bowl propped in the crook of the tree and repositioned himself in front of the mirror. "Never watch a man shave before?"

"No. Papa did not shave. He grew a beard and trimmed his mustache every Saturday afternoon with Mama's buttonhole scissors."

For some reason watching Will shave made her feel hot all over. "Did your father show you how to shave when you were young?"

"Nu-unnh." He pulled the razor up from under his jaw to his chin, then repeated the action. "By the time I sprouted fuzz, I'd left home."

"Do all men shave the same way?"

"Don't know." He splashed in the bowl. "'Lotta men, like your father, don't shave at all. Other fellas might leave sideburns or a chin goatee."

"What are *you* going to leave?"

"Nuthin' if I can help it. Unless…" He shot her an amused look. "You got some preference about it?"

Charlotte studied his features. From the remaining lather pattern she deduced his upper lip, right below his nose, would be next. Apparently he did not favor a mustache.

"No preference."

"Ever kiss a man with a mustache?" He focused hard on his chin.

She felt her cheeks grow warm. "Only my papa. And my grandfather, before he died."

"Scratchy?"

"No. Quite soft, as a matter of fact."

"My whiskers come in like barbwire. Always wanted to grow a mustache, but never had the patience. Besides, Alice—" He bit off the rest of the sentence.

So he *did* have a wife.

She turned away toward the fire pit. "I'll make some coffee."

"Already made," he called after her. "Bacon, too. We need to get an early start."

"Very well. I shall be ready."

"Charlotte…"

She turned back to him. "Yes?"

He finished a series of short strokes below his bottom lip, distorting his mouth to smooth out the scraping surface. When he dunked the blade in the water, he looked into her eyes. "Come over here."

She moved forward until the only thing between them was the enamel basin, balanced in the tree branches. "Yes?"

"Look into the mirror."

She twisted the thong-strung looking glass until it reflected her own image. Grimy skin. Eyes red-rimmed from wood smoke and dust. Sun-cracked lips. No one in Marysville would ever recognize her now. She looked nothing like Charlotte Greenfield. She looked like…like someone who would be called Charlie.

She turned her head to the side. And her hair! Even stuffed up under her hat, the unruly curls kept escaping down her back.

He met her eyes in the mirror. Charlotte looked back into the mirror and her heart plummeted. "Oh, no," she murmured. "My hair."

He turned the glass away and continued shaving. She watched his hand lifting the razor. When he finished rinsing it, she lifted the blade out of his fingers and stared down at it.

"You want me to do it?" Will asked, his voice quiet.

Biting back a sob, she nodded. *Her hair. Her long red*

hair. "Mama always said my hair was my only claim to beauty."

"Your momma was wrong."

"Couldn't I tie it up under my hat? Oh, please, Will?"

He said nothing.

"I guess not," she said softly. "How—how short must it be?"

Will splashed water over his face, mopped his cheeks and chin with the tail of his shirt. "Want to eat breakfast first?"

She shook her head. "I want to get it over with."

He tossed out the shaving water and shrugged on his shirt, leaving it unbuttoned. "Find someplace comfortable."

He began to strop the razor against a wide leather belt, tested the blade edge with his thumb and then sharpened it an additional ten strokes. Charlotte counted every one, then turned away, perched on a fallen log and waited.

Will looked down at her and swallowed. She held her head erect, but her lips were pressed together, her hands clenched at her sides. He didn't want to see her eyes.

He swallowed again. "Ready?"

"Yes," she whispered.

He lifted a handful of hair off her neck. The silky mass burned into his skin, and he hesitated.

"Go ahead," she said. "I know it must be done."

He wanted to bend and touch his face to the top of her head. Wanted to say something, but what? He let the satiny strands slide through his fingers, drew in an oddly uneven breath, and lifted the razor. "I want you to know I'm real, real sorry to have to do this."

She said nothing, just sat up straighter.

Without thinking he stepped close and pulled her head against his chest. Her hair touched his bare skin, soft as down, but against his chest it burned like a flame.

He stepped away. God, he didn't want to cut it. But she was right. It had to be done.

The blade made a soft crunch when he cut. Will flinched at the sound. He could almost feel the sharp edge of the razor slice into his gut.

She pinched her mouth tight and closed her eyes while he worked across her back. When he got to the front part, he held her jaw steady with his left hand. Tears rolled down her cheeks and wet his fingers.

"Dammit, Charlotte. I'm sorry. God, I'm sorry."

She did not reply, just laid her small hand over his and lifted it, and the blade, toward her chin.

Chapter Thirteen

Will used the razor to feather strands of Charlotte's hair so they blended together, but when he offered her the looking glass, she turned her face away. "I cannot look. I cannot."

"It doesn't look bad, honest! Makes you look kinda like…" He wiped the steel blade on his loose shirttail and snapped it back into the faded leather case Pa had given him.

"A plucked chicken," she supplied in a dismal tone.

"Not hardly. You look kinda like, well, my older brother, 'cept for the color. His hair's curly, like yours, but it's black as crow feathers."

"A plucked *curly* chicken, then." Her voice was still unsteady. She pushed off the stump and walked back toward camp, her back stiff as his rifle barrel.

She didn't put her hat on until after breakfast, and even then she didn't say anything. Her silence made him edgy.

He also felt some guilt. "Hell, Charlotte it's just hair."

"Yes. But it was *my* hair."

"It'll grow out."

"I know it will. Eventually. It's just that I don't want to look funny *now.*"

Will sighed. "You don't look funny, dammit. You look...different." He leveled a quick, appraising look at her. "Matter of fact," he said with a grin, "you look like my nephew, Charlie."

Without a word she gathered up the breakfast utensils, wiped them out and stowed them in his saddlebag. By the time they broke camp and mounted up, Will once more felt the itch under his skin. He was running out of time.

Charlotte or no Charlotte, he had to keep moving west. She'd already cost him two extra days, on a schedule that was impossible to start with. Thirty days, Captain McCray had given him. If he stayed away longer than that, he would be out of a job.

He headed the horse west and tried not to think about it.

Near dusk, the heat and the glaring sun had taken their toll on them both. Dust clogged his nostrils and sifted down inside his shirt. It wouldn't be any different for her, but she hadn't uttered one word of complaint. Her head drooped forward, exposing her sunburned neck. He figured she had a doozy of a headache, riding into the glare of the sun all day.

He wanted to stop. Make camp and rest his saddle-weary bones, but he knew he should press on, cover as many miles as possible. *Aw, hell, admit it. You also want to take care of Charlotte.* After the sacrifice of her hair this morning, he owed her that. More than that. His right shoulder no longer felt like someone was pounding the bone with a hot poker.

"We'll camp by that creek up ahead." He slowed his horse as they approached the lazy rivulet of brown-looking water.

Her head tipped up. "Thank heaven," she murmured. "I have so much sand down the front of my shirt I must weigh an extra ten pounds!"

She inspected the creek. "Not very clean water, is it?"

"We'll have to boil it before we can drink it."

"Would there be enough to…"

He knew what she was going to ask. A bath had crossed his mind, too. "Sure. You first. I'll get the fire started to heat water, then I'm goin' hunting."

"Hunting!"

"Aren't you gettin' tired of beans 'n' bacon?" he said in a weary voice.

"Not so tired I would risk someone—an Indian—hearing a gunshot."

He stuffed down a snort of impatience. "Only a damn fool would fire a shot out here without real necessity. I planned to use a snare. Should be a rabbit or two in that patch of brush."

Charlotte glared at him, then turned away to gather dry twigs and branches for the fire while Will kicked some stones into a rough circle. When he bent to ignite the dry grass kindling, he made a discovery that made his neck bristle.

The stones were already fire-warmed. Someone had

camped here recently, built a fire on this very spot. Less than six or eight hours ago, he calculated. The skin on the back of his neck began to prickle.

He laid his snares, and while he waited for their supper to stumble into his simple trap, he studied the camp and the surrounding area with the eyes of a tracker.

Two horses, judging from the hoof prints. One maybe used as a pack animal or a spare. Both fully shod. Left rear shoe nailed on crooked; either that or one horse had gone lame. No droppings, which was odd. Unless…

A squeal and a frantic scuffling noise told him the trap had been sprung. Charlotte came to her feet and stood watching, her eyes dilated until they looked more black than gray.

A jackrabbit hung upside down by one hind leg. The animal squealed again, and Charlotte clapped her hands over her ears. "It sounds like someone screaming," she cried. "A woman, screaming."

Will nodded. "Yeah, it does, some." He shut his mind to the sound, cut its throat with a single thrust of his pocketknife and set about skinning and cleaning the carcass. Jesus, she probably wouldn't eat a bite. This lady was going to survive on an Oregon Indian reservation? Fat chance. She was so green he almost felt sorry for her.

When the spitted rabbit looked done, Will sliced off a chunk and held it out to Charlotte. She looked at it for a long minute, then dropped her gaze to the empty tin plate in her lap.

"I don't think I can eat it."

"Why not?" he snapped. Damn, she could irritate him. "You're hungry, aren't you?"

"Y-yes. But somehow I cannot—"

He dropped the piece of roasted meat onto her plate. "You need to eat, dammit. Keep up your strength."

She averted her face. "I—I am afraid if I eat any, it will come right back up."

"Try," he ordered.

She picked up the meat, brought it to her mouth. Closing her eyes tight, she took a small bite. Will watched her jaws move as she chewed and felt a load lift off his shoulders. A man liked to feel he could provide for a woman.

He buried his teeth in his own piece, savored the taste of the fire-roasted flesh and washed it down with black coffee. His fatigue began to fade.

Charlotte set her plate down, rose, and walked off into the bushes, where he heard her bringing up her supper. When she resettled herself by the fire he didn't say a word, just poured fresh coffee into her mug. After some minutes, she lifted the chunk of rabbit meat off her plate and laid it onto his. He ate it, then steered his mind back to the matter of the horse manure.

No droppings could mean whoever it was had stopped only a short time at the camp. It could also mean the droppings had been purposely gathered up and disposed of by someone who wanted to cover his trail. That would explain the already warm stones, which had been deliberately separated to hide evidence of a fire. He'd bet ashes from an earlier fire, less than twelve hours old, were buried under the coals that now glowed under their coffeepot.

Will drew in a long breath. "Got us a problem, Charlie."

Charlotte shot him a look of pure fear. He'd have to

remember not to use that name unless it signaled intruders or trouble.

"What problem? Is it your shoulder? There's more salve—"

"My shoulder's fine."

How much should he tell her? He kept his eyes on her face. "Nuthin' to do with me, or you. Just a situation we need to make a decision about."

A tentative smile touched her mouth. First one since her haircut this morning, and it sure made him feel good seeing it.

"You mean the decision about who sleeps with whom?"

Will groaned. "I wish it was that simple."

Charlotte's breath stopped at the odd look on his face, half apologetic, half worried. A decision he said. What decision?

"I have had little voice in the decisions made thus far. Why ask my opinion now?"

He looked down into the flames, then at his horse picketed a few yards away, at his boots, everywhere but at her. Finally he cleared his throat and spoke carefully, weighing each word. "Well, it's like this. This camp's been used recently."

Charlotte looked at his carefully expressionless face. "What does that signify? I should think a good campsite is used many times over."

"Yeah. But whoever used this one didn't want it known. He covered up all the things that would usually be found—wood ashes, the fire ring, horse droppings. Only thing he didn't cover were the horse tracks."

"Quite possibly he forgot?"

"Maybe. More likely he left in a hurry and didn't have time to erase them."

Charlotte sniffed. "Why? Because he is trying to avoid—" Her voice rose with alarm. "You mean he is an outlaw?"

"Now don't get your knickers in a knot, Charlie."

She leaped to her feet, a hot ball of fury burning a hole in her belly. "My knickers are none of your business! And don't call me Charlie."

She wasn't sure why she was so angry, but it felt good just the same, as if she'd been holding a little ball of seething fury inside for a long time. She tried to keep her voice at a reasonable pitch. "Is this…person traveling in the same direction we are?"

"Looks like."

Charlotte snapped her jaw shut. She was learning more than she wanted to about Will Bondurant. He never said more than he had to. He was stubborn and bossy. And there was obviously a body of information he had not shared with her.

She worked to keep the annoyance out of her tone. "That does not seem surprising. Many people are traveling west. Why, before I left Independence with the wagon train, I saw ever so many—"

"Hold on a minute, will you?" He sent her an exasperated look and got to his feet.

She glared at him in frosty silence. This man was getting under her skin. She hated being left out, treated as if she didn't matter, as if she were a child. Papa had done that all her life, and now that's exactly what Will Bondurant was doing.

"Seems to me," he said in that maddeningly calm voice, "like we might want to keep movin'."

"What? You mean now? Tonight?"

He dipped his head once. "Think about it. We've got a bunch of angry Indians somewhere east of us. A suspicious traveler ahead of us. And the short man at the water hole, the one you said looked familiar."

A cold shiver marched up her spine. Instantly she recalled the image of that Indian, mounting a horse. "Just exactly what do you propose?"

"I propose we leave this camp fast as we can pack up and find another one," he said in a quiet voice. "Farther north."

"Why north?" Charlotte heard the brittle tone in her voice. Underneath she knew it was uneasiness that made her shrill, but she didn't care. Exasperation helped, too.

"Just cautious. Feel like it'd be smart. Sitting here makes me nervous."

"That is not sufficient reason to move on before we have slept. What are you *not* telling me?"

This time Will looked straight at her, his eyes cold and hard as winter ice. "I'm chasing a man who's armed and dangerous."

"I gathered that."

"It's possible I've caught up to him sooner than I planned."

A flutter of fear brushed her heart. "You think he might return to this camp?"

"Dunno for sure. Hope not. I'm not ready to take him. Not with you along."

She didn't want to admit how much that stung. She

was not wanted. An albatross around his neck. "What would you do if I were *not* along?"

"Take him."

She thought hard. Will had gone out of his way to rescue her and catch up with the wagon train at Fort Laramie. Then he'd offered to take her on to Oregon. Why would he do that?

Ah, it must be that the man he was chasing was also moving west. And that meant…

Will's first priority was not taking her to Oregon. His main goal was tracking that outlaw! He didn't care a whit about her school at Christmas Lake Valley. *She* didn't matter at all. The inescapable observation made her blood boil.

"You wretch!" She snapped out the word. "You calculating, selfish, sneaky, sorry excuse for a man."

To her surprise he didn't move. He didn't even look disturbed, just gazed at her with those cold blue eyes.

"You could at least have the decency to look guilty!" she snapped. She was so angry her whole body trembled. "At the very least you could apologize!"

"Hell, what are you so mad about? You're warm. You're full of hot coffee. You're safe. And I'm tryin' like hell to keep you that way."

"By stumbling along a trail we can barely see in the dark? I've been in the saddle since sunup. That is at least ten hours and I am tired to the bone. And now you want me to ride *more* hours?"

He came toward her. "You know what, princess? I'm not asking you, I'm telling you. Pack up and get on your horse."

"I won't do it."

"Like hell you won't." He closed his hands around her shoulders and jerked her to a standing position. "Now, git!"

He spun her toward the gray mare and gave her a slap on the backside.

Quivering with fury, Charlotte grabbed her bedroll, stomped to her horse and tied the bundle on behind the cantle. "I will *not* scrub the plates," she announced. "I will *not* empty out the cold coffee. And most particularly, I will not speak to you, Will Bondurant, ever again."

He said nothing, just moved around the camp burying the fire and kicking away the hot cooking stones, his lean face a mask of studied indifference. Charlotte decided at that moment that she detested him.

"I cannot abide men who just order people about. Men who think they always know best and run roughshod over—"

Before she could finish, Will stood before her, his hands jammed in his back pockets, his face dark with fury.

"Will you shut the hell up! I'm trying to save both our skins, and you're throwing a goddamned temper tantrum like a spoiled three-year-old."

He kept his hands seated in his pockets to keep from touching her. He wanted to, oh, Jesus, did he want to. He'd like to shake her until her teeth rattled, smack her across her blathery little mouth. Maybe toss her over his shoulder and dump her in the creek.

He also wanted to kiss her.

Lord almighty, where had that urge come from? He

wasn't an impulsive man. At least not usually. At least not in an uncontrolled way. But right now he ached to grab her, wrestle her to the ground and mold his body to hers. He ached to cover her mouth and taste her tongue, take what he wanted. *Christ, he burned with wanting her.*

He recognized the feeling underneath; it had to be fear. Fear that he was bringing her closer and closer to danger. Fear that he would lose her, like Alice. And like Pa.

And good God almighty, fear that he was falling in love with her.

Chapter Fourteen

They rode all night. At dawn Will decided they had traveled far enough north to throw off anyone following them and avoid stumbling into whoever it was moving west ahead of them. He could tell from the set of Charlotte's shoulders and the stiff way she held her neck that she was still mad as a poked rattler.

He called a halt in a sheltered stand of cottonwoods, and she slipped off her mare and made camp in silence, rolling out her pallet as far away from him as she could get. With a final sniff, she snuggled down and pulled the blanket over her face.

Well, hell. He was too exhausted to try talking sense to a woman with a mad on. Come morning, things might look better. At least the sun would warm up the air between them.

Before he crawled into his own bedroll, he fished the last dog-eared trail biscuit out of his saddlebag and laid it where she'd see it when she woke up. A peace offering of sorts. Or maybe he just felt sorry for her, knowing her belly was empty.

He lay for a while looking at the stars through the lacy canopy of tree branches, thinking about the differences between men and women. The inner differences. The physical ones were plenty clear.

Men liked to feel they were in charge. Women liked letting a man do the thinking. *Except for Charlotte.*

Men liked to prove their manhood by being good providers. Women liked being cared for. *Except for Charlotte.*

Men liked women. Women liked men. What could be simpler?

Still, he wondered what it was, exactly, that a woman felt about a man.

Especially Charlotte.

He woke to the sound of cicadas. The sun was high, the sky white with heat. He rolled over and met Charlotte's steady gaze, her gray eyes wide-open, looking into his with…what? Hell, he used to be able to read a woman just from the way she looked at him.

Not this one, *hombre.* She was as inscrutable as Pa's Chinese cook, and it nettled him worse than a thorn in his drawers. Just what did she think she was doing? *He* was the trail boss here; nothing got under his hide unless he invited it in, and he hadn't invited this—her—in.

She closed her eyes and turned over as if there wasn't a damn thing wrong. She had no right to keep him on tenterhooks! She'd talk to him, by God, if he wanted her to, and that was that.

"Wake up, dammit."

No answer.

"Charlotte, I'm sorry about your hair. Stop acting like a—"

She sprang bolt upright. "Like a what?" she challenged. "I'm acting like a human being, it's *you* who are being unreasonable. Bossy as an army colonel. You, Mr. Bondurant, are as bad tempered as a…as a…"

Will was on his feet before she could finish the sentence. He stomped over to her pallet and nudged her backside with the toe of his boot.

She leaped up so fast he wondered if she'd been snake-bit. Eyes shooting sparks, her mouth stretching into an outraged circle, she advanced on him in her stocking feet.

"Now, you listen to me, Mr. High and Mighty." She poked her stiffened forefinger into his chest. "You are being extremely rude."

"And you're actin' like a goddamn saint, I suppose?"

"Uncivilized and boorish," she continued without a pause. Her finger rap-tapped on his breastbone with each word.

"Like hell. You're the one pitchin' a fit over every little thing like—"

"Little! You call being ignored and having my opinion discounted at every turn 'little'? Let me tell you something, mister—"

"Ignored?"

"Just because I'm a woman—"

"*Ignored?* Hell, lady, one thing you are *not* is ignored."

"I said ignored, and I meant ignored. You pay no attention to anything I—"

Will grabbed her shoulders. She twisted away from him, but he held her fast, his fingers biting hard into her upper arms. "Let me set you straight on somethin', princess."

Again she tried to free herself. Will gave her a little shake and stepped in close. "Stop wiggling, dammit. Let me explain something."

Without moving, she looked up at him. Her cheeks had a pink flush over them, the exact shade of a rose his mother used to grow on the ranch. And soft, oh, God, her skin looked soft. He studied her mouth, thinking that looked mighty soft, as well.

She just stood there, gazing up at him as if she'd never seen him before. A question formed in her eyes, but before she could voice it, something in Will boiled over. The next thing he knew he was hauling her against him and dragging his mouth over hers.

At that instant every single functioning part of his body stopped working and waited, suspended outside of time, while he finished what he'd started. Her eyes might be made of ice, but her lips were made of fire. And behind her mouth lay the suggestion of dark velvet that called to him.

He closed his eyes and let himself answer.

Hell feathers and tarnation what was he doing?

The sound of an approaching horse brought his head up. Two horses. Moving slow and steady.

"Charlotte," he said, keeping his voice low.

She opened her eyes. "I hear them," she said, her voice uneven.

Will lifted his hands from her shoulders, stepped away from her and slid his Colt into his waistband. "Better put on your hat, Charlie. They're heading this way."

She reached for her hat and found the biscuit he'd left. Stuffing as much of it as she could into her mouth, she chewed, hiccupped, chewed some more. He could hear her stomach growling from where he stood.

Charlotte clamped the hat down over her short red curls and took another bite of biscuit. He moved toward her. "Try not to get between me and whoever it is."

She nodded and went on eating, a dazed look on her face, as Will came to stand beside her. Without speaking, they scanned the sage-dotted prairie in the direction of the hoofbeats and tried to calm their breathing.

Two riders. Charlotte squinted into the sun, but the figures were too far away to see clearly. When Will breathed a soft "Damn," she guessed their visitors were not friends.

"Long John and the Comanche," he intoned. "Here, have a cigar." He pulled two slightly bent Havanas from his back pocket and slipped one into her hand.

Was he crazy? Now was no time for a smoking lesson! She didn't want to struggle with a cigar; she wanted to sort out what had just happened between them. Her brain felt as if someone had mixed it up with an eggbeater.

"Watch me," he said quietly. Suddenly she understood. If the two men came into camp, she had to be Charlie, not Charlotte. Right down to smoking a smelly cigar. But first, she had to stop her heart from pounding.

Will bit off the tip of his cigar. Charlotte did the same just as a rough voice called out.

"Halloo the camp."

"Mornin' to ya'," Will drawled. "Mighty fine mornin'."

Charlotte's teeth clamped around the cigar. The two

horsemen approached at a walk. When they came into view, ice water replaced the blood surging in her veins.

The short man *did* look familiar. Where had she seen him before? On the wagon train? In Independence?

"More like afternoon, don'tcha think, friend?"

"Reckon so." Will grinned at them. "Kinda lose track of time after sunup." He spoke to the Indian in a different language and the two exchanged brief hand signs.

Will caught Charlotte's eye, touched a match to the end of his cigar and sucked in three short puffs of air. A cloud of aromatic blue smoke wreathed his face.

Oh, Lord, she had to light hers, too. At least her breathing was almost normal.

Will drew again on the cigar, removed it with a flourish and held it between his forefinger and his middle finger. "What can I do for you gents this fine day?"

Charlotte struck a match against the sandpaper end of the matchbox, but it fizzled out. She struck another. She didn't want to think about this silly cigar; she wanted to think about Will! His mouth on hers, his hard, warm body pressed against her breasts.

"We're lookin' for somebody," Long John said. His gaze slid to Charlotte. "A woman."

The match in her fingers flared. She had to bring the flame to the cigar, but her hand trembled like a windblown leaf.

"Yeah?" Will said, his tone disinterested. "What kinda woman?"

She aimed the fluttering match head at her mouth. She could do it. She *had* to do it.

Long John leaned over his saddle horn. "A redhaired woman."

Charlotte drew in a long, careful breath and saw the cigar tip glow crimson. *Thank You, Lord. Thank You!*

"Ain't seen *any* woman on the trail," Will said slowly, chewing on his cigar. "Much less a redheaded one. What's she wanted for?"

"She's not an outlaw," Long John snapped.

Will puffed out a perfect smoke ring. "Yeah? Bit of high-class calico, maybe?"

Charlotte stared at the smoke ring. Surely he didn't expect her to do *that?* She inhaled experimentally. The vile taste in her mouth made her lips pucker, and the cigar wobbled.

"Not calico, neither." Long John peered at Charlotte. "You're gonna lose that cigar, kid."

"He's just learnin' to take a ceegar," Will said. "His momma won't like it one bit, but…" He shrugged. "A boy's gotta grow up sometime."

Long John's eyes narrowed. "Don't talk much, does he?"

"Nope. Always been the quiet one in the family."

The man stepped his horse toward Charlotte. "Say something, kid."

Her throat closed. To play for time, she chewed on the cigar, even though it tasted like burnt saddle leather. She knew she couldn't do that all morning; she had to say *something.* And she had to say it now.

"Got any whiskey, mister?" She growled the words in her lowest register.

The Indian laughed.

"Hell, kid, if we had any, we'd be drinkin' it! Anyways, aren't you kinda young for hard liquor?"

"No whiskey!" Will interjected. "And that'll be your last ceegar this mornin', Charlie." He rolled his eyes at Long John. "Kid's growin' up too fast. Next thing he'll want is a bit of calico. Say, why'd you tell us you're chasin' that gal?"

"Because—" Long John settled back in his saddle and chewed the inside of his cheek "—because she's my wife."

Charlotte sucked in air past the cigar between her lips. Was she dreaming? Did he say "wife"?

"Wish ya luck," Will said with forced joviality. "Sure would hate to lose *my* wife out here in this wilderness."

"I didn't say she was lost, friend. Just said I'm lookin' for her." Long John flicked the reins and turned his mount. The Indian followed.

Charlotte watched, frozen, as the two men reined away. Just as they left the camp, the Indian said something over his shoulder. The horses trotted on, and once again the only sound was the buzzing of cicadas.

Will walked after the riders for a few paces and sat on his haunches, studying the tracks the animals left. Charlotte spit out her cigar. "What did that Indian say to you?"

Will rose and blew two more smoke rings just to steady his nerves. "He said Comanche wives never run away."

He smoked during the awkward silence, then tossed the Havana down and ground it under his boot heel. "You want to tell me about Long John? Just how familiar *does* he look to you?"

Charlotte cleared her throat. "I know nothing at all about the man."

Will wondered whether to believe her. For one thing, he was frying inside with white-hot jealousy. He didn't *want* her to belong to another man. The thought of another man touching her tied his guts in a knot.

And for another, Alice, the woman he'd known most intimately, had lied to him once. The deception had shattered his life.

Still, Charlotte hadn't seemed like the lying type. At least he hoped he'd judged her right. He'd been wrong about a woman before.

He shook off the memory and spoke in a controlled voice. "When you remember where you've seen him, let me know, will ya?"

Charlotte bristled. "Of course. What do you take me for?"

"Can't rightly decide," Will said. "Either a halfway decent actress or a mighty forgetful wife." He started for his horse, but she stepped into his path. Eyes flashing, hands on her hips, she looked mad enough to spit and shoot him afterward.

Hell, she was already mad at him. Then, to make things worse, he'd gone and kissed her. What difference did it make if she got a new burr up her...sleeve. He dug in the saddlebag for the coffeepot. He was damn hungry. He'd cook up some breakfast; maybe they'd both feel better if they ate something.

Charlotte stomped about the camp in such a fury the horses began to nicker nervously.

"Feed 'em," Will instructed from the fire he'd coaxed out of a small pile of dry sagebrush.

In stony silence, she poured two handfuls of oats

from the leather feed bag into her hat and held it out. She would never, never speak to him again. How dare he order her about like a servant? Decide everything without once consulting her?

How dare he kiss me!

While the gray nibbled up the oats, she studied the animal's teeth, imagining the powerful jaws closing over Will's forearm. Even better, around his neck.

She fumed in silence all through the meager meal of hot coffee and some unusually delicious tasting bacon, too light-headed with hunger to wonder where it came from. She gobbled down six strips, more than her share, but Will said nothing. Bound in their separate cocoons, they ate, poured coffee, scraped the frying pan and the mugs clean, and packed up their saddlebags without exchanging a word.

Will pointed north to indicate the way, and Charlotte mounted and fell in behind him. Why were they still headed north, when Long John and the Indian had galloped off to the south? She hated not knowing what was going on!

How can I find out without speaking to him?

She kicked the gray and caught up to Will, gestured north and sent him a questioning look.

"Cat's still rasslin' with your tongue, huh?" he said with a grin. "Sure hope you don't come across a rattler or step in a prairie-dog hole. Not bein' able to talk, be no way to warn me you'd lamed your horse or died along the way."

She gave him a sideways look and pressed her lips into a line.

"You're gettin' more trail smart every day, Charlie. 'Scuse me. Charlotte. Yeah, we're headin' north."

Will didn't want to tell her why. Not yet. Why add a hot rock to an already bubbling kettle? But he knew she was aching to ask him.

He reckoned it'd be a war between her curiosity and her stubbornness. The more he thought about it, the more he figured he'd enjoy watching the battle.

Chapter Fifteen

For the next eight hours Will watched Charlotte sweat as they moved north, making good time over the gradually rising plain. There'd be mountains ahead, maybe two days away. He wondered if they'd be on speaking terms by then. Sure didn't fancy sleeping separate in the windy Wyoming high country. He'd miss her soft little backside snugged tight into his groin. Hell, he probably wouldn't get any shut-eye without her.

There was another concern, too—one he tried hard not to think about. He was having trouble keeping his hands off her. What felt perfectly natural three days ago—a hand up, a touch on her shoulder, brushing a leaf out of her hair—he now found charged with tension.

His head pounded from the sun's glare, and he clamped his jaw tight against the pain. Working to get his thoughts anywhere but on her, he found himself growing short-tempered. The worst of it was that Charlotte seemed untroubled by the lack of conversation.

Sure missed hearing her voice. Kinda surprising how much it bothered him.

He jerked hard on Sandy's reins, and the mare tossed her head, then stretched her neck to peer back at him. The accusing look penetrated all the way to his boots, and he leaned forward to pat the animal's neck.

He'd never last all the way to Oregon without snapping. His head felt like a crosscut saw was slicing into his brain and it was damn lonely, talking to yourself. Maybe he'd converse with Sandy.

"Don't seem right, does it, girl? A trail companion oughtta be…a companion. She hasn't said one word to me since breakfast." *Since I kissed her.*

The mare plodded forward.

"You think she's married to Long John? I wonder. Kinda got a feeling she's not. Maybe just a wish, but she seems like a lady that hasn't got the new wore off her yet."

Sandy tossed her head as if in agreement.

"On the other hand, a woman can sure knit the wool over a man's eyes." He weighed that possibility for a full minute.

"My gut tells me there's another thing to consider here, and that is that she's not aware of herself as a female. You know what I mean, don'tcha, girl? Sure ya do. Like when a stallion covers you. Well, she doesn't feel a skosh like I'm feelin'. She thinks of me as a 'friend.' Now I ask you, wouldn't that get your bridle in a tangle?"

He rubbed one hand across his scratchy chin. "For damn sure I don't think of *her* as a 'friend.' I think of her as a woman. And by Jupiter, I think of me as a man."

Charlotte heard the muttering ahead of her, a low rumble of words she couldn't understand. Who was he talking to, his horse?

When she realized that was exactly the case, she started to laugh, then clapped her hand over her mouth.

What was he saying?

She couldn't stand not knowing. She nudged the gray mare forward, tipped her head to one side and listened intently.

Will's low voice droned on, but still she could not distinguish individual words. *Was it about her?*

She urged the gray still closer, until the animal's nose almost brushed Sandy's bushy tail. Charlotte shut her eyes to concentrate on the blur of male-voice sounds ahead of her.

"…the new wore off…"

Or for gracious sake, he was discussing a saddle? Or maybe a pair of boots? She bit her lip.

"…when a stallion covers you…"

Well! What kind of man would be interested in the intimate relations of his horse? She stepped her mare forward until the animal's muzzle drew alongside Sandy's flank.

"…don't think of her as a friend."

Her? Who is—?

Oh! Charlotte's heart dropped into her stomach.

She thought of *him* as a friend. A close friend. The first man friend she'd ever had. And he didn't think of her in that way? Then why had he kissed her?

She jerked up straight in the saddle. Well, the man was a fool. He might make some smart decisions, but when it came to people, his thinking was as scrambled up as her mother's knitting yarn. She ought to give him a piece of her mind, that's what.

If she were speaking to him, that is exactly what she would do.

Late in the day the weather turned ugly. A knife-sharp wind scudded slate-colored clouds into a lumpy mass ahead of them, and when jagged bolts of lightning flashed, Will knew they were in for a gully-washer.

They pitched camp on high ground, well away from the mix of loblolly and lodgepole pine trees, crawled into their separate bedrolls and pulled their rain ponchos over them to wait it out. Around midnight the temperature dropped and the spatter of rain turned into puffy white snowflakes. The wind drove them deeper under their rain gear, and when Will's feet began to ache from the cold he knew they'd have to move. Another three hours of this and they'd be buried under a snowdrift.

Hell's own scorpions, it was late June! Wasn't supposed to snow until late August at the earliest. He'd better think of something fast.

To the west lay more mountains. Not easy in good weather, worse in bad. North led smack into the storm, and while this squall could blow itself out or even pick up a chinook, there could be others behind it.

To the east lay… Well damn, it'd have to do. He hadn't seen his uncle since Pa died, and that was just as well, he figured. The two sides of the family never did get along. Pa's Texas kin distrusted Ma's mixed Apache-

Mexican heritage; the relatives scrapped every time they laid eyes on one another.

But come down to it, he didn't have a choice. He sat up, tossed another scrounged-up pine log on the fire and hunched his backside close enough to scorch his trousers. When he got warm, he tried to think.

What would you do if you were alone?

That was easy. He'd ride north 'til he hit sunshine and hope he didn't freeze to death on the way.

But he *wasn't* alone. He had Charlotte to think of. She wouldn't last an hour in deep snow.

He raised his head up and inspected the lumpy mound on the other side of the fire. She still wasn't speaking to him, but that didn't keep *him* from speaking to *her.* He'd tell her in the morning what he planned to do.

Hold on a minute. Might be smarter to *ask* her? Yeah, he'd ask her, not tell her. That way she wouldn't feel ignored.

He groaned aloud. Lord, if she only knew.

In the morning, snow carpeted every inch of ground with a foot of powdery white crystals, and it was still coming down. By the time he'd boiled up some coffee and baked corn dodgers on the hot rocks, he could barely see the horses.

He watched Charlotte crawl out from under the snow-covered poncho and stamp her boots to warm up her feet. Her face looked pale as the inside of an apple and pinched around the mouth. Sixty seconds in the wind and already she was cold clear through. Could she even make it the twenty miles to his uncle Chili's cabin?

"Here." He shoved a mug of hot coffee into her hand,

noting how bloodless her fingers looked as she wrapped them around the warm container.

Will drew in a slow breath of the stinging air. "Now, I'm not tellin' you, Charlotte. I'm askin'. What would you think about backtrackin' about twenty miles to get out of this storm?"

She nodded her head so vigorously Will chuckled.

"You're not gonna like it, but—" He caught himself. "Be okay with you if we hole up with…"

Jesus. How could he explain about Chili.

"There's a cabin where the Wind River range tails into the Big Horns, but it's…the man that built it…" Oh, hell.

A ghost of a smile touched her lips, and she nodded.

"C'mon and eat," Will said. He thought a moment, then rephrased it. "Would you like some breakfast?"

At that, she laughed out loud. "Of c-course I would. I d-don't even care what it is, even rabbit would be fine. I'm s-so hungry and c-cold."

Will laid his arm around her shoulders, pressed her down on the warm rocks bordering the fire pit and handed her a hot corn dodger. "I'll see to the horses."

He gathered up her bedroll blanket and wrapped it around her shivering form. Then he scooped up her felt hat and plopped it onto her head. "Keep your head covered. You'll stay warmer."

He heard the commanding tone in his voice and braced himself for a protest. But all she did was bite into the corn cake and gulp down some hot coffee. "Thank you."

Will turned away before she could see his grin. By God, she'd spoken two whole sentences to him this morning! Maybe the war was over.

A rush of something hot and sweet swirled into his chest, and for a minute he couldn't seem to get his breath.

The cold stung Charlotte's face until she could no longer feel her nose. Will had covered the lower half of his face with his neckerchief and pulled his hat down as he rode. She did the same, though her fingers were numb and clumsy. Her lips felt swollen and dry, and the tips of her ears hurt. To keep her mind off the cold, she watched the back end of his horse as the animal stumbled on through the deepening drifts.

Will Bondurant wasn't a bad man. He had volunteered to take her to Oregon, and he was protecting her, keeping her safe. He had taught her lots of things. How to keep warm. How to skin and roast a rabbit.

How a woman feels when a man kisses her.

She huddled under the blanket Will had wrapped around her and thought of his hard, hot mouth on hers. The moment had been heart-stopping, so deliciously stirring she could not get it out of her mind. As long as she lived, she would never forget it.

She had always thought kissing a man would be awkward. Where did the noses go? How did one breathe?

But when Will kissed her, it hadn't been awkward. It had been thrilling! Her body came alive in ways she had never dreamed of, all hot and languid-feeling, and afterward she felt…well, shot full of light inside and aching for more.

Stop thinking about it.

Will turned his mount and rode back to her, snow kicking up around Sandy's hooves. "You all right?" He handed her a small flask of dark gold liquid. "Drink some brandy."

She nodded, staring at his lips, then tipped the bottle under her bandanna and swallowed fire.

"It's a long pull to the Wind River," Will said.

"How long?" Her words sounded muffled.

"Six, maybe seven hours. If we keep moving." He gave her a speculative look, raising his dark eyebrows in a question.

"Why would we not?"

"For one thing, the snow could get too deep for the horses. Or one of them could go lame. Or," he said with a wry smile, "we could freeze to death."

"I have faith that we will persevere."

"Yeah? Couldn't hurt to say a few prayers, I reckon."

"I will do that," Charlotte replied. She smiled, then realized he couldn't see the lower part of her face.

"Be sure you keep warm. Sing out if you're not."

"What could you do?"

"Ride double. Drink more brandy." He reined away and took up his position in front, breaking a path through the snow to make it easier for her mare.

Charlotte's eyes stung. If they made it to the cabin— no, *when* they made it—it would be solely because of him.

Yes, he was bossy. Used to issuing orders and having them obeyed. He was rough-mannered and blunt and he took the Lord's name in vain and he shut her out, like Papa had. But Will Bondurant was a good man.

When they reached the cabin she would give him the biggest hug he'd ever received.

Chapter Sixteen

A mile from his uncle's cabin, Will felt the back of his neck prickle. He'd had a lot of thoughts about Chili Twopenny in the last ten years, but none of them ever came close to the feeling crawling up his spine at this moment.

He reined in and waited for Charlotte's mare to catch up. The icy wind had dropped, but she still sat burrowed in her blanket, her hat pulled down so low he couldn't see her eyes.

"Reckon I'd better explain some about Uncle Chili," he said as she fell in beside him. "He's my mother's brother. Half Mexicano, half Apache." He waited for her reaction, but she said nothing.

"My mother was the same, half Mex, half Apache. Her first husband was an Apache chief, Yellow Crane. After he was killed, she married a Mexican general."

"Why does he live way up here in the mountains?"

"The thing is, my momma's brother, Chili, didn't

much like the Mexican side of the family, so he left Texas. Started trapping in the Salmon and Wind River ranges, then bought himself a silver mine."

Her head jerked up. "A silver mine?"

"Near Virginia City."

She nodded. "That is east of Oregon, is it not?"

"And south some."

She tipped her head, as if trying to fit together the geography in her mind. "Which side of the family do you come from?"

"The Texan. After the Mexican general drowned in the Rio Grande, she tied up with my pa, Jackson Bondurant. I figure I'm half Anglo, and a quarter everything else. You could say my momma lived a full life."

"One could say that, I suppose. Is that how you think of her?"

Will ignored the question. "Point is, Chili doesn't cotton to most people, not just Mexicans."

"I see."

"I'm warnin' you not to be surprised by the man, or the way he lives. Won't exactly be what you might expect." Not exactly civilized, would be closer to the truth, Will acknowledged. Chili always did have an eccentric streak.

In one way he was curious how Charlotte would react to the old man. In another way, he wondered how Chili Twopenny would react to a good-looking woman dressed like a man.

He studied the cabin as they approached. No tracks marred the smooth white cover of new snow powdering the front meadow. Looked like Chili hadn't been outside since the snow started.

Then he noticed something else. No smoke curled from the stone chimney. He'd visited Chili once before, after he'd taken a slug in his chest. He'd stayed for the month of August, and hot as it was that summer his uncle always kept a fire burning. Swore it kept away evil spirits.

Will studied the small log structure. Could be Chili was off trapping somewhere. Or working his mine.

The uneasy feeling grew stronger as they dismounted and trudged up the four plank steps to the half-timbered door.

Charlotte touched his arm. "What is wrong, Will? You're frowning."

"Dunno. Just…something."

"Your uncle won't like me, being a preacher's daughter, I guess."

"Wouldn't matter if he didn't, but no, that's not my worry. He'll like you just fine."

Some instinct made him put Charlotte behind him and he heaved the door open. "Chili?" He stepped over the threshold. "Always did have an eye for a pretty—"

The old man lay faceup on the bearskin rug in front of the empty fireplace. Will knelt beside him. Dried blood matted his buckskin shirt.

"Oh, Jesus. Chili."

"Luis," a thready voice whispered.

"No, it's Will." He swallowed hard when he glimpsed the wound through the torn shirt front. A .52 caliber rifle at close range.

"Luis," the old man whispered again.

"No, it's—" Will broke off. *Chili knows who I am.*

He's naming his killer. Luis. Son of a— Cold sweat broke out between his shoulder blades.

He should have guessed. "I've been chasing him, Chili. He vamoosed out of Nogales after he—" Will purposely did not finish the sentence. Chili didn't need his final moments disturbed by old family feuds or bad news.

"How long ago?" he said quietly.

"Two days. Maybe three, I lose track."

"Before the snow," Will surmised. "There aren't any tracks outside."

"Two—" the old man labored for breath "—horses. One rider."

Will nodded. He took the weather-worn hand in his own. "I brought a pretty girl to meet you, Chili. Her name's Charlotte."

He watched Chili's dark eyes look past him to focus on Charlotte. "Ah." His cracked lips stretched into a smile. "You know what I…what I like. A pretty girl. A very pretty…"

The breath sighed out of him and Will knew he was gone. Behind him he could hear Charlotte crying. The sound of her sobs shuddering in and out sent a blade into the pit of his stomach. With a sick feeling in his gut, he reached out and closed the lids over his uncle's sightless eyes.

I'm going to kill Luis this time. It's not even going to be a fair fight.

He rose, drew a woven Indian blanket off the old man's bunk and laid it over the still form. Will's limbs felt heavy, as if he was walking through molasses.

"Charlotte?"

"Yes, Will?"

"Open the door. And stop crying."

She sniffled once and pressed her hand against her chest. "What are you going to do?"

Will's throat closed. When he could talk, he explained. "Drag Chili onto the porch."

"I will help you."

Will stared at her. She was one surprising female, all right. Wail half a day over a haircut, then stiffen up her spine and help him move a corpse.

Will saw to his uncle's body and tended to the horses. Left alone, Charlotte unknotted her fingers and surveyed the interior of the cabin. Steel animal traps hung from chains looped over the ceiling beams, and over the door a heavy-looking rifle balanced on the prongs of a mounted antelope rack. Charlotte wondered if it was loaded.

A thick black fur pelt had been nailed to the log wall and next to it hung a dusty guitar and a set of dented cowbells. A weathered wagon wheel had been mounted over the stove, kettles and frying pans dangling from hooks embedded in the spokes. The place had a certain rough charm, but the cold air in the room, and the circumstances, made her shiver.

There was no furniture other than a crudely hewn wood slab table supported on two fruit crates and two chairs made out of leveled-off tree stumps. The only place to sleep, she noted, was the square plank box bed in one corner. The realization made her breathing catch.

Had she really done the right thing, starting cross-country with Will? It would have been safer to stay with the wagon train, but that way she would have no chance at all to explore anything along the way. In particular, she reminded herself with a twinge of guilt, to investigate something near the Indian lands in eastern Oregon. For the thousandth time, she wondered if Will guessed she had not been entirely honest with him.

The door crashed open and she jumped. Will strode in, shaking snow from his hair and dusting off his trousers. "Let's get a fire started," he said in a tired voice. "Gonna be damn cold tonight."

He dropped both saddles in the corner opposite the bed, hung his hat on a set of moose antlers mounted next to the door and gestured toward her. "Wanna hang your hat up?"

He looked pointedly at her hands. Without conscious awareness she was convulsively kneading the brim of her gray felt hat. "N-no. Not yet."

"You scared?"

Charlotte stared at him. "Scared? I am half paralyzed with fear! The trouble is, I don't know exactly why."

"Maybe 'cuz there's a dead man keepin' us company?"

Charlotte nodded. "It's…awfully quiet."

"Could be you're worryin' whether that murderin' son of a—whether Luis is comin' back?"

She caught her breath. "You don't think he *would,* do you?"

"Not sure. If it doesn't keep snowing, he might hightail it into the mountains."

"And if it does?"

"He might want to hole up where it's warm."

"You mean here?" Her voice rose into a moan.

Will sighed. "He might. Depends on whether he

knows I'm on his trail or not. If he does come back, for sure he'll recognize Sandy."

Charlotte shuddered and wrapped her arms over her middle. "What are we going to do?"

Will's dark eyebrows twitched. "The usual things, I reckon. Get a fire going. Cook some supper. Get some sleep."

Charlotte opened her mouth, then quickly closed it. How could he be so maddeningly practical when things went wrong?

"Tomorrow," Will continued, "if it stops snowing long enough, I'll dig a grave."

Again, Charlotte's eyes filled with tears. "I am so sorry about your uncle. About…everything."

Will didn't answer. He knelt before the stone fireplace and laid a fire using split wood from the half barrel that served as a kindling box. When the flames rose, he rolled a thick log on top. "That should burn slow, give us heat all night."

Charlotte nodded, but she couldn't look at him. "I am hampering your search, am I not? Slowing you down. I would not want you to lose your quarry because of me. Especially now that you know he killed…" She tipped her head toward the porch.

Will scraped a match across the stone hearth. "I'm not gonna lose him. Time we reach Oregon territory, Luis will be gettin' tired of runnin'."

Flames crackled to life. Will fed it small branch trimmings and watched blue smoke curl up the chimney. "Could be Luis would get a tad careless. That would sure work to a tracker's advantage."

"Yes, I suppose so." She wondered suddenly if Long John was still trailing them. Heavens, she couldn't think about that man now. Tomorrow, when she was not so frightened. Oh, Lord, maybe she should have told Will everything.

They ate their supper of canned oysters and peas from Chili's odd collection of pantry foodstuffs and watched the fire burn to coals. Then Will rolled Charlotte's bedroll out on top of the box bed and hunkered down next to her beside the fire.

"There's no lock on the door. I'll sleep across the doorway."

"Won't you be uncomfortable? I can feel cold air blowing in under the door."

"I'll stuff a rag in the crack and sleep with a hot rock at my feet. Unless…"

She sent him a wide-eyed glance. "Unless what?"

"Unless you'd like…"

"No," she said quickly. "I am sure I will be quite comfortable on the bed."

"Wasn't *your* comfort I was considerin', princess."

The fire sparked in the silence, and neither spoke for a time. "Guess I'll turn in, then," Will said at last. "Been a long day."

"Yes, it has," she murmured. She sat staring into the flames with a faraway look, absently stroking the fingers of her right hand through her short red curls.

"Somethin' on your mind?" Will said.

"N-no. Nothing much."

He pushed to his feet. "Well, good night, then."

"Good night." She made no move toward the square

bed laden with colorful woven blankets, and for a fleeting second he thought maybe she'd change her mind and invite him—

Aw, hell, why would she? She wasn't fighting a physical need like he was.

He stuffed the dish towel under the front door to stop the air whistling in, jockeyed his saddle into place for a pillow and stretched out full-length on the bearskin rug. Even so, the plank floor seemed harder than any ground he'd ever slept on.

He closed his eyes and tried not to think of the soft bed in the corner. He heard Charlotte move away from the fireplace, heard her boots thunk on the floor as she pulled them off, then the swish of the blankets as she crawled into her bedroll.

Will laid an arm over his eyes and tried to think. Everything was out of kilter—a dead man on the porch and a killer on the loose, maybe heading back this way. Sooner or later he'd have to decide what to do about Charlotte. Especially now that Luis had revealed his whereabouts. He wanted it to be later, but he sensed he wasn't going to have it his way. Pretty plain he'd have to leave her somewhere and go on ahead without her.

Another soft blanket noise. Will cracked one eye open to see that she'd raised herself up on one elbow.

"Go to sleep, Charlotte."

But she didn't. In the flickering light he watched her toss and turn for a good quarter hour. What's eatin' her?

Then he saw her leave the bed and move toward

him. He half sat up as she crept close. "Something bothering you?"

"I can't sleep," she whispered.

"Neither can I. I keep thinkin' about…" He started to say Chili, but the word that almost escaped his lips was "you." He couldn't stop thinking about the preacher's daughter jabbing her finger into his breastbone.

She hunched motionless beside him for what seemed an unusually long time. "Will?"

"Yeah?" She didn't answer, just reached toward him, wrapped her fingers around his shirtfront and held on.

"What is it, Charlotte? What's wrong?"

"Who is Luis?"

"My half brother. His father was a Mexican general, Antonio Bajado. My father was a Tejano. Jackson Bondurant."

"Are you sure he won't come back here?"

"Not unless he's grown calluses on his brain. Luis is too smart for that."

"He is the man you are chasing? Your own brother?"

Will released a ragged sigh. "Yeah."

"Why?"

"Luis was always…different. Jealous, I guess. A year ago he went crazy. Killed my father, then shot Alice, my wife. He was aiming for me."

"Your wife! I had no idea you were married."

"I'm not, now. For a lot of years there hadn't been much between us. She was a Southern girl. She didn't like anything about Texas."

"You want to kill Luis, then?"

Will's voice hardened. "I'm gonna do more than want to."

"I wish you would not. Thou shalt not kill is the Sixth Commandment."

"Dammit, I know how you feel, Charlotte. I wish I didn't have to, but I do."

Quiet descended, broken only by the occasional spitting of the fire and their careful breathing. Suddenly she leaned toward him and snuggled her head into the crook of his shoulder.

"Hold me," she breathed. "I'm frightened. That is, if you wouldn't mind?"

Will wrapped his arms around her and pressed his face against her hair. "You know I want to. You don't have to ask."

Charlotte hesitated. "You may not want to when I tell you what I…I have to tell you."

He smoothed his hand over her soft curls. "Try me."

She was so quiet Will thought she'd fallen asleep until she drew in a jerky breath and cleared her throat. "Before I joined Mr. Ludlow's wagon train, I lived in Ohio."

"Yeah, I figured that."

"I…my father and mother died in a fire at the rectory six months ago. The day after the funeral Papa's lawyer read the will, and there was something in it I did not expect." Her voice changed and Will grew instantly alert.

"An inheritance?"

"In a way. Papa was a Methodist minister. He didn't have anything much except the house, and that burned down."

"Not money," he guessed. "Something else."

"Yes," she breathed. "This is what is so hard to tell you. Papa willed me something. A mine."

"What kinda mine?"

"Well, it can't be worth anything. Papa knew nothing about mining, so when Uncle Leo, who was an engineer, passed on and left this mine to—"

"What kinda mine?" Will repeated.

Charlotte swallowed audibly. "Copper. It's a copper mine. I'm sure it's worthless."

"Where 'bouts is this mine?"

"Oregon. Near the Indian lands. I—I have a map. Or I *had* a map. I memorized it before I left Ohio and then I destroyed it."

Will straightened and held her away from him. "Why? Why go to all that trouble?"

"So no one else could find it."

"If it's worthless, why would anyone else want it?"

"To be honest, Papa's lawyer advised me…" Her voice dropped to a whisper. "He was afraid someone would…take advantage of me."

"For the mine, you mean."

"Yes."

Will digested that. "And so?"

"And so, I left Marysville at night, without telling anyone. I took the train to Independence and found Mr. Ludlow's wagon train."

Will shifted uncomfortably. "And then you found me. You're not going to Oregon to teach, is that it?"

"Oh, yes, I intend to. The Indian agent, Mr. Stryker, has a cabin all ready for me. But…then that man, Long

John, came looking for me, and I think I know what he wants."

"Why not give it to him? Draw the map up, I mean. 'Specially if it's worthless, like you say."

"Well, because now I'm not so sure it *is* worthless."

"So once we hit the trail, you thought you'd get me to guide you to your mine."

She nodded.

"I'm having a hard time believing this, Charlotte. You planned this? All along you meant to use me for your own purposes?"

"Yes, I did," she said in a small voice.

"Well, I'll be damned. You scheming little…"

"No, it isn't like that at all."

Will snorted. "Like hell it isn't. You passed yourself off as a good Christian woman who needed help and then you— Damn, I oughtta…"

"Will, please."

"Only thing I hate more'n a woman who hoodwinks a man is one who lies. Goddammit, Charlotte, I—"

He broke off, afraid to trust his voice. "Just goddammit all to hell."

"I'm sorry, Will. I had to tell you. I couldn't stand it any longer. I didn't want to lie, but I was desperate, don't you see? That man, Long John, he must be after the mine, too. That's why he's looking for me."

"And that told you the mine must be worth something. You must have figured that out when you recognized him at the water hole."

He rose so abruptly she sprawled across his bedroll. "I'm not gonna take you to a damned mine or anyplace else. I've half a notion to leave you here in Chili's cabin until some trapper happens by. Better yet, find Ludlow's wagon train and…"

Then he remembered the hungry look in Harve Jenkins's eyes. "Aw, hell, I can't do that, no matter what."

And he couldn't leave her here in Chili's cabin, alone with no protection.

Mad as he was at her, she'd got under his skin too deep to throw her to the wolves.

Chapter Seventeen

"What about Long John?" Will growled.

Charlotte blinked. "What about him? I know nothing about the man."

"You married to him?"

"Certainly not."

Will shook his head. "You haven't been honest with me up until now. Makes a man wonder."

"I just confessed to you that I had not—"

"Then how do I know you're not lying about Long John? How do I know you aren't running away from him, like he said, not going out to Oregon to teach?"

"Will, really! Would you take his word over mine?"

"I wouldn't up until five minutes ago. Now, I don't know."

"You don't trust me? After all we have been through together?"

"You think dust and heat and thirst and bad weather is what builds trust? Just living through some misery isn't enough." He was so angry now his body trembled. In a dim corner of his brain he recognized a feeling of hurt so deep it came dangerously close to blind fury. "I guess I never realized how close love and hate could be."

"Will? What are you going to do?"

"Right this minute I don't know." He had some feelings about the matter, though. He'd like to close his fingers about her throat and strangle her where she stood. He'd also like to kiss her until she turned to jelly in his arms.

"Damn you, Charlotte."

She advanced on him, her gray eyes narrowed. "Now just one minute!" She raised her hand to jab her forefinger at his chest, but he snaked his fingers out and closed them over her arm so tight he knew he'd leave bruises.

"Let me go!"

"Hell, no."

She started to wrench free, but he pinned her wrist over her head and caught her other arm in his free hand. This time when she tried to pull free, he stepped in close and backed her up against the wall with his body. Without her boots, her forehead came just to his nose. She lowered her head and butted it against his shoulder.

He tightened his hold, pulled her so close to him he could feel her knees against his. His breath quickened, ruffling her hair every time he exhaled. When her breasts brushed against his chest, his fury turned into something else.

He wanted her. Wanted to hear her voice cry his name, feel her mouth open under his. If he stopped to think about it he knew he'd back off and stomp around outside in the cold to corral the hot hunger eating up his insides. So he wouldn't think about it.

He wouldn't stop, either. He drove his leg between her thighs. Even under the denim they felt smooth and soft.

"Will," she gasped. "What are you doing?"

"Hell if I know." He panted the words. "All I know is it feels so damn good...you feel so damn good I don't want to stop. Don't know whether I could stop, so don't ask me."

"You don't have to stop," she breathed.

"I damn well— What?" For the first time he noticed her heavy, irregular breathing matched his.

"Charlotte. Look at me."

She made a small sound and tipped her head down so he couldn't see her face. Will pressed his groin against her, hard. "Look at me, dammit!"

Slowly she raised her head. He expected defiance; what he saw sent an arrow of desire into his gut. Her pupils were dilated, her eyes so dark they looked black in the guttering firelight. He released her arms. He'd never kissed a woman against her will.

Her hands curled about his neck and tightened. Jesus and Gibraltar, she was willing. He dipped his mouth to hers and felt her burst into flame under his lips.

More than willing. She was as hungry as he was.

"Will," she murmured. "Will." Something fluttered deep in Charlotte's belly and suddenly she wanted to be closer to him. Pressed against his body as tight as she could get. "What is happening?" she said in a dazed voice.

"Damned if I know," he said against her mouth. "There's only one question, the way I see it."

"What question?" she whispered. She wanted to taste him, run her tongue over his skin, his mouth.

He lifted his chin away from her seeking lips. "Where are we going with this?"

She gave a low, soft laugh. "I think, Mr. Bondurant, that we are already there."

She couldn't explain it, couldn't even think coherently under the rush of sweet, drowsy feelings seeping through her. All she knew was what he was doing to her now, at this moment, she wanted more of, and then more. Had it been like this for Papa and Mama? So joyous and bewildering all at the same time?

It must have been, at least once. She wanted that. More than anything, she wanted that for herself.

"Charlotte. Hell, am I dreaming? What are you doing?"

"I am unbuttoning a man's shirt." She smoothed her fingers over his hard, warm chest, touched his nipples and heard him suck in air.

"Charlotte…Jesus, think a minute."

"I am thinking." She trailed her fingers to his waist, slipped them under his belt. He lifted her hand away and kissed her, long and deep. Then he started on the buttons of her shirt, yanked the tail out of her jeans and untied the ribbon that gathered her camisole across her breasts.

His fingers pushed the muslin off her shoulders, and he bent to brush his lips into the hollow of her throat. Slowly, deliberately, he kissed a path to her nipple, and she cried out in delight. Nothing in her life had ever, *ever* felt so wonderful.

He spoke against her skin, murmuring her name as he unbuckled her belt and unsnapped her jeans. Then his hands were on her hips, pushing away the fabric of her underdrawers, cupping her buttocks and—merciful heaven!—moving between her thighs. A wanton storm raged inside her. She stepped out of her jeans and drawers and opened her legs in invitation.

He went down on one knee, swirled his tongue in the depression of her navel, then with a groan he rose and shucked his jeans. They stood so close she could feel the heat from his body, but he did not touch her. What exquisite torture.

And then he stepped into her and caught her mouth under his. Their bodies touched all the way down, her skin burning against his, her movements, the sounds she made no longer under her control.

He cupped her breasts in his two hands while his tongue dipped deep into her mouth and then withdrew, over and over until she ached. She wanted to touch him, feel his manhood, but she was afraid. Such a bold thing for a preacher's daughter to do. But she felt bold! Full of the sweet, sweet juice of life here in this place, with death so near.

When he slipped a finger inside her, she moaned with pleasure. With a hoarse chuckle he swirled it once, went deeper, then moved his hand, both hands, to her swelling breasts.

Then he was lifting her, carrying her to the square bed, and kneeling over her. She reached to pull him down on top of her, but he hesitated.

Once again he used his finger to explore, his movements gentle, purposeful. With his other hand he spread her legs and positioned himself over her.

Something hard and hot pressed between her thighs, moved up to her entrance and stopped. He reached around her, spread his fingers over her backside and tipped her up to meet him. He slid forward, pressing deeper, deeper until a brief, sharp sting inside gave way to throbbing pleasure, the mystery of having a man so deep within her that his probing member touched something, and she convulsed.

He began to move, guiding her hips with his hands, pulling her toward him as he thrust into her.

She convulsed again, heard his breathing roughen and catch, drawing in and out in a steady rhythm until she felt herself rise to a pinnacle and hang there, waiting for…waiting for…

Spasms shook her. Charlotte screamed with the pleasure of it, and instantly Will's movements ceased. Then with a hoarse cry he plunged deep, his body shuddering. Her last conscious thought was how exquisite it felt.

When she opened her eyes, he was there beside her, his arms wrapped around her, his chest slick with sweat. "I'll stoke up the fire," he said in a low voice.

"Don't go," Charlotte murmured.

"We're lying on top of the blankets, naked. Sweaty. I want to keep us warm."

She watched him roll away and move to the fireplace. *I have known a man. Known him in the biblical sense.* A man who keeps me warm and safe. A wonderful man.

He laid wood on the fire, then turned toward her.

Without speaking he stretched his body beside hers and gathered her into his arms. The flames jumped and flickered in the fireplace, making the shadows writhe as if they were dancing. When he drew in an extra-deep breath, she knew he had something on his mind. She closed her eyes and waited.

"You should have told me," he said quietly.

"Told you what?" She laced her fingers into his unruly dark hair.

"That you were a virgin."

"Would it have made a difference?"

"Maybe. I would have believed you weren't married to Long John."

"Would that have stopped you?"

Will thought for some minutes. "No," he said at last. "I'd have wanted to be your first. I wouldn't have stopped unless you wanted me to."

"Well, then," she said on a sigh. "You got what you wanted." She gave a tiny laugh. "And so did I."

Will lay awake a long time, his eyes closed, breathing in the scent of Charlotte's body curled against his and listening to her soft, regular breathing. He'd thought Charlotte was different, thought she was a woman who would never lie or be dishonest. Guess he'd assumed too much about the preacher's daughter.

But Jesus, what had he done?

When he cracked his lids open, he found the cabin washed in sunlight streaming through the single window. Charlotte was studying his face with an odd expression in her eyes. He hesitated, then lifted his arm away from her waist.

"I was crazy last night," he said.

She didn't even blink, but looked steadily into his eyes. "I thought you were wonderful last night."

"I was mad as a hurt bull. Surprised. A little bit loco."

"About me?"

"Yeah, about you." Will sighed and closed his eyes again. "I was way outta line."

She laughed softly. "Oh, Will, don't brood about it. You had every right to be angry after I told you about the mine. What followed was not because of your anger."

"It was at first," he said shortly. "But it…changed. I should have backed off. Or tried to, anyway. If I'd thought about it for half a minute I'd have known you couldn't be married to Long John."

"How could you possibly have known?"

Will thought a moment. "You're an innocent when it comes to yourself as a woman."

Charlotte's cheeks flushed rose. "I am not so innocent this morning."

Will groaned. "Wasn't an honorable thing to do, takin' you to bed."

She touched his face. "What has honor to do with it?"

"For a man like me, honor's the only thing I've got."

She stared at him with wide, gray eyes. "Gracious, you really believe that, do you?"

"Yeah, I do. But I wanted you, so I went after you." Which made what he'd done even worse.

Her blush deepened. "Will…"

"And now I've got a double problem. I can't leave you here, or anywhere else. And I can't be near you, either." His concern for her well-being would always be at war with his physical hunger for her. A preacher's daughter, even one who lied to him, wasn't a light piece of calico. He couldn't bed her again. He would ruin her.

"Well, goddamn," he muttered.

"You regret it, then?" she said softly.

"More than you'll ever know, princess."

"You wish that we had not...?"

He rolled toward her and pulled her close. "Hell, no, I don't. Just wonderin' how I'm gonna get through the rest of our journey. You aren't the kind of lady a man dallies with."

Charlotte gave him a long look. She knew he was right. In the long run she would thank him. But right now she didn't want to think sensibly; she just wanted to feel him close to her.

"Well, goddamn," she echoed.

Will snorted a laugh, then cupped her chin in his hand and kissed her.

"Sure is hard to stop," he murmured. It was even harder to lift his hands away from her silky warm body and slide out of bed.

"Stay there," he ordered. "I'll get a fire going, take the chill off."

She watched him pull on his trousers and stalk around on the plank floor in his bare feet, stirring up the fireplace coals and adding more wood. His naked chest and lean, muscled back were beautiful.

Charlotte drowsed until the smell of fresh coffee

woke her. She tossed back the blanket, found the room toasty and slid her legs over the edge of the bed. Her jeans and shirt lay across one of the stump chairs. She'd have to get from here to there with nothing but the blanket around her.

Will watched her from the kitchen. Halfway across the room, she let the blanket drop away, aware of his darkening eyes. Oh, she was wicked! But she didn't care. Being admired by a man gave her an exultant feeling of being valued. A feeling of power.

She pulled on her camisole and buttoned her shirt, slowly, letting him watch. When she reached for her underdrawers, Will bolted for the door.

"'Scuse me. I'll see to the horses."

She couldn't stop smiling. Brave, strong Will Bondurant was afraid of her!

Chapter Eighteen

Will pulled the cabin door shut behind him and started across the porch. After he fed Sandy and the gray, he'd get his shovel and—

He bit off his thought when he glanced out across the expanse of snow. Silhouetted against the brilliant blue sky sat White Eagle in full feather headdress mounted on a roan. Seven mounted braves flanked him; one of them was Five Feathers.

Jesus and Jupiter, what the—?

White Eagle stepped his roan forward. "I did not think to find you here, my friend."

"You're kind of a surprise to me, too, White Eagle." Will nodded to the braves, who sat stone-faced on their painted horses. Why had they come?

"We seek the man Chili Twopenny. He has furs for trading, but he did not meet us at the place we agreed."

"Chili Twopenny is dead," Will said. He gestured toward the porch, where his uncle's body lay wrapped in the woven blanket. "Gunshot. I was gonna bury him today."

"I warned him about his guest, but he did not listen."

Will frowned. "What do you know of his guest?"

White Eagle quieted his restless horse. "That one, I have seen before. He is a bad man. He shoots first and thinks afterward. Angry men are blind."

"Yeah." Will was counting on it. He hoped Luis would stay crazy-mad and careless when he caught up to him.

White Eagle motioned toward the porch. "We will take Twopenny to our burial ground, to free his spirit."

"No. Twopenny is not of your tribe, but mine. Mescalero. I will bury him beneath the earth. It is what he would wish."

The chief grunted. "That is so. He was a good man. We will help you dig and sing over his resting place."

"He would be honored." Will went for his shovel, found one of Chili's under the porch. Purposely he pointed to an aspen copse some yards from the cabin and silently willed Charlotte to stay inside until the Indians were gone.

Will scraped away the snow. The ground underneath was hard but not frozen, and Will set to work. White Eagle and his braves watched from the backs of their horses, all except Five Feathers, who took up a shovel and joined him. Even in the crisp morning air, Will began to sweat. He'd been gone too long from the cabin. Any second Charlotte would step through the door and Five Feathers would recognize her.

The brave's sharp eyes slid over the two mares picketed on the protected side of the cabin. "Where is your woman?"

Will's hands clenched on the shovel handle. "I took her back to the wagon train," he lied. "Don't rightly know where it is by now."

"You would part from her?" Five Feathers scowled at him across the grave site. "I do not think so."

"She's a white woman. She doesn't like the plains."

Five Feathers stopped digging. "Who rides the gray horse, then?"

Will swallowed. "My nephew."

"Why does he not help bury his grandfather?"

"Still sleepin'. He's just a kid."

The brave spit to one side. "The young are lazy. You should beat him."

The cabin door cracked open and Will's stomach dropped. "Charlie?" he yelled. *Stay inside, dammit.*

"Kid's shy," Will said. "Doesn't talk much." *Don't come out. Just stay put.*

"Hunh." Five Feathers grunted.

"Chili never talked much, either. You ever hear him string five words together, White Eagle?"

The chief grunted. "Told good stories."

"Short ones, I'd guess." Will saw White Eagle's weathered face wrinkle into a smile.

Five Feathers planted the head of his shovel on the ground and watched the cabin door. "Why does your nephew not join us?"

"Scared of Indians, maybe. It's his first trip West."

"He is himself an Indian," Five Feathers shot.

"Only half," Will explained. "His ma's Mexicano."

The brave shook his head. "Let me see him."

Will gritted his teeth. "C'mon out, Charlie." *And for God's sake, look as male as possible.* If White Eagle caught him in a lie, he wouldn't live another hour.

After a long minute the cabin door swung open and Charlotte strode out onto the porch, her hands stuffed in her back pockets. A crumpled looking cigarette dangled from her lips.

Will's throat constricted. He saw with relief that her gray felt hat covered every strand of red hair. She was quick, all right. Figured out right away what she had to do—play the Charlie role.

He watched her puff away on the cigarette. She was good at acting. Damn good. In a way, it made him wonder.

White Eagle sniffed the air. "You have tobacco?"

"Not much, but you're welcome to it." Will motioned Charlotte over. "Hey, Charlie, any makin's left?"

She nodded, tramped across the snow in her best swagger and without saying a word pulled out the tobacco pouch and cigarette papers from her vest pocket and offered them to White Eagle.

"Roll him one, Charlie."

She sent him a look that would fry bacon, then set about filling a paper for the chief, her own cigarette clamped between her lips. She handed it up to the mounted Indian, then flicked a match to light it.

Not half-bad, Will thought. White Eagle bent toward the flame, puffed deeply and grinned. She'd made a hit with the chief. The preacher's daughter had real guts.

Then she handed out cigarette papers among the

braves and poured tobacco into their waiting palms. She even shared out the matches, moving from man to man lighting their smokes. Last she came to Five Feathers, who watched her every move with hard, suspicious eyes.

Will knew she was terrified. Her hand shook almost imperceptibly as she held out the flaming match. She kept her head down, concentrated on her task, and when Five Feathers puffed a cloud of blue smoke in her face, she stood her ground. The wobbly smile she managed just about burst Will's heart with pride. What an actress. *What a woman.* Scared out of her skin, but still willing to try.

When she came to Will, offering the last rolled cigarette, it was all he could do not to wrap his arms around her. He cupped his hand around hers as the match flared, bent his head toward the flame. Yeah, her fingers trembled like an old man's.

"Thanks, Charlie," he breathed on his exhale.

Charlotte removed her smoke and carefully tapped the cigarette ash onto his boot. For the rest of her life she would remember the bizarre scene she now beheld. Eight Indians and a white man puffing smoke into the clear blue sky like nine tiny chimneys. If she weren't so scared, she would laugh.

"Plenty good tobacco," grunted White Eagle. The braves nodded in agreement, except for Five Feathers, who studied Charlotte with intense black eyes.

"Hey, Charlie," Will said suddenly. "Watch me blow a smoke ring."

The Indians breathed in a collective "aaah" when three perfect rings emerged from Will's mouth. While they all tried it, jeering at each other's misshapen attempts, Will laid his arm across her shoulders and walked her off to one side.

"You've got sand, Charlie," he said near her temple.

She closed her eyes as his warm breath curled into the shell of her ear. "Just don't make me talk, Will. I can't do it."

He clapped her on the back. "Man to man, now, think you could say some words over Chili's grave?"

Charlotte stared at him. "Are you crazy?"

"Nope. Just tryin' to keep us alive. Can you?"

A burst of hilarity interrupted the pregnant silence. White Eagle had produced a perfect circle of smoke, and the clamoring braves rose to the challenge.

"I guess if I can light nine cigarettes without fainting I can recite some scripture."

"Good." Will squeezed her shoulder. "While you rustle up the Good Book, I'll think of some way to get us out of this."

He shoved her in the direction of the cabin.

"Charlie here's gonna speak to God about Chili Twopenny," Will announced. "He has a book of spells." Without looking at her, he grabbed his shovel and resumed digging.

Charlotte glared at him, then moved toward the porch, hearing the scrape and soft rhythm of the two shovels all the way to the cabin door. Good Book? Where was she going to find a Bible in Chili's crazy collection of household items?

She shut the cabin door against the sound of digging and heard instead the hammering of her heart. She couldn't do it. No matter how hard she tried to lower her voice, she would sound like a woman, not a man. Unless...

Her head came up as an idea presented itself. Why not? It would serve Will right for suggesting it in the first place.

With a determined smile, she set about planning the "service" for Chili Twopenny's funeral.

When the grave was deep enough, Will strode to the porch and gathered up the blanket-wrapped body of his uncle.

Turning back toward the cabin he shouted, "Charlie?"

The front door cracked open and a thready voice answered. "Yes, Uncle Will?"

He couldn't help grinning. "You feelin' the spirit?"

"I am ready, if that's what you mean."

"C'mon, then, kid. Let's get this over with."

Charlotte began the ceremony when White Eagle and his braves dismounted and gathered around Will at the grave site. She raised her right hand and ostentatiously opened the thickest book she could find among Chili's possessions, *Mrs. Fanny Schneider's Receipts*. Running her finger down the page she halted at "Carolina Johnnycake" and lifted her eyes to the assembled men.

Will stared at her as if he'd never before laid eyes on her. She loved surprising him. Unlike Papa, who saw her as another soul to save for the Lord, when Will looked at her, he really saw *her.*

Sending up a desperate prayer for courage, she opened her lips. "Join me on the refrain," she said to Will. He shot her a puzzled look but kept his mouth closed. Instead, he nodded and laced his hands together over his rib cage. No doubt the closest he could come to a prayerful stance.

Charlotte dropped her voice into what she hoped would come out as a tenor rather than her usual soprano and hoped the four years of experience directing the Methodist Church choir would come to her aid.

"We are gathered together to bid farewell to…my, um…grandfather, Chili Twopenny. Praise the Lord." She looked expectantly at Will.

"Praise the Lord," he quickly echoed.

"Chili was loved by his nephew, Will Bondurant, and by his grandson." *Whoever he may be.* "Therefore we will raise our voices in a mourning song."

Will's blue eyes widened. "Song?"

"Of course," she replied. "Chili would have wanted it."

He stepped close and intoned, "Hell, Charlie, I can't sing."

"Trust in the Lord, Uncle Will," she murmured. "And don't interrupt."

She began to chant on a single note. "To everything there is a season…" She nodded at Will to join her in the refrain. "Praise the Lord," they sang together on the same note.

A scratchier baritone she had never heard, but it would suffice. She lowered the tone by one note. "And a time to every purpose under the heavens…" She jabbed her elbow into Will's arm. "Praise the Lord," he sang along with her.

She dropped down another tone, praying he would not recognize the tune. "In the midst of life we are in death…" she chanted. This time the Praise the Lord came on cue, and Charlotte ignored the stinging in her eyes. Will was no singer, but he was *trying*. He cared about Chili, and he was doing his best.

"We therefore commit the body of this man, Chili Twopenny…" she sang. It was only when she started over at the beginning of her improvised chant that Will caught on. His eyes caught hers and held them while she chanted to the end of the verse. "The Lord giveth and the Lord taketh…"

He joined her on the final refrain, and Charlotte prayed he would not be angry for using "Three Blind Mice" for Chili's funeral song. It was the only tune she could think of while pacing around in the cabin, wringing her hands in desperation at the task Will had laid on her.

White Eagle and his braves murmured their approval, and as Will began shoveling dirt into the grave, they raised their voices in their own song. To Charlotte it sounded like the howling of coyotes, but then she could imagine what "Three Blind Mice" had sounded like to them. She had to respect their intent.

The grave slowly filled with soil while the Indians chanted and Will and Charlotte shoveled steadily under the warming sun. As they worked, Will began a song of his own under his breath. "When the grave's full, go back inside the cabin."

Two more shovels full of dirt plopped into the hole. "And don't come out," he sang softly. The tune reminded her of "Streets of Laredo," but it was so off-key it could be anything. "Pack up the saddlebags and…"

He straightened, made an exaggerated sign of the cross over the grave mound and collected the shovel from her hands. "And find my forty-four," he crooned.

Charlotte picked up the cookbook where she'd laid it. Just as she turned to go the Indians fell silent. White Eagle stepped forward and reached out his hand.

"He wants to touch the book," Will explained. "Holds good medicine." Charlotte started. *If the chief only knew…johnnycake and apple fritters.*

With reverence, the old man pressed his fingers on the worn blue binding, then lifted them and pointed to Charlotte. Her stomach rose and floated into her throat. Had White Eagle seen through her sham?

The chief muttered some unintelligible words, then pressed his thumb against Charlotte's forehead.

"He says you're a good man, Charlie." Will grinned at her. "Now go do what I said, and don't look back."

She shook hands with White Eagle and pivoted toward the cabin while the chief and his braves mounted their horses. At every step the sounds of men grunting and horses stamping pulled at her, but she dared not risk a look. The Indians were leaving, that was all that mattered. She kept walking.

When the rough cabin welcomed her into its safe interior, Charlotte felt an inexplicable surge of love for the place.

Will watched White Eagle's band trot out of sight before he dared to draw a full breath. Conflicting feelings roiled in his brain—fear for his life and Charlotte's; puzzlement at the Indians' actions this morning; pride in Charlotte's church savvy and inventiveness. But good God, he wouldn't want to do this dicey a dance-around twice in his lifetime.

He turned to the grave, said a quiet goodbye to Chili

and strode to the cabin. No telling what White Eagle would really do. Not for one minute did Will think they'd seen the last of the renegade band. Five Feathers hadn't taken his eyes off Charlotte until he mounted his pony and turned away.

He pushed the cabin door open to find Charlotte standing, feet apart, aiming his revolver at his middle. When she recognized him, her trembling arms lowered and the Colt clattered onto the plank floor.

"Who were you expecting, princess?"

"I-Indians," she stammered. "Oh, Will, I've never been so frightened in all my life!"

He folded her shaking body into his arms. "They're gone. Rode off to the east." No use worrying her with his suspicions about Five Feathers.

He held her until the shuddering stopped and her breathing returned to normal. "Best we mount up," he said.

"What about the cabin?"

"I'll nail the door shut. On my way back to Texas, I'll stop in and deal with it."

"Yes," she murmured. "Of course. On your way back." She swung away from him, hoisted her saddle onto her shoulder and trudged outside, her back straight as a fence post.

Chapter Nineteen

The trail to Taylor's Bridge meandered through the prettiest green countryside Will had seen since leaving Texas. The temptation to slow down and enjoy the beauty of leafy trees and green hillsides tugged at him, but he ignored it. He was wary of stopping; getting warm and comfortable after a long day in the saddle opened up his longing for Charlotte. It was all he could do to keep his hands off her in camp.

Instead, he pressed them on through Idaho's fields of purple wild flax and yellowing grasses. By the time they reached eastern Oregon, he was bone-weary and edgy with pent-up desire, and Charlotte was the quietest she'd been since they left Fort Laramie.

Will himself felt worn to a shadow, especially when he was around her at night, cooking supper, rolling out their bedrolls. He didn't know how much longer he could stand the mixture of tormenting need and carefully banked anger at himself and the situation that he'd allowed to develop.

Jupiter, he was a fool, wanting her and not allowing himself to do anything about it. Caught in a net of his own making, where he struggled, helpless as a beached trout against the pull of his body.

On the trail, they talked, off and on. Usually it led to a sharp sense of futility and loss on Will's part, and for Charlotte...hell, he wished he knew. She was quiet. Too quiet. For hours—days, even—it was like she'd turned into a statue of herself. He was getting so he could anticipate when another painful bout of words between them was coming on. When she raised her chin, like she was doing now, and straightened her spine, he knew she was going to say something.

So, okay, princess, say it. They were fifty miles into Oregon, camped by a pretty little creek; he guessed it was about time to sort some things out.

"Do you realize," she said in that controlled voice she used when she was feeling uncertain, "that we have spent thirty-seven nights together since we left your uncle's cabin in Wyoming?"

Will lifted his cooling coffee mug with a hand that shook. "Yeah. I think about it a lot."

"Why?" The directness of her tone, and the equally penetrating look in her wide gray eyes made him think carefully before he answered.

"I guess because I'm always fighting myself over how I'd like it to be."

"Which is not like it was before that night in the cabin," she said softly.

It wasn't a question, thank God. Will gritted his teeth. "Nope."

She dropped her eyes to her dusty boots. "I rather liked it when we slept…well, close to each other. The way it was in the beginning."

"Yeah. Well, dammit I can't handle that. I can't be near you without…" He caught himself. "And I can't be away from you, either."

"I understand, Will. At least I think I do. We're between a rock and a hard place, as you say."

Will snorted a laugh. "You don't know the half of it." Between a rock and a hard place was nothing compared to being stretched to breaking on the rack of desire. Days he longed to be close to her, touch her shoulder or make her smile to bring warmth to her tired eyes. Nights he longed for peace.

"I think you like me, a little," she said hesitantly. "More than just want, I mean."

"I like you more than a little, and you damn well know it," he shot. "And that's the problem. Hell, I can't wait to get you off my hands and save both our skins."

Her gasp of pain sent a shard of ice into his gut. But he'd stuck his foot in the corral, might as well ride it on out.

"I know you don't understand why I haven't touched you since that night. Eventually I'll explain, but not yet." Not until they reached Lake County and he could calculate how many days, and nights, they had left together before he saddled up and rode away from her. Rode to catch up with Luis.

The days on the trail passed in strained silence, and the nights… Will closed his eyes. The nights burned his body and his soul with the memory of her fire and the sweet, sweet taste of her body.

They drove their weary horses on through scorched hills of sagebrush and gold thistle and yellow grass, on through wide valleys where spindly trees and then tufts of green grass and jack-in-the-pulpit alternated with autumn colors of oaks and mountain laurel. Riding hard, Will could have found Luis in the thirty days Captain McCray had allotted; but traveling with Charlotte in tow had taken until mid-August.

He figured his career with the Texas Rifles was over. He'd posted a letter to McCray from the town of Vale, explaining the situation, but he knew McCray wouldn't keep him on. A Texas rifleman had to be on the scene of trouble, not halfway across the country.

He sat back and studied Charlotte on the sly where she perched on a log, gazing into the campfire. Her face was a study—streaks of dust and grime ground into her skin, smears of huckleberry juice on her chin. Her shoulders slumped in exhaustion.

From the beginning, he hadn't wanted her along but he hadn't been able to leave her behind, either. He'd had no choice. His trail and Charlotte's had linked up from the moment he'd laid eyes on her in White Eagle's camp. By the time he admitted to himself he was head over spurs in love with her, it was too late. She'd crawled into what he thought was his scarred-over, well-protected heart and pulled his soul in after her.

The thought of leaving her in Christmas Lake Valley gouged a ragged hole in the detached front he put up, but he knew he had to do it. No way would he risk putting Charlotte and his crazy half brother within a hundred miles of each other.

"Will? You're off somewhere again. The way you've been ever since…"

"Yeah, I know. Listen, Charlotte, I want to tell you something."

"Yes. I had hoped you would."

"It's hard to talk about. And maybe I shouldn't, but…"

"Just say it, Will. Be honest with me."

"Okay, here goes. At night, it's, well, it's some agony to lie next to you and not touch you."

"And it gets worse the closer we get to Christmas Lake Valley," she said in a quiet voice.

Will's head came up. Over the weeks they'd traveled together Charlotte had moved from thoughtful to angry to distant. Distant was good. It held him in check, made it easier. But what she'd just said… No, the way she'd said it, blasted through his rigid self-control.

He'd had about all he could take. His nerves stretched so taut every sinew of his body burned with unreleased tension. "Charlotte…"

She rose and tossed the rest of her coffee onto the coals. "I know," she said. "And I think we are wrong to end this way."

Will stood up to face her, the tin mug clenched in his fist. "Wrong?" He heard his voice bellow at her, but he didn't care. "What would be wrong, princess, would be to lie together."

"Why would it be wrong, Will? Aside from what the Bible says, I mean."

"You have any idea what spending your nights making love to a man would do to you? Aside from ruining your reputation, you might conceive a child. After that night at Chili's, I sweated for three weeks until your courses came."

"Did you?" She sent him a small, lopsided smile. "I did not. My 'reputation,' as you put it, is a private matter, between you and me."

He stepped in close. "Charlotte, we're not going to argue this. You don't understand enough about the ways of the West to know there are two kinds of women, the ones who marry or teach school, and the ones who whore for a living. While I hate keeping my hands off you, I'm damn glad *I'm* the one looking out for you!"

Tears welled up in her eyes. "You are walking all over my heart, do you know that?"

"And you're makin' bootlaces out of mine!"

Her mouth pressed into a tight circle. "You are a stubborn, hidebound, overrighteous…oh, dammit, wonderful man, Will Bondurant." She walked into his arms, pressing her forehead against his chest.

"I'm not so wonderful," he muttered against her hair. "I'm out to kill my own brother, and I'd like to lay you down right now and put my mouth on you and take what I want. That's not so wonderful."

Charlotte lifted her head and looked straight into his shadowed blue eyes. "Oh, yes it is, Will. Even if we may not do but what is acceptable, it is still wonderful."

She turned out of his trembling arms and dragged her pallet to the opposite side of the fire. Will was right. They had no future, therefore they had no right to the present. She would teach in her Indian school and he would ride back to Texas.

Thank the Lord that Will is as strong as he is, for I

both respect and hunger for the man, and I am sorely tempted.

Charlotte pulled her knees up to her chest and curled her body into a tense ball. She wasn't cold. Late summer air held the day's warmth until long after the fat, gold moon rose and the *skreek-skreek* of crickets subsided. An owl whirred from one tree branch to another, then sat unmoving, unblinking eyes waiting for prey— a mouse or a frog.

She sensed what it must feel like to be snatched up by relentless claws and spirited away above the tree tops. Often, thinking back on that night in the cabin when Will had taken her, she imagined her body in the grip of the same inexorable force. He had brought her to ecstasy, and it had changed her overnight. Each day her body throbbed with the memory as her mind fought to understand Will's withdrawal. Even harder was her struggle to accept it. He wanted her, but he didn't want her.

I can't wait to get you off my hands.

It wasn't only his hard, sinewy body she longed for. She missed the closeness they had shared facing the hardships of the trail west, the dangers from their enemies, Long John and the renegade Sioux band she knew was following them. She knew it because Will kept assuring her they weren't, while at the same time shielding the glow of their campfires in deep-dug pits. And because he never chose a campsite near a trail. And because he sat awake most nights, his rifle across his thighs.

Tonight she heard his regular breathing and knew he slept across the fire pit from her. He was tired out, as she was. She felt uneasy when he wasn't keeping watch, but he refused to let her sit up with the rifle. "Not until you know how to shoot it," he insisted. "Otherwise, you're as dangerous as a predator."

Charlotte had pinched her lips together. "The trouble with you, Will Bondurant—one of them, at least—is that you don't trust anyone but yourself." Remembering the words she had muttered under her breath, she had to laugh. Already she felt better.

Were all men so maddeningly self-reliant? Papa wasn't. But then Papa trusted no one but God, not even Mama. Men thought women were helpless and feather-headed. How extremely shortsighted.

She shut her eyes to think over the matter. The owl fluttered over her head just as a twig snapped. She sat bolt upright. Before she could draw breath, a hard, rough hand clamped over her mouth.

Charlotte screamed anyway, making a muffled moaning sound, and the hand tightened, closing off her nostrils. She bucked and kicked, then felt herself being dragged backward into the trees.

She tried to scream again but found she couldn't breathe. The hand over her mouth and nose smelled rank, like rancid fat and pepper. She bit down as hard as she could, and suddenly air rushed into her lungs. A ropey bare arm circled her neck, yanked her bottom across the ground.

"Will!" she shrieked.

"Roll clear," his steady voice ordered.

Oh, thank God, he was awake, aware what was happening to her. She clawed at the elbow at her throat. The man jerked to adjust his grip and she drove an elbow backward into what felt like a chest of iron. Then she tumbled sideways and curled into a ball.

The roar of a rifle cut the silence just as a terrific blow to her back made her gasp. Had she been shot? She couldn't draw air, couldn't move, and the pain…dear God, her back was on fire.

"Charlotte!"

A dead weight toppled on top of her, grinding her chin into the earth.

"Charlotte!"

Will rolled the Indian's body off her and instantly knelt beside her.

"Did you shoot me?" Her voice sounded odd, thin as paper and quavery. "Why did you, Will?"

He bent over her. "You're not shot, honey," he rasped in her ear. "Can you hear me? Five Feathers took the bullet. You're not hurt."

Charlotte groaned an unladylike protest. "Am, too. My back. Look at my back."

Will ripped her shirt out of her jeans and lifted up the soft muslin camisole underneath. "Yeah, I see it. The skin's torn. He must have kicked you."

"Hurts," she muttered.

"I'll get that salve Dr. Warburton mixed up." He rose and rummaged in his saddlebag for the brown glass jar, then hunched beside her. Dipping a forefinger into the smooth paste, he gently smoothed it over her skin with steady strokes, remembering the minty smell from the night she'd tended his shoulder.

"Right there…ouch!"

"Sorry, honey. Just lie still. I'll try not to be too rough."

She kept her head down, tucked into her collarbone while Will tended to the red, swollen scrape.

"You're gonna have a beaut of a bruise come mornin'. Like bein' kicked by a horse."

"Never been kicked by a horse," she said in a muffled voice.

"Can you breathe okay? Any ribs broken?" He pressed carefully up and down her backbone, then moved his fingers to her side, testing her rib cage. "I know it feels like hell, but nothing's broken as far as I can tell. Try to sit up."

She tried twice before she could straighten completely. Will drew her camisole and shirt down over her skinned-up back while she leaned her head forward against his shoulder.

"Put your arms around me, Will. I'm mad and I'm scared and I want to be close to you."

"Sure, honey. Let me reload first. Think I'm gonna stay awake the rest of the night. White Eagle's band can't be far behind."

He reached behind him for his rifle and every muscle and nerve in his body went still. A large muddy boot planted itself on the gun stock.

Chapter Twenty

"Too late, mister," an ugly voice rasped.

Will's gut clenched. Long John. "Now, where'd you come from?" He worked to keep his tone neutral.

"Where d'ya think? Been tracking you for weeks. Got some dandy information from that Mexican spy works for Captain Cutter at Fort Laramie. You know him. Name's Velez. Cost me a pretty penny, but looks like it was worth it."

He looked pointedly at Charlotte. "That gunshot helped, too. I's about to pass by this place until I heard that. That Indian did me a service."

"That Indian's a renegade Sioux," Will said calmly. "His band of braves will come after him when he doesn't return. Probably only half a day's ride behind us."

With his right hand, Will turned Charlotte into his chest. "I asked you what you wanted, mister?"

"Her." Long John stepped off Will's rifle and kicked it away, then nudged Charlotte with the toe of his boot.

"Sorry, she's taken."

"Actually, it's not her so much as what I figure she's carryin' with her."

Will's heartbeat tripped. "Yeah? What's that?"

Long John bent to brush Charlotte's short red curls, then rested his gloved hand on her shoulder.

"Take your hands off her," Will commanded.

The man snapped his jaw shut, but he lifted his hand away. "Look up here at me, missy. Don't remember me, do ya?"

Charlotte tilted her chin a fraction, then shook her head. Will tightened his arms around her, eyeing the distance to his rifle. Too far. If he moved suddenly she could get shot.

Goddamn, what a night. He'd better come up with a plan.

Long John spit at Charlotte's feet. "You're heading for that mine yer pa left you."

Charlotte stiffened in his arms. "She's goin' out to Oregon to teach school," Will answered for her.

"Hell no, she's not. Are you, Miss Goody-Good? You recognize me now?"

Charlotte stared at him. "You're from Marysville, I think. Yes. I believe I have seen you in town somewhere."

"That's just like all you uppity holier-than-thou folks. Never look too close at anybody beneath you."

"I do not feel anyone is 'beneath me.' God loves all His creatures."

"Maybe so. But some of His creatures think they're better than others."

Charlotte bit her lip. "That may be true, but I am not one of them."

Will figured the man's Comanche guide was concealed in the trees. Even if he could get the jump on Long John, he was still outnumbered.

"I judge people on what they do in life," Charlotte continued in a quiet but clear voice.

"Well, fancy that," Long John snarled. "You're not gonna like what I'm gonna do if you don't give over that map."

"I have no map," Charlotte said, her voice resolute.

"No?" Long John snapped. "What happened to it?"

Will eased away from her, an idea forming.

"I…I sewed it into the waistband of my skirt, but it got wet at the water hole and the ink ran. I threw it away."

"You lying little—"

Will made his move. He dove toward the rifle, rolled and came to rest with Long John square in his sights and his finger on the trigger.

With a yelp, Lohn John dropped to the earth and grabbed at Charlotte just as a bullet zinged over his head. A second shot was impossible; Long John yanked Charlotte in front of him, pinning her arms behind her back, to use her body as a shield.

Will lowered his weapon.

"That's right smart, mister. Now then, Miss Greenfield and I have some business to discuss."

Charlotte twisted her neck sideways. "H-how do you know my name?"

Long John spit again. "Don't remember, huh? I bet you remember Silas Treadwell, though."

Charlotte looked straight at Will, her gray eyes wide with fear. "Mr. Treadwell was my father's attorney. The only time I went to his office was for the reading of Papa's will."

Will held her gaze in a silent plea. *Don't move. Keep the man talking.*

"That's right, missy. Your father's will. Weren't much in it, 'cept for the map to that mine."

"How would you know about a mine?"

Long John snickered. "'Cuz I was there, little girl. Right there in the same room, but you never even noticed me. You never did."

"I believe you are lying," Charlotte returned, her voice steady.

"Nope, I ain't. I was old man Treadwell's law clerk, Amos Shrader. I knew ever'thing that went on in that office."

Charlotte's eyes sent a message back to Will. *Show me what to do.*

"Fact is," Long John continued, "that partic'lar morning I heard ever'thing that was spoke in Treadwell's office."

"The fact is, Mr. Shrader, I inherited nothing of value from either of my parents. As a minister, Papa lived on the largesse of his congregation."

Shrader grabbed her shoulder and gave her a violent shake. "Except for that mine." He squeezed his fingers until she bit her lip. Tears shone in her eyes.

Will couldn't stand it. "I said keep your hands off her!" he snapped.

Instantly Shrader released his grip, but Will knew the man's other hand held both of Charlotte's slim wrists behind her.

"About the map, now," Shrader continued. He twisted one of Charlotte's arms up toward her shoulder blade.

"There is no map. I told you, it got wet."

Shrader jerked her arm again, and she winced. Will's trigger finger twitched, but he caught himself. She blocked his firing line. He had to come up with something else.

"Okay, Charlie," he said slowly. "Tell the bastard what you told me." He prayed she would take his use of her nephew name as a cue to do some playacting.

"What do you mean, Will? About my memorizing the map?"

Shrader grinned slyly. "That's it, missy. You remember what it looked like." He tugged her arm again, hard, and she cried out. "Dont'cha, Miss Greenfield?"

Will felt a fist inside his belly begin to squeeze his gut. "Show him, Charlie."

"Y-you mean draw the map as I remember it? I can't, Will. It's all I have from Papa. I just can't."

"Sure you can, missy. You were always so smart at everything. I bet you can remember it real good." He tightened up on her awkwardly bent arm.

"No," she gasped. "I can't."

"Charlie. Just do it," Will ordered.

Her chin dropped toward her chest, but she shook her head. Will bit the inside of his jaw. Could he aim just over her head and put a bullet into Long John's chest?

He eyed the distance. No. Too risky.

"I can hurt you worse, little girl," Shrader snarled. "Worse than you ever dreamed."

Will went cold. "Charlotte," he whispered. "Please. *Please.*"

"All—all right." She sounded whipped. When Long John released her arm, Will began to breathe again.

"Got anything to draw on?"

"There's paper in my saddlebag," Will volunteered. It was brown grocer's wrapping, folded around a square of pale, hard cheese. He laid it out on the ground in front of her and shoved a charcoal-tipped twig into her fingers.

Charlotte sent him a long, questioning look, and Will nodded. "Go on, Charlie. You can do it."

She leaned over the paper, flexing her wrist, then traced a line with the charcoal and stopped as if to think. "Here's one landmark," she murmured to herself. "Farewell Bend. Then it leads toward the hills, like this…"

Will held his breath while she scratched out more lines on the map with halting strokes.

"There," she said at last. "That's the most I can recall." She straightened as Long John snatched up the crudely drawn map, folded it sloppily, then jammed it into his shirt pocket.

"Thanks, missy. Now if'n you'll just stand up in front of me so your partner won't shoot at my belly, I'll be on my way." He grabbed the back of her shirt collar and jerked to her feet. Will knew he couldn't get a clear shot until Long John reached the shadowy woods and released Charlotte, and by then it was too late. The man vanished into the dark.

He swore and lowered the gun barrel. "You all right?"

"I am quite all right, yes." Her voice was shaky.

"Sorry you had to do that, Charlotte. Seemed like the only way, once he started in on you."

Charlotte walked unsteadily toward him. "Why, Will Bondurant, what do you take me for? Surely you don't think I drew him an accurate map!"

Will stared at her. She gave him a triumphant grin, just like a kid riding his first pony.

"If he follows that map," she said with a soft giggle, "he should end up in the Pacific Ocean."

Chapter Twenty-One

Charlotte stumbled forward toward him. Will took a single long stride and caught her up in his arms. Her hands clung to his shirtfront.

"You're all right, Charlotte. You're safe."

She burrowed her face against his shoulder. "I have never in all my life been so frightened," she confessed in a muffled voice.

Will pivoted to turn her backside to the fire. "You say that every time," he said with a soft laugh. "Every single time."

She lifted her head. "Well, I *am* frightened!"

"Not so frightened you couldn't outfox Long John. You are one helluva woman, princess."

"Is that a good thing or a bad thing?" She spoke against his neck, her warm breath caressing his skin.

Will chuckled. "Yeah. It's good." He didn't trust himself to say more; already his heart felt like it was climbing out of his shirt and he wasn't sure his voice would come out steady over the chili pepper stuck in his throat.

"I want you to do something," she said.

Will frowned at the determination in her tone. "Yeah? What is it?"

"I want you to pull my bedroll over next to yours and sleep close to me tonight."

Will tightened his arms around her. "Tell you what, princess. Let's ride a couple of hours before we bed down."

She tipped her head up to look at him. "You mean tonight?"

"Now," he said. "Too many tracks leading to this place. And then there's Five Feathers's body over behind that tree." He set her on her feet, steadied her with a hand on her shoulder.

"Will, you cannot be serious."

"Mount up." He pushed her toward the horses, picketed some yards away. "I'll gather the camp."

It was all Charlotte could do to heave her saddle over the gray's back and pull her trembling body atop the animal. Still shaking from the events of the past hour, she forced her spine into a straight line and tried to control her ragged breathing.

The West was a violent, uncivilized place, full of dangers she'd never dreamed of back in Ohio. Full of mountains and ravines and barren brown plains and sagebrush and...

But now they had reached Oregon, were perhaps one or two day's ride from the Indian reservation. She knew she would never be able to persuade Will to take her to the mine first. She watched him toss his saddle onto

Sandy's back, tie both bedrolls on behind and swing his long leg over the animal's rump.

"Let's go."

They rode more than three hours, stopping only when the horses flagged and Will judged no one was following them. Long John had what he wanted; White Eagle's renegade band wouldn't ride this far into the backyards of the Umatilla and Paiute tribes. Charlotte was safe, and they were within one day's ride of Baker City, the last stop before they reached her Indian school.

He sought out a site well hidden from the trail, reined Sandy to a halt and loosened her cinch. He didn't bother to make camp, just untied the bedrolls and rolled them out next to each other. Then he reached up to pull Charlotte off the gray and into his arms.

"Will?" Her voice sounded sleepy.

"Yeah?" Very, very slowly he walked the entire perimeter of their small campsite because he didn't want to set her apart from him just yet.

"Even if I have committed Papa's map to memory, I am not going to see the mine, am I?"

"Not with me, no. I've got other business to take care of."

With a sigh of resignation she tucked her chin against his shoulder. "You are a hard man, Will. And stubborn. And just when I get used to it, you do something so gentle, so sweet, it makes me cry."

He stopped moving and just held her against him. "You think I'm hard to figure out, you oughtta take a look at yourself sometime."

"Oh. I'm not hard to understand, really I'm not. But

when I'm with you, I feel all tumbled around inside. I never know which side is up."

"When I'm with you," he said in a gravelly voice, "if I don't understand what's going on, it doesn't matter."

She tightened her arms about his neck. "Don't put me down just yet, Will."

His manhood swelled, even though he knew that's not what she meant. He wanted her so much he felt weak inside. Achy, like he hadn't eaten in a long time. *Jesus, what am I thinking?*

"Charlotte, we have to rest. Tomorrow night we'll be in Baker City, and we can sleep in a hotel, in a real bed. Right now—" he knelt and settled her onto her pallet "—you need to crawl in and get some sleep."

He tugged off her boots, retrieved their saddles and stretched out beside her. Overhead, the stars glittered white and silver, and he laid one arm over his eyes to block them out.

"Will? How many miles do you think we have ridden together?"

"Enough," he said thickly.

"I think not," she murmured. "I think not enough."

He couldn't help but smile. "Might be you think too much, princess."

She said nothing further for a long while, and then, just when he got his breathing under control, she skooched her body toward his. "I want to sleep close to you tonight."

Will couldn't answer. Instead he swallowed a groan and rolled toward her, pulled her back against him until he felt the small ridges of her spine against his chest.

Carefully he unbuttoned his shirt and spread it open so her bones pressed into his bare flesh.

Charlotte nestled her bottom into his groin. "It's just like in the beginning," she whispered. "You are warm and strong and I like being close to you."

Will said nothing.

"Tomorrow night, at the hotel, will we have a big soft bed?"

Will laughed. "Not if I can help it. Got all I can handle right here on the hard ground."

"Yes," she breathed.

He could tell by her voice she was drifting off. The last thing she uttered was a single sentence. "Isn't it wonderful?"

That thought kept him awake for another hour.

The clerk at the Baker City Hotel, a gangly redhaired man with a tic dancing in one eyelid, shoved the registry toward Will and handed him a pen. "With the rodeo in town tomorrow, this the only room I got left. Take it or leave it."

Will turned the pen over and over in his fingers. "Does it have one bed or two?"

"One," the clerk snapped. "Don't mind bunkin' with the kid, do ya?" He cut his eyes toward Charlotte, perched near the dining room entrance on a flower-print wingback chair.

"Reckon I don't have a choice," Will muttered. He signed the register W. Bondurant and son, forked over a greenback and plucked the key out of the clerk's sweaty palm.

"Supper's served 'til midnight. First rodeo event's at nine sharp. Calf roping."

Will nodded and gestured to Charlotte. "Did you ask about the bathtub?" she whispered as they climbed the stairs.

"I did. Which do you want first, food or hot water?"

"Hot water," she replied instantly. "I haven't had a proper bath since I left Independence."

"That's two thousand miles of dirt to scrub off," he joked. "Think you can do all that in one night?"

"Just you watch me!"

That, thought Will, was exactly what he didn't want to think about.

The copper tub arrived along with four buckets of steaming water, lugged up the stairs by two sweating Mexican youths. They were accompanied by a maid, who was evidently their sister from the way she ordered them about directing the water pouring and laying out soap and towels on the side table. Will tipped them each a two-bit piece.

"Gracias, señor." All three backed out the door and pulled it shut behind them.

Alone in the privacy of the hotel room, Will and Charlotte looked at each other. "You won't recognize me when I'm finished," Charlotte said.

Will cleared his throat. "I'll wait for you in the dining room. Maybe step next door for a bath myself, and a shave."

"Do it here," Charlotte offered. "I've seen you shave before."

"You haven't seen me—" Too late, he remembered.

"Oh, yes I have," she said with a grin. "First tramping around our camp with nary a stitch on." Her voice softened. "And then there was that night at the cabin."

"That's why I'm goin' next door, princess. I remember every minute of that night. Always will."

Her steady gray eyes seemed to look right into his heart. "I am glad you said that, Will. It is the same for me."

He had to get out of the room, couldn't stand here facing her one more minute without wanting to…

"We'll talk about it later, at supper," he growled.

The door banged open, then shut with a soft click, and Charlotte stood stock-still. She was completely alone for the first time in three months.

The shiny copper bathtub beckoned. She could hardly wait.

Will sank back in the bathhouse tub and let the warm, soapy water wash over his body all the way up to his chin. Every kink and ache from months of steady riding throbbed, then slowly began to ease. Spit baths in cold creek water might wash off the top layer of trail dust, but there was nothing like an unhurried hot soak to restore a man's perspective.

Something had happened to him on this trip. His mind felt more tired, his body more battered than he could ever remember, but that wasn't all. In his whole life he'd never uttered the word "please," not until he met up with Charlotte. Looking back over the years—the wrestling matches and later the rag-tag horse races with his older half brother, Luis, then the strained, lonely times with Alice after he joined the Rifles, he wished he'd done some things different. If he had, maybe Pa and Alice would still be alive.

A cowboy in the adjoining room splashed into a tub with a shouted "Hoo-rah!" Will closed his eyes to shut out the noise. Behind his lids rose an image of a slender woman floating in her own bath upstairs. He tried not to think about it.

But the mental pictures kept coming—Charlotte with her face wrinkled in distaste, pouring whiskey over his knife wound. Watching him shave, then weeping as he sheared off her hair. Laughing when he sang made-up ballads to his horse. Baking lumpy corn dogs on a hot, flat rock like he'd shown her.

He smoothed his hand over his chest where her small knobby bones had poked the night before. Damn, he wished he'd never laid eyes on her.

He knew he'd never forget her. Likely he'd never again take a woman to bed without thinking of Charlotte. He couldn't stop remembering things about her. And he couldn't stop wanting her. How the hell was he going to manage being in that hotel room with her all night?

He sat up so fast lukewarm water sloshed out onto the plank floor of the bathhouse. Through rigid control he'd managed not to compromise her further, up until now. Tonight would be their last night together. Tonight, he admitted with a barely suppressed groan, would be hell of a different color.

He'd sleep on the floor, he decided. He would *not* get a shave, nor would he have his overlong hair cut. He'd treat her the same as always; while she filled up his mind, his senses, he'd pretend otherwise. It had worked for—What had she calculated?—thirty-seven nights? He had to make it thirty-eight. Charlotte was not the kind of woman you played loose with and then rode away.

Wrapped in a bath towel, Charlotte studied the garments laid out on the double bed. Jeans, a man's plaid shirt, one intact petticoat and another in tatters, and her blue dress. Her hair was squeaky clean, her skin scented with rose water. She longed to feel soft lace against her skin, feel petticoat ruffles swish against her ankles. It had been so long since she'd worn a dress instead of masquerading as Charlie in men's britches and a cowboy hat, she wasn't sure she could revert to being Charlotte again.

She fingered the blue buttons marching up the dress front, lifted the skirt and sniffed it. It smelled of the leather saddlebag. With a sigh she hung the dress and the petticoat in the armoire to air out. She would wear it tomorrow, when she arrived at her school.

But that was tomorrow. Tonight she still had to play the role of Will's nephew, Charlie.

When she entered the dining room Will looked up from the corner table where he sat nursing a glass of some gold-colored liquid with foam on the top. His black hat rested on the adjacent chair, and he pushed it off onto the floor so she could sit down.

In the soft gaslight, his hair looked dark, the waves thicker, the silver touches at his temples brighter. He gave her a rare smile, and her breath caught.

She pointed to his tall glass. "Is that cider?"

"It's beer. Want some?"

"I do not indulge in… Oh, fiddlesticks! Let me have a taste." He pushed the glass across the table and she downed a healthy gulp.

She swallowed hard and her face wrinkled up. "It tastes perfectly dreadful!"

"Ladies usually think so. Want some lemonade?"

She stared at his face. "You didn't shave?"

"Decided not to. Lemonade?" he reminded.

"But why not? We've been traveling for weeks. Your whiskers are all, well, whiskery. Surely you are uncomfortable?"

"Nope. Gettin' so I kinda like it. Keeps my chin warm. Now, let's change the subject, Charlotte. Do you want some lemon—?"

"Yes, I do. But Will, some while ago you said…why, you have even grown a mustache! I thought you didn't—"

"I lied."

He said it too quickly. "No, you didn't," she countered, narrowing her eyes. "But you are lying now. And I am wondering why."

"You think too much, dammit. Leave it be."

She watched his mouth thin, his eyes shift away from hers. She knew that look; he was hiding something.

"After all these days—and nights," she huffed. "After all the things we have been through together, all the things we have shared—food, blankets, even…" She lowered her voice to a murmur. "*Even ourselves.* How can you hide anything from me?"

Will squirmed.

Unless… Her heart squeezed, the pain sharp and

sweet. Unless it was how he felt about her. How he *really* felt about her.

Suddenly she understood. He had not shaved on purpose because a beard served as a scratchy barrier between them. He did not want to compromise her beyond what had already happened between them. After that night at the cabin, he had withdrawn behind a mask of civility and she had wondered why.

Now she understood. He felt he was protecting her. And himself. She caught his gaze, saw his cavalier attempt at subterfuge fade into a deep, quiet hunger. She had seen it once before, at their snowbound refuge in the Wind River range. No matter what he said, he was as vulnerable as she was.

A bubble of sheer joy expanded behind her breastbone and then floated up into her throat and out of her mouth. "You love me!" she blurted.

Instantly she clapped her hand over her lips. *Had she really said that?*

Will thunked his glass onto the table so hard half the beer sloshed out. "Are you crazy?"

His voice was harsh. Defensive, she decided with a happy little sigh. Evasive of him, turning it back on her.

She smiled. He was unnerved. "Quite," she said crisply. And then she laughed.

"What's so damn funny?"

"Everything," she choked out. "You. Me. That black horse you insist on calling Sandy. Your beer flying all over the tablecloth. The look on your face. Oh, Will, it's all wonderfully funny!"

"Good thing there's nobody else eatin' supper at this

hour," he grumbled. "Somebody'd think you'd ridden right off your rocker."

Charlotte couldn't contain the bubble of happiness suffusing her being. "Well, have I not?" Her smile turned into a grin. "And what about you, Mister Brand-New Mustache? What about you?" she said more softly.

"This isn't about me," Will snapped.

"Of course it is. It's all about you. And me. Me, rubbing scented soap all over myself, hoping you'd notice. And you, keeping your beard to protect yourself."

Under the table Will knotted his fingers into a fist. "It's you I'm trying to protect, Charlotte."

"No, it isn't, Will. It is *you* you are trying to protect." Her gray eyes looked straight into his, and in their depths he saw an expression of amused accusation.

"And now that the matter has been clarified," she added in a calm voice, "I find I am most ravenously hungry. I'd like a steak, a big juicy one, with lots of fried potatoes and a whole bowlful of—"

"Exactly what I ordered," Will interrupted. "For both of us."

"That makes two very hungry people at this table, does it not?"

"Yeah, it sure does." He found himself grinning back at her like a fool cowpoke lusting after the rancher's daughter. Jesus H. Jupiter, she *did* smell good, and he damn well *had* noticed. He noticed so much his head was spinning.

He would never make it through the night.

A stringy-looking waitress in a pink apron plopped down two thick white china plates of steak and potatoes, poured coffee into the cups and propped one hand on her hip. "Cream?"

Will and Charlotte looked at each other across the table. "Later," Will said. "Close the kitchen door on your way."

The woman shot a glance at him, but he didn't notice. Neither of them noticed. They were engrossed in each other.

She did as he asked. The instant the door slapped shut Will stood up, hauled Charlotte out of her chair, and wrapped his arms around her. "Whatever I feel about you, it's not gonna change anything about tonight. I'll sleep at the livery stable with Sandy if I have to." He brushed his mouth against her temple and sat her down at the table again.

"It will make no difference," she said. "There is room for me at the livery, as well."

"Shut up and eat," he ordered.

"Oh, yes, *sir*," she quipped. She saluted him with her fork. "You don't even have to say 'please.'"

Chapter Twenty-Two

Will laid his coffee spoon on the china saucer, then picked it up again and stirred the brew for the fifth time in the last five minutes. If he kept his hands busy, he could control the need to touch her. Looking at her was hard enough.

All through supper, he found himself desperately making conversation just to keep his mind off the fact that she was sitting a scant arm's length away from him and in another fourteen hours he would never see her again. His throat tightened at the realization.

He'd thought this would be easy, taking Charlotte to Oregon and leaving her at the school. *Easy.* Now he was sweating silently at how *not* easy it was turning out to be.

What a damn fool he was. He wanted her so much he ached, but he knew he couldn't push it. Wouldn't even if he could. He had nothing to offer Charlotte except himself for one night, and that wasn't enough. Yeah, they liked each other. More than liked, maybe.

But it—he—would never be enough for a lady like Charlotte.

He had to keep her talking; and he didn't dare watch her mouth while she did it.

He forced his voice out over the lumpy rock in his gullet.

"I know about your pa. Wanna tell me about your mother?"

"Mama?" Charlotte lifted her cup, cradled it in her fingers. "Mama was…quiet. One of the meek who are destined to inherit the earth. She did every single thing Papa asked and never questioned it." She sipped a mouthful of coffee and cocked her head. "I resolved never to be like her."

Will chuckled until she voiced her own query.

"What was *your* mother like?"

His mother! The question caught him like a fist to his gut. "I told you before, she was…I guess you'd call her a half-breed. That makes me a breed, too."

Charlotte studied his face with such intensity he thought he must have gravy dribbled down his whiskers. "Half-breed of what?"

"Half-white. Tejano. Quarter Mex, a quarter Apache."

She nodded. "Your hair is dark, but your eyes are blue. It is a most handsome combination."

Instantly she lowered her lashes and bit her lower lip. Then her tongue came out and traced over the spot.

Will shifted uncomfortably. He wasn't sure how much more he could take before…

"You go to school back in Ohio?" he asked in a hoarse voice.

"Of course. Everyone did, except the Negro children and the white trash down behind the train station."

"You ever wonder why those children didn't?"

Charlotte frowned. "I never did when I was young, no. Papa said it was part of God's plan. When I got older, I asked Papa again. He said such people were the descendants of Cain."

"That's one way to look at it, all right."

She stiffened her spine. "I did not believe him." With that she sat up even straighter. His mouth went dry as her breasts swelled under the thin cotton shirt.

"My whole family, 'cept for my white father, would be considered the same. Descendants of Cain."

She said something, but he had trouble concentrating on her words; his gaze kept drifting to the curling tendrils of red hair at her temples, to her lips. To the little hollow at the base of her throat. What was she wearing under that plaid shirt, something soft and lacy? Or maybe nothing at all?

He cleared his throat. "My older brother, Luis…"

Her eyes met and held his. "Yes. The man you are tracking. What about him?"

"Luis is three-quarters Apache, one-quarter Mexicano. Even down in Texas they wouldn't let him in the schoolhouse door."

Her cup clunked down onto the saucer. "That is exactly why I am needed in Oregon. There must always be teachers who are willing to civilize the sav—"

"Hold it right there, princess. Indians, Mexicans, or any combination of them are not necessarily savages."

"You told me Luis killed your uncle."

"And my pa, and my wife," Will grated. "That makes him crazy-insane, not a savage. Something got left out of Luis from the beginning."

"Or perhaps God is not yet finished with him?"

"Yeah, I'll just bet." It wasn't working. Even provoking an argument hadn't cooled him down any.

"Charlotte…"

She looked up and their gazes locked. The look in her eyes sent a bolt of pure, driving desire through him; his resolve began to crack. He needed her, body and soul. Now.

"Let's go up to bed," he said, his voice quiet.

Her eyes stayed riveted on his. "Oh, Will, I thought you would never ask."

The second the door shut behind them, Will reached for her. "Charlotte…goddammit, Charlotte." He buried his face in her soft curls, breathed in the spicy-sweet scent that rose from her skin. She tipped her face up.

"Will," she whispered.

His hands went to her neck, working her shirt open button by button. "I can't leave you without… Oh, Jesus, I want you so much. So damn much. I don't want to do this, Charlotte, but—"

"Yes, you do, Will," she said with a smile.

"Yeah, I sure as hell do. I don't want to stop, honey." His fingers pulled her shirt free, then went to work on her trouser fastenings.

"Don't stop, Will. I want you to touch me and touch me, and kiss me, and touch me some more." She stepped free of her trousers, then felt her underdrawers slide down over her hips.

Her fingers at his belt made him suck in his breath. He couldn't wait.

He caught her up, lifted her onto the bed, and stripped.

"My…" His kiss swallowed her words. As his mouth moved over hers, his hand found her soft, moist entrance.

"…courses are due in a few days," she gasped. She arched her hips once and he was ready. More than ready.

His body throbbed for release. "Charlotte, what are you telling me?"

"That you need not fear that I will conceive. It is a safe time."

But he did fear. Not for a child, but for his own heart and now his soul, which now belonged to her. Would always belong to her.

He could no longer reason, could only feel. She was all silk and fine bones, and he prolonged each thrust, listening to her cries. His throat, even his chest caught fire and something burned on his neck. Only then did he realize it was his own tears.

Charlotte writhed under him, whispering to him as he moved. "Yes. *Oh, yes.*" He covered her mouth with his and took her over the edge with him. God in heaven, he would never be whole again without this. Without her.

Later, he took her again, and then again, and she screamed in ecstasy, weeping, calling out his name.

At last, near dawn, they slept.

"Morning to ya, Mr. Bondurant," the desk clerk sang as Will descended the stairs into the hotel lobby. "Past noon already. You'n yer son have missed some of the rodeo, ropin' and other athletic events. Bull riding's next. If you hurry you can catch it."

"Not in a hurry," Will said amiably. His whole world was spinning slower today. Not too surprising, considering last night.

He turned toward Charlotte, descending the staircase behind him dressed in her usual jeans and plaid shirt. "How 'bout you, Charlie? Interested in fancy ridin'?"

Her eyes dancing, she sent him her *are-you-crazy?* look, then stepped in close. "I have had a sufficiency of 'athletic events,'" she murmured. "I should think that would be the last thing on your mind this morning."

"Matter of fact," he breathed near her temple, "it was the first thing on my mind this morning. It still is."

She flushed scarlet and pushed past him to the dining room. "Last one seated is a horse's—" Her hand smacked over her mouth. Will laughed while her gray eyes widened in horror at what she'd almost said, then good-naturedly slapped her on the shoulder and strode past.

"A 'horse's aster' is what we say in Texas. It's a kinda flower, grows six, eight feet tall in the panhandle."

Despite her gaffe, Charlotte ate with relish, devouring three eggs, a plateful of crisp bacon, three pancakes and a pot of coffee in short order. No meal had ever tasted so good.

Will ate slowly, watching her with darkened eyes, his mouth—oh, that marvelously skilled mouth—quirked in a lopsided smile. She would remember that smile, and the past twenty-four hours, for the rest of her days.

He pushed back his plate and rose. "Let's go."

She caught her breath. "Back to bed?"

His eyes sobered. "I wish we could, honey, but it's over."

Over? The word ricocheted around in her brain while she fought for comprehension. Then, with understanding, came a shard of pain like an ice pick clawing into her chest. She half turned away from him.

Of course it was over. What had she thought would happen when Will delivered her to her destination? He would ride on. Leave her at the school and ride away, out of her life.

Her throat closed. *Yes, it is what I want.* What she wanted, anyway, before Will. Before…

No, that wasn't true. She still wanted to teach, to help civilize the Indians. But now she wanted something more, as well. She wanted Will.

Deep in her bone marrow she knew he wasn't for the asking. He'd never led her to believe he was, or ever would be. He had never lied about it; it was she who had deceived herself. She'd thought that, since he loved her, he would change his plans.

I am a foolish, green girl. It had never occurred to her that loving someone did not necessarily mean staying with them. When they reached the reservation, Will would leave her.

She composed her face, then turned back to him. "Last one mounted is—" her voice faltered "—an aster's horse."

Will stared at her retreating figure. He didn't quite get the joke; an aster's horse? And for sure he didn't know what had caused her eyes to turn to gray granite all of a sudden. The only thing he did know was that he'd never seen her back so rigid. Hell, it looked stiffer than his rifle barrel.

The "school" turned out to be a weathered shack with an attached lean-to constructed of leafy cotton-wood branches that offered shade from the searing late-afternoon sun. Half a mile outside the barbwire-marked boundary of the Paiute Indian reservation stood a small log cabin, across the road from a rundown trading post of some sort. "Indian Agent" was hand-lettered on the front door.

"Looks like we're here," Will said. They walked the horses to the hitching rail in front of the post and dis-mounted in unison. An hour ago, Charlotte had changed from jeans into her blue dress; now she had a bit of trouble when her petticoat snagged on a dangling stirrup.

Will was the first one up the single step and onto the wide porch. He turned the rusted knob and pushed on through into the dim interior of the building. Charlotte was right behind him.

"Mr. Matthews?" Will called.

"Yes," a man's voice answered. Footsteps, and then a bulky form emerged from behind a tan canvas curtain. "Ah'm Sam Matthews. What can I do for you folks?"

Will sized up the man. Thinning red hair, a pleasant, somewhat shiny face. A "good" face, he decided. Kind, intelligent eyes.

"Miss Greenfield has accepted a teaching position in the school yonder. Here she is."

"Ah'm deeply honored, ma'am." Matthews took her

hand and gently shook it, his appreciation of the blue dress apparent.

"Mr. Matthews," Charlotte responded.

"Sure don't get many ladies out this way. Y'all thirsty? Ah've got good clear water out back, and—"

"Not thirsty, thanks," Will said shortly.

"Ah expect you'll be wantin' to see your house, Miss Greenfield. Just let me close up my office and—"

"No need," Will interjected. "We can see it from here."

Matthews studied Will. "Somethin' eating you, mister?"

Will jerked. "Sorry. Didn't think it showed."

"Oh, it shows all right. Ah'd say your sorts have trickled out of your pocket, and now you're all out of 'em. Sorts, Ah mean." The man grinned, waiting for Will to get the joke.

Will didn't.

But Charlotte did. Her laughter crawled under his skin and set up a prickly itch right over his heart.

"Sorry, Matthews," Will offered. "Got a lot on my mind."

"You two married?"

Will jerked again, just as Charlotte brought out a dignified "No."

"Nope," he added in the same instant. "Just…friends. Partners," he amended.

Sam Matthews rocked back on his heels and grinned. "Makes no never mind to me, or to the Indians, either, if y'all don't have the blessing of the church. But Father Montrose, now, he might pay some pointed calls after you've settled in."

"We're not 'settling in,'" Will said. "Leastways, not together."

Charlotte nodded. "You see, Mr. Matthews, within the hour, we are going our separate ways."

"Aah." The older man looked at Will, then shifted his gaze to Charlotte. "In that case, folks, make yourself at home and take your time about it. Ah have a distaste for goodbyes, so Ah'm going back to my office and have a drink in your honor. Water, of course. Gave up spirits when… Never mind, 'tain't important. You two just go along, now."

Will took Charlotte's hand and walked her to the door.

The sky turned rose and purple as the day faded and the sun slipped toward the horizon. Charlotte had always liked sunsets; back in Ohio they signaled a cooling off as twilight fell, softening the harsh light of midsummer.

From this day forward, she would hate this hour. It would always remind her of this moment, standing on the narrow plank porch of the house she would occupy while she taught school, watching Will's mouth twist as he tried to smile.

"I'm leaving the gray with you. Don't want you to be alone out here without a horse. I'll pay John for it when I get back to Fort Laramie."

She stepped toward him. "Will." She could not keep her voice steady.

"I want to kiss you," he said quietly. "Think Mr. Matthews is watchin'?"

"I don't care if he is." She spoke softly, watching pain

cloud his dark eyes and anguish replace his carefully impassive expression. Her heart wrenched.

"Charlotte." He pulled her hard against him and stood, breathing unevenly, his chin against her hair, as the sun slipped away into lavender and then gray dusk. "Pa used to say this was the time the day dies."

She tried to smile. "And tomorrow a rooster somewhere will think he's turned night into day again." She turned her face into his shoulder. "We are such little bits of insignificant matter in the universe. Does it matter to God whether one man and one woman see each other again before they die?"

He set her apart from him, reached out and touched her cheek with his curved hand, kept it there while he struggled to speak. "I don't know, honey. It matters to me."

Her throat closed. Speech was impossible.

"I didn't want to love you," he whispered. "But I do."

Charlotte closed her eyes in agony.

"Look at me, Charlotte." When she opened her lids he bent toward her. "Kiss me."

He caught her mouth under his and let his lips tell her everything he could not put into words. When he lifted his head, tears burned in his eyes.

"Oh, Will. Will." Her throat ached with the need to cry, but she would not let herself. Not until he was gone.

Abruptly he released her, pivoted and tramped down the single porch step, his hands jammed in his trouser pockets. Charlotte watched him move to the black mare, snug up the cinch and climb into the saddle. He touched the brim of his hat, turned the horse and was gone.

She watched until she could no longer see the speck

of black moving away from her, or the dust cloud in his wake. After a long minute, she dashed her hand over her brimming eyes and grabbed up the splayed straw broom tucked into the far corner of the porch.

Her back straight as the broom handle, she walked into her house.

Chapter Twenty-Three

The minute the Golden Belle saloon caught Will's attention, he slowed Sandy to a walk along the pitted main street of Twist. Tied to the hitching rail in front of the saloon was a roan gelding with a white slash on its forehead. Will swore when he recognized the animal. Just the kind of place he'd expect to find Luis.

Wearily he swung his leg over Sandy's hindquarters, looped the reins over the rail and punched open the swinging doors. He didn't know which he wanted to enjoy first—a stiff shot of whiskey burning down his throat or the expression on his half brother's face when he looked down the barrel of Will's Colt.

A single coal-oil lantern illuminated the scarred oak bar. Will stepped toward it and froze at the sound of his brother's voice behind him.

"Will! *Mi hermano!*" The familiar, muscular figure strode out of the shadows and threw his arms around Will. "Little brother, where did you come from?"

"Texas, where do you think."

The dark, hawklike face broke into a grin. "From Tejas? To Oregon? What are you doing here?"

Will disengaged himself from his brother's grip. "I came to see you."

"All the way from Tejas for me? I am honored, little brother. Truly."

Will stared at him. Luis hadn't changed. The same dark good looks, the same charming, almost silky, manner. Only his eyes looked different; an odd, almost feral light burned in the dilated black pupils.

"Roberto! A drink for my little brother."

The rotund bartender shuffled forward. "What'll it be, mister?"

"He will have the same as me," Luis said with a happy laugh. "We haf shared everything since we are *niños.*" Again he enveloped Will in a smothering embrace.

"Come. Sit with me. We will talk." Luis sat Will down at a table in the corner. "Remember when you had your first whiskey? At Señorita Maria's, it was. You remember Maria?"

Will nodded. The barkeep set two fingerprint-smeared glasses on the table and splashed in some whiskey. Luis lifted his drink, saluted Will, then tossed back the liquor in one gulp.

"I still cannot believe what my eyes tell me. You haf come to see me! Ah, little brother, that makes me so happy."

Will sipped his whiskey and said nothing. His brother's guileless smile sent a chill up Will's spine. Didn't Luis realize why he'd come? To take revenge? *To kill him?*

"Maria, she was also your first woman, eh?" Playfully, Luis punched Will's shoulder.

What was his brother's game? "Luis—"

"Ah, *no, mi hermano.* Do not speak in that voice, *por favor.* I remember that voice. You use it when you want someone to do something."

"*Sí.* Luis, what the hell are you doing?"

Luis looked blank. "Doing? Yesterday I get drunk with my friend, Roberto. Today I get drunk with my little brother."

Will studied the dark face across from him. Something was wrong with Luis. Very wrong. He set his glass on the table and leaned forward. "Luis, what—"

"Ah, Will, what for you want to spoil this beautiful day with your frowns and heavy words? Always you are too serious. You must learn to enjoy life, little brother. Like I do."

"Sometimes a man has to be serious, Luis. A man has to face up to what he does in life."

"*Que?* It is you who must face up, Will. And it is I who must teach you."

"Dammit, Luis, what are you talkin' about?"

His brother's grin lit up his face. "Always you are so, you know, 'right.' There is no softness, no understanding. There is only the law. Only what is 'right.'"

The hot, sticky air inside the saloon pressed Will's breath back into his lungs. He began to sweat. "How else should a man live?"

"It is not for one man to say how another shall live. But I will tell you, because you are my brother. Always a man should love his brother and help him."

"Quit stalling, Luis. I want some answers."

"Answers? But that is not what you need, little brother. What you need is…how you say in *Inglése*…compassion. That is it, compassion. You are a very selfish man, Will. Everything has to be your way, or it is not enough."

"You're crazy, Luis."

"*Sí*, perhaps I am. Sometimes. It comes and goes. But I see how you live *your* life, how you hide behind your honor because you are afraid you will lose something."

"Lose what?" Will growled.

"Ah, *mi hermano*," Luis sighed in apparent exasperation. "Lose something you love."

Will flinched. "Shut your lying mouth, Luis. I lost Alice because you stole her. And then you shot her."

Luis cocked his dark head. "That is only partly true. You had already lost your wife when she died. You lose her before she came to me. You do not want to face the truth, little brother."

The urge to level his revolver at Luis's smiling face was almost overpowering. Will licked his lips and wondered if Luis was armed.

Of course he was armed. Luis was always armed. Even if he wore no gun belt, there would be the pistol in his waistband, the knife inside his shiny leather boot.

Under the table, Will closed his hand over the butt of his Colt. Slowly he eased it free of the holster and held it against his thigh.

Luis rambled on, unaware of the danger.

Or was he? Luis was like a fox. He could smell death and smile his way out of it.

Suddenly the dark face sobered, and Luis bent toward Will. "I know that you are want to kill me. But you should not."

"Why the hell shouldn't I? You're a killer."

"As are we all, given the right circumstances. But that is not the point. You should not kill me because if you do not accept your part in the death of your wife, you will be an angry *hombre,* like this, all your life. No bend. No compromise. A man like that, he is always alone."

"What about Pa?"

Luis shook his head. "You know the truth of that, I think. I was aiming for you, but your *padre* got in the way. You know that. So it is not me you hate, little brother. It is yourself."

"And Chili?"

"Ah, *sí,* there was also Chili." Again the strange, almost luminous light flared in Luis' eyes. "He would not drink with me."

"So you shot him?"

"For such an insult, yes." Luis shifted his gaze to the bar where Roberto wiped the wood with a soiled towel. "And for other things."

Will tipped the gun barrel up. The bullet would plow through the thin pine table and enter Luis chest-high. His thumb slippery with sweat, he eased off the safety.

"I tell you what, little brother," Luis said amiably. "I will buy you another whiskey and you tell me all about your women, eh? Then I will tell you about mine."

Will's finger tightened on the trigger. "Nothin' to tell."

Luis opened his eyes wide. "Nothing? *Nada?* You think I, Luis Bajado Black Hawk, believe that?"

"I met a girl on a wagon train. I left her on the Paiute reservation." The instant the words were out of his mouth, the hair on his neck bristled.

Luis grinned at him. "That I do not believe. Or…" He peered into Will's face. "Maybe so I do believe. You have the look of a man who—"

The door smacked open and two men stumbled in. Luis tilted his head toward the bar. "Those two, they are stewed like ripe tomatoes," he said in an undertone. *"Vamanos."*

He rose and ambled toward the door. Will fingered his revolver, then eased the safety back on. He couldn't do it. Couldn't kill his own brother in cold blood, no matter what.

Out on the dusty street, Luis clapped an arm about Will's shoulder. "You look tired, little brother. You come to my place and rest."

Will clenched his jaw so hard his teeth ached. Luis *was* crazy. So far from sanity it made Will's skin crawl. But he still couldn't kill him.

"Your place," Will agreed. He'd wait until morning, take Luis into custody and ride him back to Texas for trial.

But at dawn, Will woke to find Luis gone. The tracks led south, toward the reservation.

Charlotte surveyed her young students, sitting respectfully in the shade of the lean-to. Holding class inside the shack was impossible; it was so stifling she had felt the flimsy walls press in on her, and though the seven young boys managed to stay awake through the long afternoons, Charlotte found herself yawning continually in the suffocating heat.

"Now," she urged. "Who can remember the English word for a big animal with four legs and a trunk? John?"

"My name is not John," the boy responded. "I am called Yellow Bird."

"Yes." Charlotte nodded. "But John Yellow Bird is your name now. Your Christian name."

The boy did not raise his voice, but his eyes flashed. "My name is Yellow Bird. It is an Indian name, not a Christian name."

Charlotte shook her head. She'd had the same argument every morning for a week, not only with John Yellow Bird but with Matthew Black Buck and Samuel Runs With Moon and the other boys, as well. "Our language is very old, very beautiful to hear. To us, English sounds ugly, like the squawking of chickens."

She mopped her forehead and the back of her neck with her only handkerchief. She was determined not to give up. They resisted their new Christian names. They resisted her efforts to teach them English. They resisted every bit of what she had to offer.

And as for civilized manners, saying "please" and "thank you" instead of uttering a grunt or, worse, simply making a sign with their hand, after hours of explanation and pleading, she decided to set that task aside for the moment.

She was learning that the Indians, whom she had once thought of as savages, were as different from one another as white men were. Some were savages; some were not.

"The Paiute people are a peace-loving tribe," John had explained. "We do not want to be like the white man."

Charlotte liked the students who rode out to her school each morning; they were intelligent, with inquiring minds and much good common sense. And they had a highly developed sense of personal honor and fair play. There was nothing "wrong" with them, as she had been led to believe back East. Nor did she find them lacking in worth. Their beadwork and the woven blankets they shared with each other were beautifully crafted.

"But if you are to survive in the white man's world, you must learn. You must adapt to new ways."

"Why should we do this thing?" John's young, proud face darkened. "The white man took our land. If the white man has his way, he will destroy our way of life. We must preserve *our* way."

"Of course," Charlotte replied. "But don't you see? You must also learn to fit in. You must integrate yourself into the white man's world. Otherwise, you, and your people, will not survive."

"Why," the young Indian pursued with his usual tenacity, "are the white man's customs and beliefs better than the red man's?"

"I—I am not sure that they are, John." In fact, she was not sure of anything lately. Matters that were perfectly obvious back in Ohio were not that simple out here in the West.

"It is not your fault, Flaming Hair," John said gallantly. "Perhaps when you grow older, you will understand these things."

Charlotte burst out laughing. All the students used the Indian name they had given her, Flaming Hair. She liked it, she acknowledged. But exactly who was the teacher here?

She had to smile at John's assumption that *she* would grow out of *her* strange ideas, at the same time that she expected *them* to grow out of *theirs*.

"I think, Yellow Bird…" Charlotte caught the quick look of astonishment and then approval at her use of his Indian name. His real name. "I think we have battled the matter to a draw. Perhaps we should agree to disagree on some issues?"

"I agree," John said with a gracious wave of his hand. "May we still be permitted to come to school? To look at your picture books?"

The other boys nodded with enthusiasm. One of the six, Peter Flying Duck, raised his head and addressed her in halting English. "Is not Flaming Hair we do not like."

"Not Mister Sam, either," John added. "He is a good man."

"You," Peter continued, his black eyes shining with admiration, "have a good heart."

Charlotte's heart catapulted into her throat. "Why, thank you, Peter." She might not teach them what the church elders had insisted upon, but she was having a good effect. She and her students were communicating honestly. Much good could come of such beginnings, she reasoned. In the wider world, understanding was necessary among different nations, even among different cultures.

By your students you shall be taught, she recalled from her Sunday school lessons in Marysville. And so she would learn.

"Now, Yellow Bird and Flying Duck, I see that your ponies are cleverly painted with designs and images. Such things take skill. Would you like to make a picture book of your own?"

She left the boys excitedly murmuring among themselves and set off for her house to retrieve paper and colored ink. One step beyond the screen door Sam Matthews had attached the day before and her hand flew to her mouth. Long John and the Comanche crouched inside, waiting for her.

Before she could cry out, Long John knocked her to the floor with a blow to her jaw. Dazed, she struggled to her knees, then felt a hard, sour-smelling hand close over her nose and mouth, cutting off her breath.

When she regained consciousness she was seated on a horse, an unfamiliar horse, and Long John was speaking into her ear.

"You little bitch, you tried to fool me. But I figured it out, and now—" he grabbed a handful of her loosened hair and yanked her head back "—now, you're gonna draw up a new map and then we're gonna follow it to that mine of yours."

A cloth of some sort had been stuffed into her mouth and tied tight behind her neck. She shook her head violently.

Long John doubled up one fist and crashed it into her cheek. "Oh, yes you will, missy. 'Cuz if you don't I'll dump your corpse where even the buzzards won't find it."

Charlotte shut her eyes and tried to think. Her students! Surely they would come to investigate when she did not return? And Sam. Was he closeted in his office, or had he been watching through the window?

Dear God, help me!

Chapter Twenty-Four

Will squinted at the set of faint tracks through the dust-blown gully, and a vise of iron tightened around his pounding temples. There it was, plain as a platter of sliced spuds: hoof prints with the left rear shoe canted off center.

Any blacksmith with half an eye would've straightened that in a heartbeat, but Luis didn't like anyone else handling his horse. He'd probably done the shoeing himself and gotten careless.

Just as Will had hoped. He tilted his hat down against the harsh sunlight. Still, his half brother was crafty. Even a careless Luis was dangerous.

It was a hard day's ride to the Paiute reservation; Will knew he had to stop soon and rest or he'd kill his horse. He slowed Sandy to a walk, then dismounted in a sparse stand of cottonwoods and let the mare snuffle the last of his canteen water from his cupped hands. Another hour and he'd reach the trading post. He hoped to God he wouldn't find Luis there, as well. When it came to women, his brother was a predator. When it came to a *pretty* woman, Luis could be an animal.

Will remounted and spurred the mare into a fast gallop. He'd learned as a boy never to tell his half brother anything of his feelings or his private life. Even mentioning a girl on a wagon train had been a mistake. How could he have been so thickheaded? Luis would guess she meant something to Will.

His brother, God blast his slippery hide, would want her, would take her just because Luis always wanted what Will had, whether it was horses, or guns, or women. A pretty woman worked on his brother like a mare in heat.

Sweat trickled down the back of his neck. He should never have left Charlotte at the reservation. Should never have given her up to chase Luis for revenge. Jesus, he should have claimed her then. Married her, even. And then spent his life protecting her. But he'd let his anger get in the way.

The small cluster of buildings that made up the trading post came into view ahead of him. No sign of the roan gelding, but Charlotte's gray mare was hitched to her porch railing. Will let out a heavy breath and felt his heart lift. She was here, thank God. He would see her again. And when he did, he might have to refigure what was most important in his life.

On the other hand, his years of experience playing fox and coyote with Luis told him it might be too soon to make any plans. His wily, soft-footed brother could be anywhere—at the trading post, inside Charlotte's little log house, even behind him, sighting down his gun barrel.

Before he could dismount, the Indian agent, Sam Matthews, stepped out the door, buckling a gun belt around his hips.

"Matthews! What's wrong?"

"Get down, Bondurant. Come inside where we can talk."

Will's eyes slowly adjusted to the dim interior of the agent's office as Sam sat him down and started talking. He stopped the man midsentence.

"Gone? Whaddya mean, she's gone?" An icy wind seemed to blow into his chest.

"Indian kids, her students, told me. Seems she left them in the lean-to and went into her house for something and didn't come back."

"You believe 'em?"

"Hell, yes, Ah believe 'em. The kids may be Indians, but they're not likely to make up a yarn like that."

"How long before they came to you?"

"'Bout half an hour. Ah swear Ah heard a couple of horses earlier, but those Paiute boys, her students, they ride their ponies to school, so Ah thought… And right about then that other fella—"

Will's entire body went cold. "What other fellow?"

Sam Matthews bent clear hazel eyes on Will. "Tall fella. Said he was your brother. Said you'd sent him."

"Sent him to what?" Will shot.

"To bring the lady back to Twist so's you two could get married up."

"That bastard," Will said under his breath.

"Ah shoulda caught on, but he kinda looked like you 'cept for his eyes." The agent shuddered. "Right queer eyes."

"He is my brother. My half brother."

"He was lyin', wasn't he? About bringing Miss Charlotte back to Twist."

"He was lying." Will clenched his jaw.

"Anyway, when he went into her house to fetch her, she was gone."

Will shook his head, torn between relief and dread. At least Luis didn't have her. Yet.

But somebody did.

"Anybody ever come to visit her?"

"Not since she got arrived that day, with you. Jeeze, Will, Ah feel awful about this."

"Her horse is still here, so I'd guess she was forced. Any idea who took her?"

"Nary a one, and Ah'm sorry for it. Shoulda kept a sharper eye on her."

"Never mind, Sam. I can make a pretty good guess who took her. And why. Name's Amos Shrader, and he's travelin' with a Comanche."

"Jesus and Joseph, we'd best get after them!"

"Not so fast. You reckon Luis, my brother, is on their trail?"

"Dunno. He took off like he was shot out of a cannon."

Will nodded. He knew what Luis would do if he wanted something. He went after it and just took it, any way he could.

"Mount up. That is if you're goin' with me."

"'Course Ah'm goin' with you. That's where Ah was

headed when you rode up. Miss Charlotte, she's real good people."

The two men strode outside to their mounts to find a cluster of young Indian boys waiting. One of the boys stepped forward.

"Mister Sam?"

"Ah'm listenin', Yellow Bird. What is it?"

"My brothers and I— " he swept his small arm out to indicate the circle of tense, dark faces "—we think the one who rides the red horse with the mark here..." He touched his forehead.

"Yeah? What do you think, Yellow Bird?"

"We think he follows tracks when he goes."

"Why do you think so?" Will said slowly. He met the boy's steady black eyes and held them. "Why?"

"Because he ride in very fast, from the east." Yellow Bird pointed back the way Will had come. "But when he ride away, he slow down and goes to the south."

"South," Will echoed. "Like he was trackin' someone?"

"Yes." Yellow Bird nodded. "The way my people would."

"That figures," Will muttered. Luis always was more Apache than Mexicano. Maybe that was why he was crazy for killing; he never really belonged in either camp.

"There is nothing to the south," Yellow Bird continued. "Only rocks and sand. Not even any beargrass. Why would a man ride in that direction?"

"Wonderin' the same thing mahself," Sam said.

Will said nothing for a full minute. Most likely Long John and the Comanche had trailed Charlotte here to the trading post, then kidnapped her. They would force her to guide them to her mine. Then they'd…

He pushed the thought away and tried to think clearly. Luis was trailing Long John and the Comanche. Will hadn't a clue about the location of Charlotte's mine, but maybe he didn't need it. All he had to do was track Luis and his slew-footed gelding.

"Sam, you know anything about a mine south of here?"

"Not 'xactly. Rumors only. Somewhere around Sheep Rock. Nobody's ever found it, and wouldn't matter if they did. Somebody from back East s'posed to own it."

"Don't think so," Will said as he swung into his saddle. "Miss Greenfield owns it."

"Well, Ah'll be…"

Will reined Sandy away. "Close your mouth, Sam," he called over his shoulder. "And mount up, if you're comin'."

The young Indian, Yellow Bird, stepped forward, blocking the path of Will's mare. Will pulled up and stared down at the boy. "You got some say-so here?"

Yellow Bird drew himself up as tall as he could and propped his small hands at the waist of his deerskin britches. "Flaming Hair…" he said. Then the boy swallowed hard.

"Yeah? What about her?"

"You will find her?" The expression in the dark eyes was not the least bit childlike; it was damned determined.

"Yeah, I will. Step aside, now."

The boy stood his ground. "You will take care of her?"

"I give you my word, son. Or I'll die tryin'."

Yellow bird pivoted out of Will's path, then turned back. "Do not beat her for her disobedience. She is not very old. Not grown up yet."

In spite of the hard knot in his gut, Will chuckled until Sam caught up to him and the two men spurred their horses away to the south.

Charlotte huddled before the meager cook fire Long John had built, chafing her wrists where the confining ropes burned.

"You sure this is the place, missy? Don't look like a mine to me, just a big sand wash."

"I am as sure as I can be, considering that I am relying entirely on my memory. May I have some water now?"

"Later. You think real hard. Fifty paces south of that big rock yonder, that right?"

Charlotte nodded, too weary to argue. She was positive she remembered the landmarks correctly, but Long John was right. As far as she could see there was no structure that looked remotely like a mine.

"Please, a drink of water?"

Long John tossed the canteen at her. "Stop whining."

Charlotte unscrewed the cap and wet her tongue with the metallic-tasting water. She wasn't whining. She *never* whined. That's what Mama had done when she wanted something, and Charlotte detested it.

She got down a single swallow before the Comanche yanked the canteen out of her hands. Fighting the urge to scream, she rested her head on her raised knees. She hadn't spent thirty-seven nights on the trail with Will without learning the dangers of not having enough water. She could die. Will would never know what had happened to her.

Was that what Long John planned for her? Let her die of thirst out here in this broiling heat? Her mouth felt parched, her tongue sluggish. He wouldn't let her die until he found the mine, would he?

He would, she decided. It wouldn't matter if they never found the mine; she would not survive the ordeal. Long John would never believe her memory of the map was accurate. Or, worse, he would assume she had purposely misled him once again.

The Comanche drank deep and handed the container to Long John, then grunted and pointed at the sky. The harsh blue overhead had begun to turn salmon and gold as the sun sank toward the west.

Long John stopped gulping water and looked up. "Yeah, I see it. Even if that blasted mine is here, we aren't gonna find it in the dark." He prowled a circle around the sputtering campfire, passing so close to Charlotte she could feel the movement of air against the back of her neck.

On his next circuit he paused behind her and prodded her backside with his boot. "Better get some sleep, missy. We'll do some more looking in the morning."

Hungry and tired as she was, Charlotte knew better than to protest. Her stomach hurt and she felt lightheaded. Her head throbbed from hours of riding into the sun, and she desperately needed water. At least night would bring cooler air.

Maybe she wouldn't die yet. Long John might keep her alive until tomorrow, or maybe even another whole day.

The last thought she allowed herself before drifting into an exhausted sleep was the memory of Will's mouth on hers and his rusty-voiced goodbye. Her breath hitched in.

He cared for her. She knew it as sure as... Her cracked lips twitched into a smile...as sure as her name was Charlie.

"Look yonder," Sam murmured at Will's side. They had ridden through the night, following the fresh hoof-prints in the faint moonlight. Will was so tired his vision was blurry, but he knew he couldn't stop.

"Where?"

"Big shape over by that pointed rock. Horse, you think?"

"Could be. Big horse." Will narrowed his eyes. "No rider."

"No wild horses around these parts, Will."

Will licked his dry lips. "It's Luis. He's on foot. Musta seen something."

Sam whistled under his breath. "Can't follow tracks a horse don't make. What do we do now?"

"First thing is, watch your back. Luis can walk real soft."

"Okay," Sam muttered.

"Second, let's backtrack a ways. Take cover and wait 'til there's light to see by."

"Ah like the way you think, son," the agent murmured. "My butt's so sore it feels like my momma's pincushion."

"Let's go," Will said. "Slow and quiet."

"Right." Sam turned his horse.

"And like I said, Sam, watch your back."

Ten minutes later, crouching behind a lumpy rock screened by a tangle of sparse sage and a single wind-twisted pine, Will positioned himself facing Sam, rifle across his thighs. Sam kept his eye on the murky shadows behind Will, his revolver drawn and ready. Other than the occasional call of a night bird, the night was so quiet Will could hear his heart thumping.

And hot as Texas, Will noted. At least Charlotte would be warm, wherever Long John had taken her. *Just keep your spirits up, princess.*

He looked up at the glittering stars. *Lord, I'm askin' You. Begging You. Keep her safe.*

At the first pale blush of dawn, Will and Sam resumed the search. At Will's insistence, they took the bridles off the horses, guiding them with makeshift harnesses improvised out of rope. "Quieter this way," Will said.

After an hour, he pulled up. "Wish Luis had a crooked boot. Sure would make tracking him easier."

Sam surveyed the barren terrain. "Not many places to hide out here. Our man should be easy to spot."

"Don't count on it," Will said in a dry voice. "Luis is like one of those lizards, the kind that blend into their surroundings."

"Sounds kinda like he's been on the run before."

Will said nothing.

"What's your brother wanted for, anyway?"

"Murder," Will said, keeping his voice even.

Sam sent him an assessing look. "And you're his brother. Ah'd guess you're a lawman, as well."

"Not in Oregon. But I'd fake it if I could catch up to him. My first thought was to kill him, but— I ought to take him back to Texas for trial."

"Jesus. Probably get yourself killed instead."

"I wouldn't bet on it," Will said, an edge in his tone. "Luis is three years older than me. When we were growin' up, I learned everything he learned. I know his tricks. Most of 'em, anyway."

Sam swore again. "How come he's so wild?"

"He's more'n half Apache. Leastways, that's how his momma explained it."

Sam chortled. "Ah'd shore hate to go up against a man like that."

"Don't worry about it, Sam. I'm part Apache, too."

Sam eyed him curiously, then turned his gaze back to the flat, dry land surrounding them. "Ah'd give my right arm for a few trees about now. Maybe even some water nearby."

Will gestured with his chin. "Up ahead. Scrawny and sunbaked, but they're trees."

Sam bent forward and squinted without speaking, then straightened. "Cottonwoods. Let's go."

Will reached over and grabbed the older man's make-shift harness. "Not so fast. Let's circle around, come in from behind."

"How's that gonna make a difference?"

"On our bellies. We need to be close to the ground."

They dismounted quietly, picketed the horses behind an outcropping of red rock and crept forward, shirt-fronts in the dirt. The sparse stand of cottonwoods seemed unnaturally quiet the closer they drew, and Will's senses sharpened. When birds were quiet at sunup there was usually a reason.

Fifty yards from the first tree, both Will and Sam removed their hats and stuffed them under their belts. Hugging the sandy ground, Will crawled noiselessly forward, wishing Sam, behind him, didn't breathe so heavily. Luis had ears like a cougar.

Hell, it probably wouldn't make a damn bit of difference. If Luis sighted them first, they were dead men.

Chapter Twenty-Five

Charlotte stood in the center of the dish-shaped ravine, withdrew the scrap of brown wrapping paper from her skirt pocket and unfolded it once again. Shielding her eyes from the blinding sun, she studied the marks she had laboriously made.

Could she be mistaken? Could she have misremembered the landmarks of rocks and trees she had memorized months ago? Her mind was so tired, her thoughts so tumbled, she was no longer sure.

She stepped off the distance for the third time that morning: fifty paces from the odd-shaped overhanging rock, moving straight south. Long John and the Comanche followed on horseback, the muffled thunk of hoofbeats at her heels prodding her forward. The mine had to be here. It had to be!

She halted and gazed at the sandy wash where she inevitably ended up each time she measured off the distance. Nothing. Not a telltale scrap of wood or a cave entrance in the semicircular sand-rock wall she faced. She stared at the red-brown pocket of earth where she stood until her eyes burned. *Where is the mine?*

"Give me that!" Long John snatched the map out of her hand. He studied the paper, his puffy face growing red with fury on top of his sunburn. Charlotte stepped out of his way. While he muttered and swore atop his horse, she focused on his boot.

He rode like an Easterner, she observed. Only a greenhorn jammed his foot all the way into the stirrup; Will had taught her to just "toe the arch." If the horse bolted or threw her, she could disengage. "More than one pilgrim has been dragged to death behind a spooked horse."

To Will, all Easterners were "pilgrims," and he did not mean it in a religious sense. A dart of pain lanced her chest. She had grown to like Will's barbed comments. And oh, Lord God, how she missed them. And him!

Something about Long John's boot caught her attention. The man's feet must be enormous! The oversize boot alone must weigh…

With a cry she jerked to life. His foot! A man's foot. Uncle Gus's foot! Why had she not seen it before? Uncle Gus had drawn the original map after his visit out West before Papa died. The fifty paces were measured with Uncle Gus–size steps!

"What's wrong, missy? See a snake?"

Charlotte clenched her fists. The only snake she saw was sitting on the horse in front of her.

"I just thought of something," she said, keeping her voice neutral.

"Whazzat?" Long John spit out the word, his eyes hard. *Oh, my. Do I explain and die afterward, or keep silent and die now?* Either way she was edging closer and closer to not surviving this day. The look on Long John's face told her his patience was wearing out. The man's lips were thinned into a mean-looking line, and his eyes glittered with a murderous light.

If she told him what she had reasoned out, he might yet find the mine. But to claim it, or work it, he would have to share the location with someone in a town somewhere. Would a sheriff or a marshal connect her disappearance with a stranger claiming a mine that was, she hoped, registered in her name?

At least she prayed it was in her name. Papa's attorney would surely have seen to that, would he not? But she remembered suddenly that Long John had been Mr. Treadwell's law clerk. She guessed he had purposely failed to record the deed when the attorney asked him to. Or, worse, he had surreptitiously torn it up. Why had Mr. Treadwell not given *her* the deed, along with the map?

She would probably never know the answer to that question; she would have to be satisfied with finding the mine and trusting that the truth would eventually come out when someone found her body.

"Speak up, missy! Haven't got all day."

Yes, she decided. She would tell him. It was the only thing she could do.

"I have had an idea," Charlotte announced. "The person who drew the original map, my uncle Gustave Greenfield, had rather large feet." She paused for Long John to make the connection.

He stared at her with a blank look.

"Like yours," she prompted.

"So what?"

Charlotte took a deep breath and sealed her fate. "Fifty paces in a man's stride would be far longer than fifty paces in mine. My feet, even in these boots, are small."

The Comanche laughed, and then silence dropped over the three of them as Long John digested this. He dismounted, handed the reins to the Indian and strode toward the landmark rock. When he reached it, he pivoted and started back, heading straight south and counting off his steps aloud.

Just when he reached thirty-nine, Charlotte saw a flicker of motion at the high edge of the wash. She bent her head to brush off her skirt and surreptitiously watched the spot. There it was again, so subtle it was like a shadow falling on a rock, then evaporating into nothing. The hair on her forearms prickled.

She shot a glance at Long John and the Comanche, but both were absorbed in the measured pacing.

Charlotte swallowed a cry of relief. It was Sam Matthews. It had to be. Sam was the only person, other than her students, who would know she was missing. In the next instant, an ice pick twisted into her belly. Sam was a gentle soul who never wore a gun. He would be no match for Long John and the Comanche.

The pace count reached forty-four before she glimpsed another movement, this time on the lip of the slightly elevated edge of the sand pit.

Then everything happened at once. A man's head

appeared at the edge of the wash. It was not Sam Matthews, Charlotte realized. The Comanche's head
snapped up, his gaze swinging away from Long John to
the perimeter of the pit. At that moment Long John
reached the count of forty-nine; as he uttered "fifty," the
ground caved in beneath him.

The Comanche's hand closed around her upper arm.
With a grunt, he kicked his horse and lunged forward,
dragging her over the ground to where Long John stumbled out of a sand-covered structure of broken timber.
The mine!

The Indian shouted something and hurled Charlotte
in front of him, where she sprawled facedown, her chin
scraping the sand. A rough hand jerked her into a sitting
position and Long John crouched behind her, one hand
across her throat, the other fumbling for his revolver.

Another flicker of movement on the edge of the pit.
Charlotte cried a warning, but it came too late.

A dark, whip-thin man she did not recognize rose to
a standing position, arms ostentatiously uplifted away
from his holstered revolvers.

"Do not shoot, *amigo*. Let us talk."

Long John motioned the man down into the pit. He
was tall, bronze-skinned, with dark eyes that shone
oddly. There was something familiar about him, but
Charlotte couldn't think clearly enough to explore the
thought.

The Comanche drew a rifle from a deerskin roll and
trained it on the stranger as he strode into the wash.

Long John's cold steel gun barrel pressed under
Charlotte's chin. "Who the hell are you?" he shouted.

A dazzling smile lit up the dark man's face. "I am Luis Martin Bajado, at your service."

Charlotte went cold all over. Will's half brother. The killer.

He bowed with surprising grace, then tipped his black feather banded hat toward her. "*Señorita.* One so lovely should not look so frightened."

"What do you want?" Long John snapped.

The smile flashed again. "Why, it is obvious, is it not? I want the *señorita.*"

The barrel tip pinched into Charlotte's flesh. "What for?"

"*Mi amigo,* I should think that is obvious, as well."

"That all you want?"

Luis made a show of scanning the sand wash and the now-exposed cracked timbers of the mine. "No, my friend, there is nothing here to my liking, except for her. Not even whatever is hiding under the earth there." He gestured to the mine entrance. "A mine, I think. But I do not want it—too much work. The lady, she will be work enough, and much more enjoyable, eh *señor?*"

Charlotte's stomach turned over. For a moment she thought she might be sick.

"Not sure you can have her," Long John said. "You prepared to bargain?"

Bargain! Charlotte jerked and the gun jabbed harder.

"*Sí,* I will bargain. She is very pretty, no? I offer one hundred dollars."

Long John laughed. "Not enough. The lady has some…information I don't want made public."

Luis lifted his hand. "It is not information that interests me, *señor.* Two hundred dollars. In gold."

Long John's guttural panting near her ear stopped short. In the heavy silence Charlotte set her fear aside and prepared to bargain for her life. She could die from Long John's bullet, or she could accompany Luis to a fate she could not contemplate. She decided on Long John.

No sooner had she opened her lips than a shadow fell across her face and a low voice spoke.

"She's not for sale."

Chapter Twenty-Six

At the sound of Will's voice, Charlotte felt an over-whelming urge to sob with relief. A thousand thoughts swirled around and around in her brain. Where had he come from? How had he known she so desperately needed help?

Will had his revolver aimed at Luis, and for the first time she was glad—so thankfully glad—he was armed. Luis's left hand inched toward his gun belt.

"Drop 'em, Luis."

"A moment, little brother. Let me speak."

"Drop 'em," Will repeated. Charlotte had never heard his voice so hard and cold. She watched the dark man casually unbuckle his weapons and let them fall where he stood.

"And the pistol in your belt," Will said.

With a shrug, Luis drew out a smaller weapon and dropped it onto the pile. "I am glad to see you, *mi hermano*."

"Sure y'are," Will said softly. "And the knife in your boot. Both boots."

"Little brother, you would pluck me like a chicken?"

"You're lucky that's all I'm doin', Luis. Shoulda shot you when I found you at the Golden Belle."

Long John brandished his own revolver in the hot, still air to catch Will's attention, then with studied care he brought the barrel back to Charlotte's chin and forced her head up. "I'll kill her if you make a move, Bondurant. Take your brother and go."

"Not so fast, Shrader. It's not Luis I want."

Charlotte blinked twice at the unreality of the scene. Surely she was hallucinating. Will and Luis faced each other, Will on the edge of the wash, armed; Luis not a yard to her left, unarmed. And the Comanche, still mounted, his back to Will, watched Long John with an expressionless face. A rifle lay across his lap.

It was like an awful dream. Sitting on the ground, locked in Long John's sweaty embrace, Charlotte saw it all as if outside of herself, the men frozen in place as if caught in a photograph.

"I repeat, Bondurant, make a move and I'll kill her." At her back, Long John twitched.

Will looked down at him for a long moment. "You all right, Charlie?"

"Yes. Just thirsty."

"Give her some water," Will ordered.

"Why should I? She led us on a helluva wild-goose chase. 'Bout cost me my last penny."

"Just do what the man asks." This time the voice came from behind her. She twisted her head to see Sam

Matthews, pointing a rifle at the Comanche. The Indian sat his horse without moving.

A standoff. Charlotte closed her eyes and tried to pray. *Dear Lord, as sure as I'm sitting here, someone is going to shoot someone. Please, please don't let it be Will.*

"Charlie?" Will called again.

Her lids snapped open. "Yes, Will?"

"Can you walk?"

"I—I think so."

"She's not going anywhere," Long John snarled. "I'll shoot her if she tries anything. Or," he added with a glance at Sam, behind him, "if anyone tries to shoot."

Luis grinned up at Will. "You have caught me in a sandbox, little brother. But I have nothing to do with this business." He gestured toward the exposed mine timbers. "All I want is the pretty *señorita.*"

"Then you've got business with me, Luis. You lay one finger on her and I'll drop you where you stand."

Luis raised his arms in mock helplessness. "What are we to do, *mi hermano?* Both of us want the lady, but another man holds the pistol under her chin."

Will thought it over. He didn't trust Luis; he'd learned that from his growing-up years. And he couldn't trust that lying law clerk, Shrader. He calculated the odds, based on their positions.

Sam, at the edge of the sandy depression, had the mounted Comanche in the pit covered. He himself had his Colt trained on Luis, where he stood near Charlotte's huddled form. A standoff.

He had to act, and he had to do it now. If he swung

his revolver to Long John, could he kill him before he put a bullet into Charlotte?

"Charlie?"

"Yes, Will?" Her voice was getting shaky.

"Remember that mornin' you got bucked off your horse?"

"Y-yes." She had landed on her rump and was sore for a week. Will had spent an entire morning teaching her how to survive a fall from a horse. *Keep your head down and roll clear.*

Oh, God. He wanted her to do that? *Now?* If she even twitched a hand, Long John would shoot her.

"Whaddya want to know that for?" Long John was growing nervous. Charlotte could feel his arm begin to tremble.

"Just reminiscing. We traveled a long ways together. Just makin' conversation with an old friend." Will's tone was so amiable she wondered if she had misinterpreted his message. But his eyes were not amiable. They held hers in a steady gaze, and slowly their meaning came clear to her. *You can do it.*

"Charlie?"

She had known Will less than three months, but she would trust him with her life. She looked up at him and nodded her head once. Slowly, so Long John wouldn't panic and pull the trigger.

"You two can stop your remembering," Long John barked.

Luis turned an interested face toward Charlotte. "I would like to hear more about the lady's horseman-ship." He spoke calmly and deliberately, addressing the remark to Charlotte. For a split second the gun barrel at her throat slipped. Now was her chance.

She threw herself sideways and curled into a ball. Two gun shots rang out simultaneously, and something heavy, a man's body she guessed, fell on top of her.

When she opened her eyes, Long John lay sprawled on the sand an arm's length away. Will must have killed him when she rolled to the side, leaving him a clear shot.

But the second shot? What was that? This weight pressing down on her, who was it?

Using all her strength, she pushed her head out from under a thick shoulder. Will was scrambling down the steep-sided wall toward her, and at the same moment, the Comanche dropped a smoking rifle onto the sand and raised both hands. Sam Matthews strode forward, kicked the rifle away, and spoke to the Indian in his language.

The man lying on top of her groaned. A warm sticky substance soaked into the bodice of her dress, and Charlotte froze in horror.

"Charlotte!" Will's tense face swam into view. Had *she* been hit?

He lifted the man off her, and when she crawled free she saw that it was Luis. Will rolled him faceup and she gasped. His dark face looked a sickly gray.

Will bent over him. "Luis?"

"Ay, little brother," came the fading voice. "I try to protect the pretty *señorita*. She is safe?"

Will touched his brother's blood-drenched shoulder. "She is safe. You have done a fine thing, Luis."

Luis's grin was uneven. "I did not do it for you, *mi hermano*. I did it because—" his breath rasped in, then flowed out in a sigh "—because she is *muy bonita*." Another soft sigh and he was gone.

Charlotte's breath caught in a sob. She watched Will kneel beside the body, his mouth twisting in anguish. "Luis. It was still a fine thing. The finest thing you have ever done." Swallowing hard, he bowed his head. "Thank you, brother."

Suddenly Sam yelled something, and Will grabbed Charlotte, pulling her beneath him.

Three mounted Indian braves ringed the sand wash, lances poised.

"Red Wolf," Sam called. "Little Bear." He made a sign with his hand.

"Will, let me up," Charlotte said. "I know those men."

Will jerked. "Are you crazy? You're scared to death of Indians."

"They are the fathers of my students. They are Paiute."

Will stared at her. Her face was dirt-streaked, one sleeve of her blue dress ripped at the shoulder seam, her fiery hair a tangle of curls and snarls.

She had never looked so beautiful.

"Will, you don't have to carry me. Put me down."

"Not on your life, Charlie." Without slowing, he strode over the parched landscape to the rock where his horse waited. She had to be feeling his heart pound right through her dress. He tightened his arms around her.

"Will, really. I can certainly walk."

"So can I. Faster than you."

She sighed and snuggled her head against his neck. Even all tangled up, her hair felt silky on his skin. He couldn't explain what he was doing, tramping over the ground with her held tight in his arms. Maybe he just wanted to feel her body safe and warm and close to his.

"Will, am I not heavy?"

"Yeah, some."

"Then put me down!"

"Nope."

"Oh, you are such a stubborn man!"

"Sometimes. I figure we're about equal in the stubborn department."

Charlotte sighed once more, curved her free arm about his neck and peeked over his shoulder. Behind her, Sam Matthews and two of the Paiute braves were lashing the bodies of Luis and Long John onto their horses. The third brave stood guard over the Comanche.

How very odd it seemed, one Indian helping to bring another to justice. Perhaps that is what she should address in her classroom, not teaching one culture to succumb to another, but seeking fair treatment for all under the law. Of course it was the white man's law, she conceded.

"I can hear your brain buzzing," Will said. "You know you kinda hum when you're thinkin'?"

"No, I didn't know."

"And you do some fancy moaning when we—"

"Will!"

He chuckled, bent his head and kissed her bare shoulder where the sleeve had torn away.

"Will, stop. Sam will see us!"

"Can't." He kissed her throat where the neckline of her dress stopped, then strode on a few paces and kissed her temple.

"Will, what are you doing?"

"Laying my claim, what does it look like?"

Charlotte said nothing. What a funny kind of pro-posal. Or *was* it a proposal?

"Why are you laying a—?"

His rumbling laugh cut off her words. And then he coughed and fell silent. After a long minute he cleared his throat.

"Why?" he echoed.

"I, yes, well, I thought we had made a decision. I would teach here in Oregon, and you would—"

"Yeah, I thought so, too, Charlotte. But now there's something I need to tell you."

"Oh." Her voice sounded flat, but she couldn't help it. He had that "you're not going to like this" tone.

"It's about my wife. Alice."

"Oh," she said again. Her heart squeezed once and plummeted into her stomach.

"See, Alice was raised on a sugar plantation in Lou-isiana. She hated Texas, and after a while she decided she hated me, too. I guess I left her alone too much. Closed myself off from her."

Charlotte came instantly alert at the change in his voice. "You tried the same tactic on me, as well," she said.

"That's the part I had a hard time accepting, that I was more than half to blame for what happened. Any-way, she ended up in Luis's bed. When I came after her, he shot at me and hit her instead."

"You wanted Alice to love you, not Luis, is that it?"

"I'd sure like to think so, but truth is, there's more to it." He sucked in a lungful of air and blew it out in a rush.

"Go on, Will. I'm listening." She heard him swallow twice.

"Alice was pretty. Real pretty. I hate to admit this, Charlotte, but when I got to know her inside, I didn't like her too much. But even so, I didn't want Luis to have her. All the years we were growing up together, Luis always had to have every single thing I wanted."

Charlotte went perfectly still.

"Well, then you came along. I liked you. A lot. On the outside *and* on the inside. And it scared the hell out of me."

Charlotte thought while Will closed the distance to his black mare. "What about the mine?"

He stumbled, almost dropping her. "The mine! Haven't you heard anything I said?"

"Of course I have. You are afraid because now there is more at stake."

He stopped short. "But it's not the mine that matters here. It's, well, it's…oh, hell, Charlotte, it's because I'm never gonna be able to leave you alone. Ignore you, like I did Alice."

"I should certainly hope not!"

She started to hum and Will walked on, unable to suppress his smile. "You like Oregon?"

"I like teaching. I hate getting sunburned when I hang up my washing. Do you like Texas?"

Will's movements checked momentarily. "Never lived anywhere else."

"I imagine we'll have to return to Baker City."

Will set her gently on her feet, turned her to face him and closed her in his arms. He held her, saying nothing. At last he dipped his head and caught her mouth under his.

After a long, long moment, he raised his head. "Baker City?" he said in a low voice. "What for?"

Charlotte leaned her forehead against his chin. "First, it's the county seat. I want to check the records on my mine."

"Charlotte, I don't ever want you to set foot anywhere near that stove-up old mine."

"Second," she continued, her voice unruffled, "I will need to find a mining engineer and hire some miners."

Will busied himself settling the bridle he'd removed over Sandy's muzzle and kept his head down.

"Third—" she hummed a short tune she wasn't sure Will recognized "—Baker City has a hotel. A private room. With a double bed. And—"

"Sold." Will lifted her into the saddle, climbed on behind and bent forward to press his lips to her neck.

Despite the late-morning heat, Charlotte shivered. Will wrapped his arms around her and lifted the reins.

"Fourth," Charlotte murmured almost inaudibly, "Baker City will have a preacher."

Will dug his heels into Sandy's side, and the horse jolted forward.

Chapter Twenty-Seven

The Baker City courthouse, a white-painted stone building in the center of town, looked to Charlotte like a three-story loaf cake with windows between the layers. After the long, hot ride from the reservation trading post, just seeing the cool paint-frosted bricks made her thirsty. And hungry.

Atop the structure, a blue and gold flag alternately billowed and hung limp from the iron pole as the scorching late-afternoon air gusted and ebbed. Oddly, it smelled not of dust, but of something sweet.

"Rain comin'," Will remarked as they walked their horses past the barber shop. "Smell it?"

Charlotte slowed the gray and sniffed the breeze. She caught the scent of honeysuckle and something else, something sharp and spicy, but it wasn't rain. "I don't think so. I smell cookies!"

A wave of homesickness engulfed her. "Mama used to make such good cookies," she said with a sigh. "Oatmeal and lemon."

Will sent her a quick look. "You miss the East?"

"Oh, no. I could never go back to Ohio. I've changed too much."

Will studied her face. "Because you've camped thirty-eight nights with a rough-edged Texan with a beard and no manners?"

"No, not because of that. Well, maybe a little bit. It certainly was educational!"

Will laughed. "Educational," he repeated under his breath. "That's a bit like calling a green horse an animal you wouldn't want to milk."

"Marysville is quite staid, really. In some ways I guess I was always an outsider. Now I would shock them out of their high-button shoes. Fitting into a 'back East' way of thinking would be impossible now."

"Where do you figure you fit now?" he said, his voice careful.

Charlotte turned narrowed eyes on him. "With you, of course! Don't tell me you haven't been thinking just that?"

"Yeah, I been thinkin', all right." Will swiped off his hat and ran the fingers of one hand through his dark hair. "Problem is, I don't know where *I* belong anymore."

"Do you not plan to return to Texas?"

Will gave her a long look. "Got no real family left in Texas. And I don't have a calling outside of the Rifles. Been thinkin' maybe I'd buy a ranch…" He eyed the wind-bitten buildings lining the town's main street. "Someplace where there's good water. Someplace where it greens up in the spring."

"Oh?" Charlotte waited, biting the inside of her cheek.

"That'd make a fine journey, don'tcha think? Ramblin' around lookin' for a pretty piece of land?" He replaced his hat, then bent his head to study Sandy's twitching ears. "You interested?" he said in a low voice.

She smiled at his gently probing question and twisted in the saddle to look at him. His hair was mussed and hung below his ears, his chin darkened with a three-day growth of whiskers. And his eyes, blue as mountain lupine, held hers in a steady gaze, waiting for her answer.

A man could be so dense at times!

Charlotte reached over and grasped his hand. "Am I *interested?* Will Bondurant, just you try and stop me!"

"Hell, honey, I don't want to stop you. I want you to come with me. Help find our place."

Charlotte's heart cartwheeled inside her chest. "'Our' place? As in you-and-me-together-on-the-same-place place?"

A slow smile curved his lips. "Yeah."

"I thought we came to Baker City to see whether I really own the mine?"

"That's one reason."

"And maybe hire a mining engineer and a crew."

"That's a good reason, too. But I figure the most important reason is that inside this courthouse is a judge who can marry people."

"Yes," Charlotte agreed softly.

Will looked at her with darkening eyes. "Matter of fact, I think we should settle it now. Are you gonna marry me?"

"Of course I am, Will. I wouldn't let you run a ranch without me. I can roll my own cigarettes, patch up your injuries, and…"

Will grinned. "Guess I'm lucky to have you."

Charlotte straightened her spine. "You are so right, Will Bondurant." Holding her head at a queenly angle, Charlotte felt tears of pride burn into her eyes. "You are so damn right."

During the brief, simple ceremony in Judge Madison Whitcomb's chambers, Will held Charlotte's hand tight in his own, and when they turned toward each other to pledge their vows, both pairs of eyes shone with tears.

The judge looked from one to the other, swallowed and went on with the ceremony. When he pronounced them man and wife, his voice cracked.

Afterward, they walked to the Baker City Hotel, hands still clasped.

"Hello, Mr. Bondurant," the redhaired hotel clerk said when they approached the registry. "I seen you ride into town a while back, an' I got your room all ready for you. And your—"

He shifted his gaze to Charlotte and stopped.

"My wife," Will supplied quietly. His fingers squeezed Charlotte's. "We'd like a bathtub, a big one, hot water and a bottle of champagne."

"Oh, yessir. Big tub and champagne." The clerk turned scarlet and bobbed his head. "Comin' right up."

"Do you wish more towels, *señor?*" The young Mexican chambermaid's dark eyes looked expectantly at Will.

"*Gracias,*" Will said. He couldn't seem to get his voice to sound normal, but then a man didn't get married every day. Funny, he wasn't nervous during the ceremony in the judge's chambers; then he knew exactly what he was doing.

That soft, buoyant feeling in his chest was humbling. He knew that marrying Charlotte was the best thing he'd ever done, but he was unprepared for how it made him feel inside.

He gazed at the tub of steaming water, then sought Charlotte's eyes. She sat primly on the edge of the double bed, her bare toes peeking out from under the hem of her skirt. What would she think about sharing the oversize copper tub? And the champagne. And…his heart wobbled crazily and flipped over…the rest of his life.

"Some scented soap, *señor?*"

"What? Oh, sure."

"And for the champagne, you would like two glasses?"

"No glasses," Charlotte pronounced from the bed. She caught Will's gaze and grinned crookedly. "I've always wanted to—"

She broke off, her cheeks flushing crimson.

Will pressed a two-bit piece into the maid's hand, ushered her to the door and locked it after her. The rustle of a petticoat behind him told Will his bride had started to undress.

"Wait," he said, his voice thick. He turned to see her hands flutter at the buttons on her dress.

"Wait? The water will get cold, Will."

"The water will be fine. I want to undress you."

Without a word, she lifted her arms to her sides, and Will stepped nearer and began to slip the mother-of-pearl buttons free.

"Will," she breathed as her dress fell away over her hips. "Touch me."

"Not yet." His hands trembled over the petticoat tie at her waist. She raised her arms again.

"Undo me," she said in a quiet voice.

He worked the ribbon knot free, watched the soft muslin garment drop to her feet and felt his chest squeeze. Lifting the camisole over her head, he caught the light, sweet scent of her skin. Kinda lemony, with something spicy underneath. He released another button and her lace-edged drawers slid to the floor. If his groin got any tighter, he wouldn't be able to sit down in the tub.

Will cupped her face between his palms and tipped her chin up. He'd never felt so awkward. "How come you don't smell like dust and horse, like I do?"

Charlotte pressed her nose into his neck and inhaled. "You don't. You smell like leather and camp smoke." Then she grinned and added, "And dust and horse."

"Kiss me, honey." He caught her mouth under his and let himself taste her the way he'd been thinking about ever since that day in White Eagle's camp, dipping his tongue deep, rimming her bottom lip with her own moisture.

"Damn, you taste good," he whispered. His hand shaking, he slowly drew his palms down her rib cage to her waist, then splayed his fingers over her softly rounded backside. "You feel good, too." He kissed her again and moved one hand to his belt buckle.

She said nothing as he shrugged out of his shirt and trousers, but her breathing grew increasingly shallow and uneven. He liked it, the sound of her breathing. When he stood naked before her, she stepped in close and wound her arms around his neck.

Lord, he could feel her warm breasts burn against his bare chest, her gentle breath flowing into his ear. It made him crazy. And so hard he knew she could feel him rise against her belly.

She swirled her tongue over one nipple, moved up into his mouth, then into his ear. "Last one in the tub is a…"

She darted away and headed for the bathtub, but Will blocked her path. Laughing, she tried to dodge around him, but he caught her easily, lifted her into his arms and plopped her into the water. "Too cold?" he said as he watched her breasts disappear under the water.

"No. It's just right. But," she said with an impish grin, "there is no room for you."

"That so?" Without waiting for her response, Will strode to the chest of drawers next to the bed, puffed out the kerosene lamp, and lit the fat green candle in the ceramic holder. Then, moving to the window, he raised the sash and let the warm, fragrant air circulate through the room.

Last he lifted the champagne out of the brass bucket and stepped to the tub. "I'm comin' in behind you, Charlie. Skooch forward a bit so I can…yeah, that's it." He splashed into the water, champagne in hand. "Now lean back against my chest," he whispered.

Charlotte pressed her knobby little backbone against him. It felt like a strand of perfect pearls pressed against his chest. Her bottom fit into his groin, and with a little gasp she allowed his legs to stretch out on either side of hers. He leaned his head back, and with his thumbs began working the champagne cork free. When it fizzed and bubbled over, he directed the foam into the hollow between her breasts.

"Oh, a bath in champagne! I've always wondered… Oh, Will, I have wondered about so many things."

He tipped the bottle into his mouth. "Yeah? What things?" The wine felt cold and stinging going down, and sinfully good when it got there. Suddenly he couldn't stop smiling.

"Wow," he said with a chuckle. "Ever tasted champagne before? Try some." Carefully he guided the tip of the bottle into Charlotte's open mouth. She swallowed a small sip, then took a bigger mouthful.

"Oh, my!"

"You like it?"

"Oh, my, yes," she said on a sigh.

"Good." He tightened his legs about hers and bent forward to kiss the back of her neck.

"Will, do you know what the word *decadent* means?"

"Nope," he lied. "Don't care, either. I love you, Charlie. I'm half-crazy with it. You're what matters most in my life."

Charlotte's breath caught in a hiccup. "Oh, Will, I think I'm going to cry."

Again Will leaned his head back, and this time he closed his eyes. He could feel every inch of her wet skin against him, feel her feathery curls brush his Adam's apple. Her warm tears rolled down over the hand he'd laid against her throat.

"This isn't decadent, honey. It's what a man and a woman do."

A little sob shook her body. "Then do some more."

For a long while all was quiet. Then he heard another sound, coming from across the room, from the open window.

"Listen, Charlotte," he murmured. "It's rainin'."

As long as he lived he would never forget this night, the two of them so close together, the warmth of candle glow washing the room.

And the sound of the gentle, nourishing rain.

They patted each other dry with the towels left on the side table, and then Charlotte felt Will's arms gather her close. "You ready for bed?" he breathed.

"I've been ready for the past hour," she whispered. "I thought you would have noticed."

"I noticed. Didn't want to rush you."

She kissed the underside of his jaw. "Rush me," she murmured.

Will made a low, satisfied sound in his throat and scooped her into his arms. He laid her on the bed, turned back for the champagne bottle, then changed his mind. "Hell, I'm drunk already on the way you smell with soap bubbles all over you."

Charlotte laughed. "I, however, am stone-cold sober," she lied.

"Guess we're not well-suited. But if that's so, how come you're smiling and I'm so damn happy I could float right off this bed?"

"Maybe it's the champagne?" She felt like teasing him. Touching him. Making him want her.

"Champagne's got nuthin' to do with it." He smoothed his fingers over her breast, lingered, then bent to kiss her. "You do, though. You've got everything to do with it."

His mouth showed her exactly what he meant, moving from her lips to her throat, then to her aching nipples. As his lips closed over one bud she made a small moan and threaded her fingers through his still-damp dark hair.

He moved again, lower, and she arched convulsively. He made love like he rode his horse, Charlotte thought. His motions calm, purposeful, gentle. Even graceful. How could a man so untutored in the fine points of genteel behavior be so…so…artful? So skilled. So beautiful in what he did to her?

His slow pleasuring emboldened her to touch him. When he groaned, Charlotte smiled into his eyes and stroked the tip of his shaft. It was deliciously warm and hard at the same time, his skin silky smooth to her touch.

"Charlotte." The low, rumbly groan came again when she brushed the tip a second time. She liked stirring him physically this way, just her hand on his body.

In the next few moments she learned something new about Will: she could tease him just so much and then his face changed and his movements because less playful and more deliberate.

He pulled her beneath him, slid one hand between her thighs and spread her legs. His mouth closed over hers as he entered her, slowly. Steadily. When he began to move, gently at first, Charlotte sighed with the pleasure of it, feeling him deep, deep inside her.

"I don't want this to ever end," she murmured. "Ever."

"It has to, honey." He thrust rapidly for a few seconds, then slowed for three long, deliberate strokes that brought her to the brink.

"Come with me," he breathed near her ear. "Let go and come."

Again he quickened his rhythm, then continued with three more long, deep thrusts that pushed her breathing into gasps. When he did that, moved as slowly as he was, something deep inside her curled in pleasure. Suddenly the wonderful feeling swept her up and hung there, until she tumbled over the edge. Will tensed, then cried out and spilled himself into her.

"Yes," he whispered when their heartbeats returned to normal. "Charlotte, I feel things with you, inside you, I've never felt before."

She stretched sinuously, like a sated cat, enjoying the loose, satisfied way her body felt, and watched his deep blue eyes darken again with desire.

"There is a time for every purpose under the heavens," she quoted, her voice drowsy with love. "Now is the time—" with a lazy smile she captured his hand, brought it to the juncture between her thighs "—to make love again."

The following morning they rode west. Gradually the dry landscape turned green, with lush meadows of wild barley grass and gentle hills dotted with sugar pine and red maples. Ranches and farms were starting up everywhere. They passed trim white clapboard houses, apple and cherry orchards, big red barns with sleepy-eyed cows in the yard. The spreads looked so peaceful, so downright beautiful, Will often blinked moisture out of his eyes.

Ranchers on horseback tipped their hats as they rode by. Wives—some old and plump, some so young their faces looked shiny and new, stood along fences in their bibbed gingham aprons and waved.

"It looks nice here," Charlotte remarked more than once.

"Not green enough," Will replied. "Besides, we can't afford a spread that big. Not and build a house without scratchin' the bottom of the barrel."

They moved on, continuing their search.

Then one morning they rode up a long, gentle slope and dismounted at the top of the hill. Below them spread a wide green valley with a stream meandering through it.

"Grass," Will said softly.

"Trees, too. And three windmills," Charlotte added. "Even a little town."

They looked at each other for a long moment. Then, without a word, they joined hands. "Yeah?" Will murmured.

Charlotte didn't answer, just stretched up on tiptoe and kissed him, hard.

Chapter Twenty-Eight

$\infty\!\!\infty\!\!\infty\!\!\infty$

They settled on a small spread in the Willamette Valley with a year-round spring and a duck pond. Will started clearing trees for the ranch house, marveling at Charlotte, who worked alongside him as he felled the oak and cedar, helping him skin them out and plane them. He planned on six bedrooms, but when he told her she went white as the canvas tent they were living in.

"Six!" she squealed.

Will scuffed the toe of his boot in the dirt. "Well, yeah, honey. I figured we'd need them. Eventually."

Charlotte gave him a look he couldn't decipher.

When the split shake roof was finished, with the help of two men Will hired from town, Charlotte packed up the tent and began planning how to use the small but tidy bedrooms upstairs. One room for sewing, she decided. Another for the library they were slowly building with books on horse breeding and mining, rounded out by Shakespeare and Longfellow. At night, they read to each other. After going to bed, they lay in each other arms, limbs entwined, whispering.

In the crisp fall mornings, Will rose, poked up the fire in the kitchen stove and brewed a pot of coffee. While Charlotte sipped it, propped up in their tumbled bed, he would announce his plans for the day. "Today I'm gonna build a spring house…a pigsty…a chicken pen." Charlotte was amazed at how the ranch buildings multiplied over the months.

One cloudless November day, Will rode into town for supplies and the mail, which was delivered to the Maple Falls post office. When he returned, Charlotte was bent over the stove, putting up applesauce and baking oatmeal cookies.

"Got two parcels here, addressed to you," Will said.

Charlotte dried her hands on a huck towel, and while Will unloaded the sacks of coffee beans and sugar, she carefully undid the twine knots. What tumbled out of the first package brought a puzzled look from Charlotte and a whoop of delight from Will.

"It's copper," he chortled. "Must be from the mine. Look at it, honey. It's pure copper!"

He turned the lumpy mass of red-brown ore over and over, then presented it, along with a folded letter, to Charlotte. "Charlie, I think we may be rich."

"What nonsense, Will. We are already rich."

"I mean money-rich. Read what Iversen says."

Charlotte unfolded the paper and scanned it. "Oh, my. Mr. Iversen says he'll need to hire three more men. The assayer's report says it's 'the highest quality copper he's ever seen.'"

She sank onto the wood-backed kitchen chair and looked up at Will. "I cannot believe it."

"Nuthin' wrong with a bank account that doesn't squeak, is there? We're down to nuthin' but rocks and pennies."

Absently, Charlotte bit her lower lip. "I don't need money to be happy, Will."

Will laughed. "Sure helps, though. Just borrowed money from the bank for the horses we're gonna breed. Tomorrow I'll start building the barn we're gonna breed 'em in."

She folded up the letter and laid the hunk of copper ore on top of it. "Move, Will. You're blocking the stove and my cookies will burn."

Will stepped aside and watched her fly to the oven, wrap a towel around her hand and slide out a pan of big, fat oatmeal cookies.

"Aren't you gonna open the other package?" He propelled it across the kitchen table with his forefinger. "It's from the trading post. Maybe Sam sent us a wedding present."

Charlotte scooped the cookies onto a thick green plate and set it on the table before Will. Perching on the chair across from him, she addressed the knots on the parcel, pulling and tugging at the twine until Will reached over and cut the string with his pocketknife.

Charlotte unwrapped the brown paper and gasped when a hand-sewn book fell into her hands. The front and back covers were made of polished wood, held together by cleverly twisted rafia grass. "Will, look!"

Printed on the cover in large black letters was the title: *Flaming Hair's Story*.

"It's from my students at the reservation," she cried. "Oh, Will, look—they've drawn pictures! All the things I told them about how I came to Oregon."

Charlotte turned over the flyleaf with reverent fingers. "Written and illustrated by John Yellow Bird, Samuel Runs With Moon, Matthew Black Bear and Peter Flying Duck." Her eyes filled. "Oh, Will!"

Will touched her shoulder and bent to look at the unusual volume. The first drawing showed Charlotte at the Sioux camp, looking on as Will fought Five Feathers. He read the caption aloud. "Flaming Hair is rescued by Will Texas Star."

Charlotte laughed through her tears. "I told them about most of our adventures. The stories captured their attention and helped me convince the boys to come to school each day, if for no other reason than to hear another tale. The paper and colored inks I ordered from Sam, to teach them writing."

She ran her fingers over the pages. There were pictures of the camp scenes with rabbits roasting on skewers, Will shaving, then a drawing of Will cutting Charlotte's hair. She lifted the page.

"Oh, look, it's Chili's cabin in the snow." Then came a picture of Chief White Eagle and his seven braves gathered about Chili's gravesite, another of Charlotte spraddle-legged on a log in her jeans and blue plaid shirt, smoking a cigar—even a picture of Will and Charlotte blowing smoke rings at each other.

"All the things I told them about," Charlotte murmured. She turned page after page, reliving every hour of their journey with a lemon-size lump in her throat. Toward the end there were drawings of Charlotte teaching school in the cottonwood branch lean-to, mounted on her gray mare and standing on the trading post porch with Will on one side and Sam Matthews on the other.

"But how can this be?" Charlotte murmured. "There are illustrations here of things my students couldn't possibly know about. Our horseback trip to Baker City…look, there's the Baker City Hotel! Here we are at the courthouse, getting m-married. See? The man is putting a ring on the woman's hand."

"Sam must have told them the rest," Will said.

She turned another page. "And just look! Here's our beautiful ranch house!"

She wiped her eyes with the hem of her apron. "Here we are on the front steps. Why, they even remembered my blue dress! And…"

She turned the final page and her heart caught. A man, tall and dark with long hair and a distinctive green shirt with a big silver star pinned to the shoulder, stood facing a woman with flame-red hair and a grossly swollen belly pushing out the front of her blue skirt.

"Oh, my," Charlotte said. She read the caption. "Flaming Hair and Will Texas Star await their child."

Will leaned over her shoulder for a closer look. "Gettin' a little ahead of things, I guess."

"Oh." Charlotte pressed her fingers against her mouth and began to sob. "Yes. I mean, no, they aren't," she said in a watery voice. "I mean…"

Will folded his arms about her and pressed his lips to her hair. "Well, Charlie, I'll be damned."

"Oh, Will..."

"Yeah, honey?" His voice was unsteady, his eyes wet.

Charlotte looked up into his face. "How could they possibly know this even before I did?"

Epilogue

Leah Marie Bondurant was born six months later, on June 23, 1862. Eventually all the bedrooms at the big white ranch house filled up, but it was Leah, their first-born, who caused the most commotion in the otherwise peaceful valley.

Neighbors from all over Golden Valley came to see Will and Charlotte's daughter. "Lordy, lookit that red hair," the men said. "And those big blue eyes," the women echoed. "What a fine mix of the two of you."

And at the end of every visit to see Leah and, over the years, to welcome the four brothers who followed her, Will would lay his arm across Charlotte's shoulder and whisper into her ear.

"Let's go up to bed, Charlie." Charlotte would smile up at him and say, "I thought you would never ask."

Then, after a brief pause, they would always add, in unison, the word "Please."

* * * * *

If you enjoyed what you just read,
then we've got an offer you can't resist!

Take 2 bestselling love stories FREE!

Plus get a FREE surprise gift!

Clip this page and mail it to Harlequin Reader Service®

IN U.S.A.	IN CANADA
3010 Walden Ave.	P.O. Box 609
P.O. Box 1867	Fort Erie, Ontario
Buffalo, N.Y. 14240-1867	L2A 5X3

YES! Please send me 2 free Harlequin Historicals® novels and my free surprise gift. After receiving them, if I don't wish to receive anymore, I can return the shipping statement marked cancel. If I don't cancel, I will receive 6 brand-new novels every month, before they're available in stores! In the U.S.A., bill me at the bargain price of $4.69 plus 25¢ shipping and handling per book and applicable sales tax, if any*. In Canada, bill me at the bargain price of $5.24 plus 25¢ shipping and handling per book and applicable taxes**. That's the complete price and a savings of over 10% off the cover prices—what a great deal! I understand that accepting the 2 free books and gift places me under no obligation ever to buy any books. I can always return a shipment and cancel at any time. Even if I never buy another book from Harlequin, the 2 free books and gift are mine to keep forever.

246 HDN DZ7Q
349 HDN DZ7R

Name	(PLEASE PRINT)	
Address	Apt.#	
City	State/Prov.	Zip/Postal Code

Not valid to current Harlequin Historicals® subscribers.

Want to try two free books from another series?
Call 1-800-873-8635 or visit www.morefreebooks.com.

* Terms and prices subject to change without notice. Sales tax applicable in N.Y.
** Canadian residents will be charged applicable provincial taxes and GST.
   All orders subject to approval. Offer limited to one per household.
   ® are registered trademarks owned and used by the trademark owner and or its licensee.

HIST04R   ©2004 Harlequin Enterprises Limited

e**HARLEQUIN**.com

The Ultimate Destination for Women's Fiction

For **FREE online reading,** visit
www.eHarlequin.com now and enjoy:

Online Reads
Read **Daily** and **Weekly** chapters from
our Internet-exclusive stories by your
favorite authors.

Interactive Novels
Cast your vote to help decide how these
stories unfold…then stay tuned!

Quick Reads
For shorter romantic reads, try our
collection of Poems, Toasts, & More!

Online Read Library
Miss one of our online reads?
Come here to catch up!

Reading Groups
Discuss, share and rave with other
community members!

For great reading online,
visit www.eHarlequin.com today!

A BRAND-NEW BOOK IN
THE DE WARENNE DYNASTY SERIES
BY *NEW YORK TIMES* BESTSELLING AUTHOR

BRENDA JOYCE

On the evening of her first masquerade, shy Elizabeth Anne
Fitzgerald is stunned by Tyrell de Warenne's whispered suggestion
of a midnight rendezvous in the gardens. Lizzie has secretly
worshiped the unattainable lord for years. When fortune
takes a maddening turn, she is prevented from meeting Tyrell.
But Lizzie has not seen the last of him....

Tyrell de Warenne is shocked when, two years later, Lizzie
arrives on his doorstep with a child she claims is his. He
remembers her well—and knows that he could not possibly
be the father. Is Elizabeth Anne Fitzgerald a woman of
experience, or the gentle innocent she seems?

THE MASQUERADE

"A powerhouse of emotion and sensuality."—*Romantic Times*

Available the first week of September 2005
wherever paperbacks are sold!

www.MIRABooks.com

MBJ2209